C000005461

MURDER
AT
MAYPOLE MANOR

A POSIE PARKER MYSTERY #3

L. B. HATHAWAY

WHITEHAVEN

WHITEHAVEN MAN PRESS
London

First published in Great Britain in 2016
by Whitehaven Man Press, London

Copyright © L.B. Hathaway 2016

(http://www.lbhathaway.com, email: permissions@lbhathaway.com)

The moral right of the author, L.B. Hathaway, has been asserted.

*All characters and events in this publication, other than those clearly in the
public domain, or specifically mentioned in the Historical Note at the end
of this publication, are fictitious and any resemblance to any real persons,
living or dead, is purely coincidental.*

All rights reserved.

No part of this publication may be reproduced, stored in a retrieval
system, or transmitted, in any form or by any means, without the prior
permission in writing of the author, nor be otherwise circulated in any
form of binding or cover other than that in which it is published and
without a similar condition including this condition being imposed on
the subsequent purchaser. Sale or provision of this publication by any
bookshop, retailer or e-book platform or website without the express
written permission of the author is in direct breach of copyright and
the author's moral rights, and such rights will be enforced legally.
Thank you for respecting the author's rights.

A CIP catalogue record for this book is available
from the British Library.

ISBN (e-book:) 978-0-9929254-7-5
ISBN (paperback:) 978-0-9929254-8-2

Jacket illustration by Red Gate Arts.
Formatting and design by J.D. Smith.

For Ingrid, with love

By L.B. Hathaway

The Posie Parker Mystery Series

1. *Murder Offstage: A Posie Parker Mystery*

2. *The Tomb of the Honey Bee: A Posie Parker Mystery*

3. *Murder at Maypole Manor: A Posie Parker Mystery*

4. *The Vanishing of Dr Winter: A Posie Parker Mystery*

PART ONE

An Unexpected Invite

One

The shrill ringing of the telephone cut through the warm, velvety quiet of the office waiting room. A fire was smouldering in the hearth and the lamps were turned down low.

After some delay and with a great deal of muttering, Posie Parker, Private Detective and owner of the Grape Street Bureau snatched up the receiver with an ill grace. The dulcet tones of the Operator trilled out across the London airwaves like a cheery budgerigar.

'Will you please hold the line for Scotland Yard, modom?'

What a thoroughly stupid question, Posie thought to herself, twitching the telephone cord in irritation and rubbing sleep out of her eyes. *As if you could say no to the most senior Police Department in England!*

Posie was standing in her secretary's empty office. She idly flicked the cards on Prudence Smythe's desk calendar to make the correct date, Friday 30th December 1921 – pointlessly perhaps, as it was only her in the office, so what did it matter? – and then she started to pick things up off the desk: a piece of withered mistletoe; a blue paper party hat; a packet of Rowntree's dark chocolate. After a couple of seconds a familiar voice came on the line:

'That you, Posie?'

'The very same.'

'You sound different. You haven't got a bally cold, have you?'

'No. I was sleeping. You woke me.'

'At four in the afternoon?' Detective Inspector Richard Lovelace's clear, authoritative voice sounded incredulous. At her silence he continued uneasily.

'Er, well, never mind. You must have your reasons, I daresay. Did you have a good Christmas? Lots of parties?'

'No. Not really.' Posie opened the chocolate and crammed it into her mouth in one go. She was starving. Food stocks at the Grape Street Bureau were running low. Prudence wouldn't mind: needs must and all that.

'It was very quiet.' *Not to mention lonely.* With only a cat and a borrowed dog for company, in fact. Not that she'd admit *that* to Inspector Lovelace. Or the fact that she hadn't bothered to change out of her pyjamas for more than three days in a row, just throwing a coat on over the top when she had needed to walk the dog around the block.

'Where's Len?'

'Wales, I think. Somewhere by the sea with his wife, Aggie. A family gathering. *Out* of London anyhow. Just about everyone is out of London right now. Since the war everyone seems to make a real fuss about Christmas, don't they? Like they never did before. It's all been blown right out of proportion if you ask me.'

'Hmmm, perhaps. And what about Alaric?'

Posie sighed. Her famous explorer boyfriend and his whereabouts were not a good topic of conversation just now. 'South Africa. For another month or so. It was a last-minute thing. He got an offer he couldn't refuse; to speak to some learned society about his adventures. It was ridiculously well-paid, and easy money. He took off on Christmas Eve.'

'What about his city bees? Don't tell me *you're* looking after them?' The Inspector was referring to a few experimental beehives which Alaric Boynton-Dale had set up on the roof terrace of Posie's Bloomsbury block of flats, Museum Chambers. Inspector Lovelace had been instrumental in procuring Alaric a special licence for the beehives in September, and had shown a very slight interest ever since.

'Bees sleep through the winter, Inspector. So fortunately *I* don't have to do anything. Although right now I wish I was a bee, sleeping through the winter.'

'You sound a bit down, old girl; not quite yourself. Everything all right? Where's Dolly and Rufus?'

'Dolly's busy being pregnant and is miles away at Rebburn Abbey and Rufus has been called to Balmoral to wait upon the Royal Family or something. That's what happens when you're one of the biggest landowners in the country. Lord Rufus Cardigeon is probably making himself indispensable to old King George as we speak.'

'I see.'

A very small note of cajoling lent itself to the Inspector's voice. 'Well I'm dashed glad I found you, Posie. I've sent a few telegrams and notes to Museum Chambers today. But they've all been returned to me, unread. Ted the Porter said you'd left. I thought you'd gone off on a toot somewhere…'

'No. Unfortunately not. The central heating at Museum Chambers broke down on Christmas Eve. And we're not allowed open fires there. So I moved in here.'

'You're kidding me. You spent Christmas in your office?'

'Yep. At least it was warm.' Posie looked around her. She had already taken down the Christmas decorations, not bothering to wait for Twelfth Night, but the usually neat waiting room was a mess: a pink foil-covered package of Fry's Turkish Delight sat melting by the fire; a stack of paperback novels were propped against the couch; a sleeping bag and a pillow were sprawled all over the floor and an occupied dog basket was tucked over in the corner. The dog, Bikram, a handsome pointer, was snoozing in the heat from the fire.

'No wonder you're a good deal pipped. Can't say I blame you. But what about tomorrow? New Year's Eve? Have you any plans?'

Posie sighed: it seemed that she was quite alone in the world, tucked up high above the London rooftops. To make matters worse, the storm which had blown itself out earlier in the day was whipping itself up again outside, and heavy rain was lashing against the windowpane like a bevy of small stones being thrown repeatedly at the glass.

'Nope. No plans. Not a sausage.'

'Well, that's what I hoped you'd say. I need your help. So no more of this feeling sorry for yourself flimflam, old girl. I need you tomorrow and the day after. Top-secret mission from Scotland Yard. Seriously undercover. What do you say?'

Posie was gripping the telephone cord in excitement. *Anything; I'll do anything to get out of here.*

'Mnnn, well. I might consider it,' she replied mock-cagily. 'What is it you want me to do?'

'I need you to pretend to be my wife at a New Year's Eve party tomorrow evening. Mine won't do. And in fact, you're eminently more suitable for this than my own wife would be.'

'That sounds a little odd. Dashed familiar if you don't mind me saying so.'

'No, no. It's not like that,' said the Inspector hastily. 'Molly, my *real* wife, is pregnant, so she can't come. But she wouldn't have been suitable anyhow. Not subtle enough, and not bothered enough. She'd rather be home knitting tiny lemon-yellow booties or whatever it is that babies wear nowadays. She certainly wouldn't be up to coming along to a glamorous New Year's Eve party down in Kent and acting out a part.'

'What "part" would that be, Inspector? I don't follow you.'

'I can't explain on the telephone. It's too risky. This

should be a secure line, but you never know. I've probably said too much already.'

'It sounds a bit odd, Inspector.'

'I totally agree. You'll just have to use that famous Posie Parker gut instinct about whether to accept or not. But know this: you'd be helping me out no end; not to mention serving your country. There's a question of national security at stake. So are you in, or not?'

Just then an almighty ruckus broke out in the corner of the waiting room. Posie's brand new copy of Agatha Christie's *The Mysterious Affair at Styles* came a cropper. She sighed heavily. Bikram the dog and Mr Minks the office Siamese cat were hissing and tearing at each other. Actually, it was Mr Minks doing all the hissing and tearing. Bikram was just defending his dog basket. Over a week in a confined space had done nothing for dog-cat relations.

'It depends, Inspector. On two things.'

'Go on.'

'One – is there central heating? And two – can I bring a dog?'

Inspector Lovelace laughed in relief. 'Yes to both,' he said certainly. 'Meet me at Victoria Station, Platform 3 tomorrow. Twelve noon. And thanks, Posie. I owe you one.'

No, thought Posie as she replaced the receiver. *She* owed *him* big time. She had been on the verge of getting cabin fever, or worse. And after all, there was only so much Turkish Delight a girl could eat.

* * * *

The call from the Inspector galvanised Posie into action and she felt like she had woken from a bad, fuggy dream.

She snapped to work clearing up the office, as the

following Monday, 2nd January, would be the start of a normal working week and she couldn't imagine anything worse than Prudence Smythe and Len Irving arriving back at work and witnessing the detritus of her week's sloppy stopover. Besides, she didn't want to have to explain to either of them that she had taken shelter at the Grape Street Bureau over Christmas, with simply nowhere else to go.

She changed out of her flannelette pyjamas, opened a new bar of Yardley's soap and washed in the tiny office bathroom with the cracked sink. She threw on some real clothes at last and put her old mackintosh on and then took Bikram for his evening walk through the dark, rainy streets of Bloomsbury.

The weather outside was filthy and both Posie and Bikram were blown around no end. The pavements were totally empty of course, and it wasn't until Posie was on the Tottenham Court Road that she noticed anyone else about. The cafés and shops were all closed and had been for the whole week, but in some windows shop girls could be seen lit up in fleeting glimpses behind screens, manoeuvring precariously on ladders with large 'JANUARY SALE' signs, getting things ready for the next day, when crowds would flock to Oxford Street and Regent Street to try and pick up a bargain on the first day of the sales. On the junction with the Charing Cross Road a man with an old white caravan was doing a roaring trade selling fish and chips, despite the weather, and the hot vinegary scent drifted temptingly over.

Posie queued for a portion patiently in the rain and then ate her fish and chip supper back at the Grape Street Bureau, in front of the fire, sharing it begrudgingly with Mr Minks. As she did so, the telephone rang again. The wind was shaking the window-casements like crazy and whistling through the doorways, and Posie could hardly hear what the Operator was telling her. It was a bad, stormy line, with a great deal of strange ghostly noises, taps and hissings in the background.

'Posie?'

'Who is this?'

'Rainbird speaking. I thought the Operator announced me? I'm calling on behalf of the Inspector.'

'Oh, hello, Sergeant. Everything all right, is it?' She gripped the receiver nervously. She hadn't realised quite how much the invitation from the Inspector meant to her. Had it been cancelled, worse luck?

'Has there been a change of plan?'

'No, no. But the Inspector forgot to tell you something. He told me to tell you to bring a very nice frock. Apparently it's going to be a seriously fancy affair. If it's no trouble, that is?'

There was a flurry of fuzzy hissings down the line. 'No, of course it's no trouble. Well, if that's everything? This really is a terrible line, Sergeant. I'll wish you a Happy New Year and ring off. Hope you have a good evening tomorrow, wherever you are.'

'Oh, no need for that, Miss Parker, but thank you all the same. Didn't the Inspector tell you?' came the Sergeant's muffled voice, as if he were speaking into a large goldfish bowl with the fish still *in situ*. 'I'm coming with you tomorrow. I'm to be valet and general dogsbody. My name will be Perkins, by the way. Better get used to it; you'll have to pretend I've been your servant for years. I'm looking forward to this little jaunt.' He paused, and when he spoke next it was in the tones of one who is privy to special, secret knowledge. 'Did you happen to know that Amory Laine is going to be one of the guests?'

'No!' Posie gasped aloud. Amory Laine was the current English film star *du jour*, and had recently become very famous. 'Golly. The Inspector told me nothing! Is there anything else which I should know about?'

'Oh, stacks. Until tomorrow at Victoria,' replied the policeman maddeningly, before ringing off.

* * * *

Two

Saturday the 31st of December, the very last day of 1921, dawned grey and bitterly cold after the storm of the night before.

A shivery sort of day, thought Posie wistfully as she picked her way through the early-morning streets. London was looking particularly ugly, in fact. Several roof tiles were down and bits of broken twig and smatterings of rubbish were draped along the roads at regular intervals, souvenirs of the storm the previous night, lending Bloomsbury a particularly shipwrecked, flooded look.

Posie dashed back home to Museum Chambers to pick out a dress. On entering the common hallway she whistled under her breath as she contemplated just how cold the building actually was. No-one was about, sensibly, and it seemed as if the very air was actually made up of freshly formed ice particles. Trying not to shiver, and wrapping her thick tweed coat tightly around herself for warmth, Posie took the birdcage lift to the top floor and entered her apartment, clenching her teeth together to stop them from chattering.

You could have cut the air inside with a knife, it was that cold. As fast as she could, Posie ran to her bedroom and changed quickly into a smart brown Harris Tweed day suit with matching beret. She started throwing make-up and perfume into her nice leather overnight bag willy-nilly.

The Inspector had said they would be working undercover, and he had said it would be a glamorous affair, but Posie was dashed glad she had spoken to Sergeant Rainbird. After all, there was glamour and then there was *glamour*. If Amory Laine the film star was gracing the place with her presence then this New Year's Eve party belonged firmly in the second category.

Amory Laine was a dark smouldering waif of a girl, the darling of the Icon Film Company. There didn't seem to be a magazine cover or a newspaper on a news-stand these days which didn't feature Amory's little heart-shaped face somewhere on it, with her trademark raise of the left eyebrow and surprised-looking cupid's bow pout. She had starred earlier that summer in a smash hit of a silent movie, *Innocent and Naïve*, playing the lead role; a sweet, fragile country girl seduced by the bright lights of the city, who then gets into trouble and realises the error of her ways too late. Posie had seen the film with her friend Dolly, and had enjoyed the box of truffles she had purchased far more than the film itself.

If truth were told, Posie had found the look of Amory Laine very annoying, but she told herself to reserve judgement now until she had actually met the girl: Posie knew that part of her inherent hostility was no doubt a case of the old green-eyed monster rearing its ugly head, and that pangs of jealousy on her part about the girl's beauty and trimness of figure wouldn't help Inspector Lovelace at all on whatever undercover work they were to be engaged upon.

So just what sort of party was it to be if a very famous film star was attending? One with lots of film stars and famous people, perhaps? It seemed likely.

It wasn't Posie's world at all. She found herself wishing wholeheartedly that she had her good friend Dolly Price, now Lady Cardigeon by marriage, to talk to: Dolly was a lover of all things cinema-related and could have provided her with a veritable mine of handy information on Amory Laine, including any skeletons which might be lurking in her closet. Posie decided it would be prudent to buy a movie magazine and gen up on who was who in the film world: *forearmed is forewarned*, she told herself sagely.

Scurrying around in her bedroom Posie packed hastily, her fingers almost turning blue from cold. It sounded as if the glamorous party would be no place for her old carpet bag, and fondly Posie shook out her bits and pieces from it and tucked it away in the cupboard. She selected her only other handbag, a ridiculously expensive and vastly underused black patent leather bag from Bally of Switzerland, a birthday present from her first fiancée, from before the war, and transferred her vital things across. She grabbed her only real jewellery, a single strand of large real cream pearls, and then took out of the cupboard a floor-length red velvet dress from Harrods, still in its shop wrappings. The dress was sumptuous and had been very expensive. Posie smiled to herself: she had intended to wear this tonight all along, but she had expected to be spending the night with different people, or a different *person*, at any rate, and in wildly different circumstances. *If* South Africa hadn't cropped up, that was…

But who was she to stop Alaric from going where he wanted to? Thank goodness the dress was going to get an outing, in any case. She packed the matching red shoes and headed for the door.

As she locked up, Posie suddenly realised she hadn't packed anything warm to wear. The Inspector had said there would be central heating where they were going, but you never knew. Coming back inside the flat, Posie caught sight of Alaric's favourite thick grey jumper lying on the brand new American Lloyd Loom hall chair, along with a good deal of his other travelling clothes which were heaped around it in discarded piles.

The vivid green chair was almost buried in the clothes, and Posie was glad of it. The fashionable seat was Alaric's Christmas present to Posie, but she had hated it from the word go. She reminded herself to move it to a less visible place in the New Year.

As she left the apartment block, Posie ran head-on into Ted, the Chief Porter.

'I thought you'd left here long ago, Miss. Don't hang around; it's like sittin' in an igloo! And folks say it's only goin' to get colder; some thinks snow is on the way. And you can't get a plumber for love nor money round here 'til Monday morning. Would you believe it?'

Posie fished in the Bally bag and drew out a few coins and a key on a piece of string. She pressed the items on him.

'But you've already given me a nice Christmas tip, Miss Parker. What's all this about?'

'Are you able to feed my cat, Ted? Grape Street, on the corner. Top floor office. Just two streets away – and just for tonight and tomorrow. I'm back on Monday, latest. That's the key to let you in.'

'Course I can, Miss. But that's way too much money there. What you feeding him on – lucky beggar – prime cuts?'

'Exactly,' said Posie.

* * * *

Thoughts of Amory Laine led Posie to grab a motor taxi and head over to Curzon Street in Mayfair to have her hair newly shingled at Geo. F. Trumper. She took her overnight bag and Bikram, too, planning to go straight on and catch the train at Victoria.

Feeling spruce and fashionable and with a neat half an hour to spare, she dawdled through Shepherd Market in Mayfair. She then bought several copies of penny movie magazines at the news-stand outside Green Park Underground Station, and, lingering, for good measure she bought a copy of *The Times* and *The Lady*, too.

But then time seemed to run away from her somehow, and before she knew it Posie was on the verge of being late. Heart in her mouth, she scanned Piccadilly frantically for a cab. But none came.

A note of sharp panic gripped her; she couldn't afford to miss the train and mess this up for the Inspector, and it was too far to walk to Victoria from here. Now encumbered with her collection of heavy papers, with Bikram straining uncomfortably on the leash beside her, uneasy among all the shoppers and tourists, Posie searched the wide boulevard for a cab of any sort.

It was just then that she experienced that old unwelcome sensation of the hairs standing up on the back of her neck. Sure as bread was bread someone nearby was watching her.

Posie gulped uneasily, checking the crowds on the other side of the road; people in their weekend best were teeming in and out of Green Park's main entrance, and gathering around a chestnut seller plying his wares outside the wrought iron railings, doing a good trade because of the cold snap. But she couldn't see anyone watching her at all.

At last she spied a rickety old hansom cab coming her way. Posie sighed with relief and stepped out into the main thoroughfare of Piccadilly.

'I say! STOP! Driver!'

It was getting much, much colder quickly now and Posie noticed that the driver was shivering inside his sheepskin coat. Just as she was giving instructions and manoeuvring Bikram up into the tight carriage, she caught sight of the man who had been watching her.

Posie stared back defiantly.

He was standing on the other side of the road, near the arches of the Ritz Hotel, next to a newspaper boy with a sandwich board advertising the latest adventures of Ernest Shackleton. The man was dressed in nondescript black clothes and wore a homburg hat pulled well down over his face, and a scarf drawn up. He had a cigarette or a cigar clamped tightly in his mouth. He looked like virtually every man in the city on this freezing cold day, which was very unhelpful.

Except that when he saw Posie meet his gaze, he melted away guiltily into the dark shadows of the arches around him. But not before Posie had registered a sense of the man's height, of his wariness.

Who on earth was the man? And why was he watching her? What sort of trouble was she attracting now? But she didn't have time to think on it. It was a quarter-to twelve.

Rats.

'Fast as you can, please, driver. I'll make it worth your while,' Posie called up through the trapdoor to the man on the sprung seat behind the fly carriage.

'This is one time I *really* can't be late.'

* * * *

Three

Dashing along Platform 3 at two minutes to noon, Posie cursed under her breath. She was obviously in the wrong place.

The train to Dover had been listed as leaving at 11.58 from Platform 1, so she had missed that. But the Inspector had said Platform 3. *This* was the platform for the Golden Arrow, that ridiculously expensive, first-class only train, and the announcer repeated over and over through the loudspeakers that the Golden Arrow would be departing at a quarter-past the hour to Dover, for the Paris connection. There were no other trains leaving from Platform 3.

Flummoxed, she came to a standstill. Sweaty and all out of sorts, Posie started to cast her eyes up and down the dim platform, all the while balancing her luggage and trying not to be pulled over by the dog, who wanted to run everywhere. The platform was busy with exceptionally well-dressed people saying their goodbyes next to the train.

At that very moment a small crush of people came along the platform, almost knocking her and Bikram over. In all the confusion Posie only really noted that the fawning green-liveried Golden Arrow staff who swarmed along were focused on one individual at the very centre of the crowd, and she or he was so small that they were entirely swallowed up by other, nondescript, taller people carrying vast amounts of luggage. There was a buzz of raucous laughter and cameras were being clicked, too. The bright light of a journalist's flashlight dazzled Posie. She craned her neck to catch a better glimpse of who it was, but saw that the crowd, *en masse*, was already heading up some shiny gold steps into one of the beautifully glossy cream-and-green carriages.

How the other half live, Posie thought to herself with a half-laugh.

'Mrs Grosvenor, can I take your luggage from you, ma'am?' said a voice very close by. 'And the dog, too?'

She turned instinctively, ready to disabuse whoever the person was who had got the wrong woman. And then she froze, for she saw it was Sergeant Rainbird. But wearing the very smart black of a professional manservant. She stopped herself from goggling stupidly. Whatever charade she was to be involved in obviously started here, on the platform.

'Ah, yes, er, Perkins. There's a good fellow.' She passed everything over and then almost gasped again as she saw a figure bowling up to her, familiar yet unrecognisable at the same time. Detective Inspector Lovelace of New Scotland Yard.

'Hildegard, darling. How was your writers' retreat? How quaint of you to wear your *country* clothes. Will you change on the train? Was it *very* cold up in the north?'

The Inspector grabbed Posie and made as if to kiss her, his lips coming to rest in her shingled hair. Shocked, Posie said nothing and tried to keep herself from gasping like a fish out of water.

'Just keep quiet,' he hissed into her ear. 'We don't know who's watching. Smile but don't say a word.'

Inspector Richard Lovelace was done up like a member of the upper classes. His normal slightly fusty brown homburg hat and tweedy suit were nowhere in evidence, and his dark navy three-piece suit and burgundy silk cravat obviously came from Savile Row's finest. A black legal cape made of lightweight wool was draped around his large, fairly stocky frame, adding a surprising note of elegance. Shiny black shoes with spats completed the look. His head was bare and Posie noted his normally slightly wild red hair had been shorn very short all over and there were streaks of grey at his temples. He wore round golden spectacles and he looked like a judge who had forgotten his wig. The look suited him.

'Trust you to just be in the nick of time, my love,' the Inspector said loudly, falsely jolly, leading Posie towards one of the gleaming carriages and presenting a uniformed lad with a pair of purple tickets.

'Here we are then.'

* * * *

As the train started to move off, Posie settled back into the comfy green cushions of her chair. *The Golden Arrow!*

'It's only as far as Dover. Don't get carried away, darling, and fall asleep expecting to end up on the outskirts of Paris or somewhere.'

Opposite her sat the Inspector, his cape and jacket now removed. The blinds of their private compartment were drawn down on both sides, and outside their door in the communal corridor Sergeant Rainbird was loitering, supposedly checking off a luggage list but ostensibly making sure the coast stayed clear. Bikram was snoozing underneath the seat, under Posie's legs.

There was a sudden strange knock on the glass of the compartment door. Two short knocks, then a third long one: *Rap-Rap. Raaap.*

'Okay.' The Inspector breathed a visible sigh of relief. 'We can speak now.'

'Thank goodness for that,' Posie whispered. 'I don't know whether I'm coming or going, and on the Golden Arrow at that. Talk about pushing the boat out; I didn't know Scotland Yard had such reserves of wealth up their sleeves! And look at you all dolled up! Some dressing up box you've got there.'

'Mnnn. Speaking of which, this is for you.' The Inspector pulled a large, bulky, brown-paper wrapped parcel out from under his seat and passed it over.

'Is this what I'm meant to be changing into?' said Posie, a touch icily. 'And what was all that about country clothes? Cheek! This is my nice brown tweed suit. I got it at Peter Jones on Sloane Square!'

'Yes, well. Sorry about that, Posie. But we're meant to be *rich*. Rich, and showy with it. You can wear *this* for the daytime, and I trust you've bought your own evening attire? Good. Oh, and don't forget we're meant to be married, too.'

He fished in his waistcoat pocket and brought out a small brown envelope and shook out its contents. Two rings. He passed them over. Posie's jaw dropped. One was a plain band of rose gold. But the other was a square-cut emerald the size of a quail's egg. It sparkled threateningly at Posie, as if willing her to lose it in an instant.

'Paste,' said Lovelace reassuringly. 'Stick them on and forget about them.'

'If I don't gouge my own eye out first,' said Posie. 'Now tell me *who* I am. And what's going on.'

In a few brief sentences, the Inspector sketched out a character description for the fictional couple they were pretending to be: *he* was James Grosvenor KC ('you should call me Jimmie'), a barrister at the top of his profession, a King's Counsel, waiting to be appointed a High Court Judge. *She* was Hildegarde ('call me Hilda'), his wife; a mother of one and a would-be crime novelist. They lived in Pelham Place in South Kensington and their daughter, Lucy, attended the nearby school on Queen's Gate. Hilda Grosvenor had just been off on a short writers' retreat in Yorkshire.

Posie gave a slight moue of distaste but then she nodded in agreement.

'That's fine. Hilda Grosvenor sounds dreary and dull as ditch-water but I suppose it makes sense: you know enough about law to blag it as a barrister and I'm nosy enough about people to want to write about them. Now tell me where we're off to. Something to do with film stars, is it? I know Amory Laine is going wherever we are, too.'

'Did you see her getting on the train, then? With all those journalists at her heels? Is that how you know she's coming with us? I didn't tell you, so how else would you know?'

Mindful of Rainbird's position and not wanting to name him as a blabbermouth, Posie held her tongue and just nodded vaguely. The Inspector leant closer.

'Well, you're right. She *is* coming with us. We're off to a party at Maypole Manor. It's at St Margaret's Bay, near Dover. This train was much quicker than the regular train to Dover, it only takes an hour and a half, which is why we're on it. It's a beautiful spot there, but lonely as hell, perched right out on a cliff overlooking the English Channel. It's the most southerly tip of England, actually.'

'I've never heard of it,' said Posie, frowning.

'No. You wouldn't have. But you *would* have heard of its owner. Or Alaric would have done. How is he, by the way?'

'Conspicuous by his very absence. I don't want to talk about him. You were saying?'

'Ah, yes. Lord Robin Glaysayer. He's the owner.'

'Robin Glaysayer, the famous adventurer?'

'Well, famous in his day. But yes, the very same. The famously wealthy Scottish Lord who sold up everything to go and spend his time rummaging around in foreign countries, getting a bit of a tan.'

'Yes. Alaric knows him a bit. But I thought he lived in Africa or somewhere wild, or on a ranch or something? Isn't St Margaret's Bay in Kent a bit tame for him, sir?'

'You'd think so, wouldn't you? But he had this place restored and done up a few years ago as somewhere he could retire to. Loves it there, apparently. He doesn't do that much adventuring anymore. Bit old and sick now. Anyhow, he lives at Maypole Manor with his two daughters, who drop by sometimes. He gives the most amazing house parties, both at Midsummer and New Year. Never the same people twice, apparently. You know, guests finding emeralds in their soup and that kind of lark. An invitation is like gold dust.'

'No wife, sir?'

The Inspector frowned and rubbed at his grey-tinged temple. He got out a blue legal notebook which was half-filled with scribblings. He ran a finger down a page.

'Nope. As I thought. The wife died many years ago. Oh, and another interesting thing is that the two daughters, Jacinta and Jocasta, are both adopted. Adopted by the Glaysayers as babies, though. I've got all the details here. They must both be about your age, I'm guessing.'

'Oh? And what age is that?' Posie was pushing thirty and feeling sensitive about it.

'Old enough not to ask stupid rhetorical questions, *darling*.'

A knock came at the door. Four sharp raps.

'I say, Mr Grosvenor, sir,' said Rainbird loudly, putting his head into the compartment and pulling a face. It was obviously a pre-arranged signal. 'I hadn't closed your small trunk just as tightly as I thought I had, sir. Could I ask you to help me for a second? It needs two to fix it, and I can't see any other servants around the place. I'm ever so sorry, sir.'

'Of course, Perkins. Bring it here.'

Rainbird came shuffling into the compartment heaving the small trunk behind him.

'Something funny's going on in that bathroom,' he hissed. 'A fella went in, but didn't come out. A woman came out who must have been in there the whole time and now she's gone back in there again.'

The Inspector groaned. 'Sounds like a spot of hanky-panky to me. Is that all, Rainbird?'

'You told me to tell you if there was any funny business going on, sir. I just thought I should make you aware.'

'*I'll* go and have a look,' said Posie, getting to her feet and swaying a little with the rhythm of the train. She grabbed the bulky package. 'I might as well go and change out of my *country* clothes.'

Out in the green-carpeted corridor there was no-one about and Posie passed an empty compartment next to their own, which she felt had been left vacant on purpose somehow, and then two occupied compartments, both with their blinds lowered, like their own. The corridor was dimly lit with little tulip-shaped yellow bulb lights, as if for the evening, even though it was barely afternoon. The windows facing the outside of the train all had their blinds down too. Striped gold and green against the rich lacquered wood.

The bathroom was at the very end of the carriage and as she struggled along with her package Posie was suddenly caught unawares by a freezing cold sharp draught of air. The outside window next to the bathroom cubicle was wide open, and the blind was up and flapping around wildly in the wind. The air which came pouring in at high speed felt like it was full of ice. Shivering, Posie caught the wooden sash and pulled the window up with one sharp bang.

A middle-aged man passed her in the corridor. He was tall with a neat clipped beard and a Russian-looking warm winter hat, black and tassely. In fact, he had something slightly of the old Tsar Nicholas about him. It could have been the icy blue eyes. He nodded politely at Posie.

'Goodness, I was just on my way to get that! I could

feel the draught all the way back down there in my compartment.' He indicated further along, away from the direction Posie had come from.

'They say it's about to snow. That breeze certainly promises cold weather!' He tipped his hat at Posie: 'Good day to you, madam.'

Posie nodded back but was preoccupied. She had expected to have to wait for the bathroom, or to force open the door or something, but the door had been left ajar. Peering inside, it was obvious that it was vacant. Posie stepped in and latched the door behind her. The tiny room was freezing cold.

Something glittered on the floor. Bending down, Posie saw that it was a shard of mirror. Next to it was a small stick of red greasepaint without a cover, as if a lipstick cylinder had broken and the actual make-up had come loose from it. A tiny stub of a black cigarillo had been ground underfoot and, turning it over, Posie found it was still warm and smouldering.

Standing up quickly, Posie saw that the sumptuously decorated mirror above the tiny bathroom sink was shattered into hundreds of pieces, and that even as she watched, tiny slivers were coming away and falling into the sink below.

That's seven years bad luck for someone, she thought to herself, frowning, seeing her face reflected many, many times over in the splintered glass.

She looked around but there seemed nothing else amiss; everything else was in order, with the window closed and the green and gold blind pulled down too. Sighing, Posie tore open the brown-paper package and shook out three tissue-wrapped parcels inside. The tissue was stamped all over with a tiny 'H' emblem, and the parcels were fastened with a sticker saying 'HOUSE OF HARLOW'.

'Goodness me,' she breathed. The House of Harlow was perhaps the most fashionable, most expensive women's fashion house in London right now. When the House of Harlow made something, the newspapers and magazines took note; within days seamstresses all over England were trying their hands at imitating the Harlow style.

Unfolding the paper, Posie shook out a bright green drop-waisted dress, the colour of jade. It was made of a light worsted wool of the finest quality Posie had ever held. It was deceptively simple, but the devil was in the detail: hours had been taken ensuring the cut was just right, that the bias-cut seams were perfect. The deep V-neck was finished with an inlay of sparkling gold and silver tweed, and a tiny 'H' embossed jade button was sewn into the collar. A matching gold and silver tweed jacket lay under the dress, and underneath that, a beautifully impractical pair of green suede pumps. Posie realised everything exactly matched her 'new' ring.

The funny thing was that the outfit looked like it might be a perfect fit; it looked just the right size. And that *was* funny because Posie usually had to get her clothes either specially made for her, or else bought off the peg after having spent hours and hours looking for just the right thing. She was an 'odd' size, but she dressed nicely and so no-one ever realised.

So how on earth had Inspector Lovelace managed to get an outfit so exactly right for her?

Bemused, and still very cold in the little cubicle, Posie changed quickly and sure enough, the new outfit fitted her like a glove. She didn't need to look into the shattered mirror to know that she looked like a dream; she *felt* like a dream. The shoes on her feet felt light enough to dance in. Her Peter Jones Harris Tweed suit looked and felt coarse and lumpy by comparison and she shoved it haphazardly into the ripped paper bag with her matching beret. Definitely 'country clothes'.

She stepped out into the corridor feeling like a swan metamorphosed from the ugly duckling.

'You took yer time, lovey,' a little cockney voice snapped beside her, shattering her illusion. 'You kept me waitin' ages. It might be a fancy train, but there's still only one lav in this carriage, an' I'm dyin' for a pee.'

Posie jumped: she hadn't been expecting anyone to be outside and had been in a world of her own. She opened her mouth to apologise but no words came. She was shocked into silence. She saw that the tiny girl standing there was Amory Laine, the film star.

The limpid dark-brown eyes decorated with lashings of black mascara looked up at Posie, but rather than being coquettish and teasing, they were irritable and accusing and they blazed wildly. The trademark raised eyebrow was nowhere in sight. The girl was smoking a Sobranie through a long pink glass holder, tapping the ash on the varnished wooden wall of the train. The girl suddenly stared at Posie's new green dress with a modicum of interest and wrinkled her nose. She leered:

'Don't *you* look the part, in yer hoighty-toighty clothes.'

Posie flushed with real embarrassment, but managed to draw herself up to her full height and started to walk off without saying anything by way of retort. *Good job the cinema is silent*, she thought to herself in wonder: the girl was cheap as chips, and a potty-mouth to boot. If people could only hear her voice for real they would run for the hills, sure as bread was bread. Posie thought of the movie which had made Amory's name that summer: *Innocent and Naïve*. How ironic! There was nothing innocent about the girl at all, let alone naïve.

She was aware of a slight movement behind her as a man came out into the corridor and stood with the film star for a moment. Next she heard a snide comment, deliberately delivered to be overheard, and to sting:

'Some people think they're so fancy; prancin' about in House of Harlow clothes. More money than sense, I'd say. Certainly more money than *looks*. Keepin' me waitin'! Cheek of it!'

'Hush, darling,' came the man's voice, soothing, smooth as silk. 'Don't be so rude.'

Her face smarting with anger, Posie edged her way back up the corridor.

* * * *

'Anything odd happening out there?' asked the Inspector quickly.

Posie shook her head and told him what she had seen in the bathroom, and about her horrid confrontation with Amory Laine. The Inspector nodded knowingly.

'Sounds like the girl was in the bathroom before you and trashed the place; throwing her lipstick and all sorts about. She probably flew into a rage and threw something at the mirror, too.'

'But why? Why is she so out of sorts? You don't sound surprised. That's shocking behaviour, even for a film star!'

'Well, let's just say she has quite a *reputation*, does Miss Laine. Rages and wild fits and all sorts. So no, I'm not surprised. And nor am I surprised to hear she's loitering around outside the bathroom.'

Posie raised an eyebrow.

The Inspector pinched the top of his nose dramatically and made a snorting noise. Posie looked blankly back at him.

'Oh, Posie, sometimes you are so very naïve,' the Inspector said, almost fondly. '*Cocaine*, Posie. And stacks of it. The girl's as high as a kite almost all the time, apparently. So she probably hadn't got a clue what she was saying to you. Not really. All a lot of hot air.'

'Goodness,' said Posie, digesting this surprising news and settling back down into her chair again.

'By the way, you look very nice.' The Inspector smiled approvingly.

'You'd better tell me,' said Posie, suddenly remembering her green dress and its beautiful and bemusing fit, 'how on earth do I happen to be wearing an outfit which fits me better than anything I have ever worn in my life? As far as I know I have never given my measurements to anyone other than my seamstress. Bribe her, did you?'

'Ah,' said the Inspector, giving an apologetic shrug. 'No. Nothing to do with your seamstress. But I have to admit to a rather, er, unusual approach being taken. Unconventional, even. But needs must, you know.'

'Explain.'

'Well, your flat was empty, wasn't it? And we needed you to look the part. First impressions count. So yesterday evening, after you had agreed to come with me on this little outing to Maypole Manor, MI5 opened up your apartment and took a few bits and pieces from your cupboard over to the House of Harlow so that one of the Harlow sisters could run you up something suitable overnight, based on your real clothes. Cost us a packet but I didn't think you'd mind.'

Posie's mind was reeling. But only one thing stood out.

'*MI5?* The British Intelligence Agency? In my flat? What on earth do they have to do with all of this? And they do, don't they?'

The Inspector grimaced and nodded, splaying his hands.

'This isn't some little cosy country jaunt, is it, if MI5 are crawling all over it? Including in my wardrobe, by all accounts.'

'I was just about to explain *everything*.'

Posie crossed her arms huffily. 'Yep,' she said firmly. 'You better had. And quickly.'

* * * *

Four

They were interrupted by an unfamiliar, unrehearsed type of knocking.

'Tea, sir? Tea, madam?'

Inspector Lovelace waved away the boy with the tea trolley and waited until Rainbird gave his 'good-to-go' signal again. *Rap-Rap. Raaap.*

'I could have done with a cuppa and a sandwich,' said Posie belligerently. 'I haven't eaten all day.'

'I'll send Rainbird along to the dining car in a bit.'

The Inspector rolled up the blind and looked out as the train clattered along. The sky was bleached of colour and the light held all the muddiness of a bruise. Tell-tale hailstones started to smatter against the glass.

The Inspector snapped the blind down irritably. Bikram stirred in his sleep.

'What's wrong?'

'The weather. Snow. It's not really ideal.'

'For a house party? I wouldn't have thought it mattered that much. We'll all be inside.'

The Inspector splayed his hands.

'I'll explain. Until a few weeks ago Robin Glaysayer was giving his usual sparkling New Year's Eve party. He'd invited the crème de la crème of English society; a few aristocrats, theatre actresses, film stars, artists, writers and a few politicians and businessmen thrown in for good measure. You get the picture. There was no way a policeman like myself would be attending. Probably even a barrister such as Jimmie Grosvenor, my alter ego, would have been too boring a guest.'

'Oh? So what happened?'

'MI5. They asked Lord Glaysayer to cancel the party he had planned: tell most of the invitees that the thing was off; hoped they'd all understand.'

'But it's not off, is it? It's still going ahead. And Amory Laine is here, isn't she? So what happened? She didn't get the telegram cancelling it?'

'The party being held now is a much smaller, reduced version of what would have been going on. It's the kind of party MI5 want. There will only be twelve of us in all, including the host and his daughters. The word went out that Lord Glaysayer was quite ill, and that only a few people, mainly family, would be attending at Maypole Manor for the New Year's party this year.'

'So it's a dummy party? It's staged, you mean?'

The Inspector nodded. 'Basically, yes. But MI5 thought it best that some of the original guests, those on the first guest list should still attend; make it look like a proper party, if you will. The icing on the pretend cake.'

'Hence Amory Laine, sir?'

'Yes. And her husband, too. He's a portrait artist, a well-known one too by all accounts. Heard of him? His name is Julian Carter.'

Posie shook her head, remembering the silky reassuring voice in the corridor a few minutes before.

'I didn't know she was married. I pity him. Poor sausage.'

'Mnnn, yes. I expect he has a lot to deal with. But there's another couple coming from the original guest list, too,' the Inspector continued, looking at his blue legal notebook.

'An Italian nobleman, a Duke, by the name of Luca Del

Angelo and his current paramour, an It-girl called Lehni Brandenberger. A beauty, apparently. Don't suppose you know them, either?'

Posie shook her head, fingering the fine tissue-like wool of her glittery jacket with satisfaction.

'Good. Then our cover won't be blown. Will it?'

'You said that this was "*the kind of party MI5 want*". So *who* exactly is attending that MI5 want to be there? Can you tell me? Or is that a top secret?'

'I can tell you,' said the Inspector. He ran his thick index finger down a list in front of him. 'They've sent me all the details so I'm well briefed. So, as well as the three hosts, and the delightful Amory Laine and Julian, and the Italian Duke and his girlfriend, and us of course, there's the MI5 contact; his name is Bryn Cardinal. Jolly good chap, actually; one of their best. Got covered in ridiculous amounts of silverware in the last war, but decent with it. He's a personal friend of Assistant Commissioner Scabbes, one of the most senior men at Scotland Yard. It seems that Cardinal will be pretending to be a big shot businessman specialising in mining. There will also be a government chappie there by the name of Edwin Goodman.'

The Inspector frowned, then spied a tiny note he had made in a margin.

'Oh, yes. I forgot. There's a twelfth man, too. But I can't tell you his name; I don't have it. He's a new addition; only found out he was going to be attending this morning, so we'll have to find out who he is when we get there. The man will have been vetted of course by MI5. Apparently Old Robin Glaysayer insisted on having at least one old school friend or someone he was pally with there for himself as company.'

'I can't say I blame him, sir. He's effectively had his party hijacked from underneath him. I'm surprised he agreed to it at all. Aren't you?'

Lovelace shook his head. 'No. We had him in a tight

spot. He hadn't paid a bally lot of taxes or duties or some such rot. Anyhow, the Customs and Excise boys had a field day reporting all the many instances and amounts he owed. MI5 were rubbing their hands in glee when they realised they could make him bend to their will. Poor old Glaysayer simply *had* to agree to it all. Didn't have much of a choice.'

'Does he know who everyone is, sir? That you are really a Scotland Yard Inspector, I mean?'

'Oh, yes. Man's sharp as a razor beneath the charm. Wouldn't do to pull the wool over old Glaysayer's eyes. He's been sworn to secrecy, of course.'

Posie puffed her cheeks out. Her stomach was beginning to rumble badly and she hadn't thought to pack anything to eat at all. Like an idiot. But mainly her brain was working overtime. So many questions. And so far, no real answers.

The Inspector got up and opened the compartment door. He bellowed out to Rainbird, who seemed to be loitering further along the corridor.

'Perkins, we'd like some refreshments, please. Fast as you can, man. China tea for two and whatever they've got which is easy to transport. Maybe some sandwiches. Oh, and some chocolates. A box. You know how Mrs Grosvenor has a terribly sweet tooth. Humour her.'

'Right you are, sir.'

Posie looked up and grinned as the Inspector slammed the door shut behind him. She was mightily cheered by the thought of some chocolate. It was bound to be good quality too, here of all places. 'Good job I'm in a good mood and don't mind your rotten cheek, sir.'

She had ferreted around in her Bally bag and brought out her own smart black notepad where she had scribbled down a few lines.

'A few questions, sir, if I'm allowed?'

'Fire away while the coast's clear.'

'Let me get this right. So MI5 want to use Maypole

Manor for a staged party particularly because the place belongs to Robin Glaysayer, and he'd be having a party there anyhow?'

'Sort of correct. But it's more a question of *where the house is* which is important. But it provides a nice fuzzy backdrop of course, to have a party going on in the background. A distraction.'

'A distraction from what, sir? And what do you mean "*where the house is...*" I don't get you, sir.'

'Think carefully, Posie.'

Posie screwed up her nose and nibbled her pen-lid. She puffed in irritation and swung the blind open. She saw that the train was crossing over the bridge on the River Medway, giving a splendid view of Rochester Cathedral and the castle there on the very edge of the great grey river, the vast expanse of water glittering like silver in the sparse winter sunlight.

That was it!

Water.

'Ah! You said Maypole Manor is virtually on the southernmost part of England, that it juts right out into the English Channel! So it's very near France. And that's important. Am I correct? Is that what this is all about?'

Inspector Lovelace grinned and nodded encouragingly. 'I knew you'd get there in the end.'

Her brain raced: 'What-ho! Exciting stuff, eh?'

She thought for a second before gushing on:

'So what is it that MI5 have got their knickers in a twist about? An international smuggling ring? It must be! What are they dealing in? Drugs? Jewels? Black market foodstuffs?'

The Inspector shook his head, suddenly serious.

'Much worse,' he said soberly. 'We're dealing with a traitor, Posie. Or traitors. And a secret of such national importance that men will kill for it, and *have* killed for it.

It's not a joke. We're here to make sure that no-one dies tonight. Not on our watch, at any rate.'

* * * *

Five

Over tinned-salmon sandwiches and slices of slightly dry Dundee cake the Inspector outlined the background to Posie as he understood it.

Britain and Germany were still, unofficially at any rate, at loggerheads since the Great War, despite the truce and the treaties. There was talk among the men working in Whitehall of a simmering animosity barely contained below the surface; of the two countries being sworn enemies still, no matter how many men had died or what sort of treaties had been signed after the Great War. In fact, the animosity had got worse precisely *because* of those wretched treaties.

Many of the men who stalked the corridors of power in Parliament were whispering about *another war* looming in the future: a need for Britain to protect itself *now*; to keep itself ready and alert; to collect weapons while it could.

'Another war!' gasped Posie, incredulous. 'I don't believe you for a minute! They said that the Great War was the war to end all wars!'

'*Who* said that?' asked the Inspector quizzically, a ghost of a smile playing around his lips. 'Were "they" the same ones who said that the war would be a short and glorious one? That it would be over by Christmas in 1914, when in fact it dragged on until 1918? Sometimes you have to get real, Posie. We both lost loved ones in that war, I know. I'm the last person to want another war, believe me. They don't think it's immediate, but it could escalate. It's a *potential* war on the horizon. In the near future.'

'Goodness! That's terrible.'

Lovelace nodded.

'Several months ago now an American engineer by the name of Dick Wainwright and two engineering colleagues of his from the United States approached the British government. They wanted to make serious money with some plans they had been working on: a blueprint for an aircraft which could drop bombs so efficiently that it quite took the breath away. They called it 'The Guillotine', as it promised certain death; precision bombing, one hundred per cent accuracy, on a vast scale. Nothing like it had ever been known before. Certainly the bombing campaigns of the Great War would pale into a disorganised, haphazard insignificance compared to what could be achieved by this monster. Whole areas could be annihilated.'

Posie gasped. 'What sort of scale are we talking about?'

'I'd say 'the Guillotine' was capable of bombing whole villages and parts of towns. Such a weapon in the hands of a country at war would mean that the other side would be put at a significant disadvantage. In fact, I'd go as far as to say that this new aircraft would be a game-changer: any country which had this blueprint of Dick Wainwright's in their possession would certainly win any war they felt like waging.'

Posie nodded, still shocked. 'Go on.'

'The British government spoke with Air Chief Marshall Trenchard, Head of the Royal Air Force, and he decided we simply *had* to have the plans: they were exactly what the Royal Air Force needed; he's all about strategic bombing. The government agreed and decided to pay the American engineers a whopping great amount for the blueprint of 'the Guillotine'. But then, after the money had been wired, on the evening that Dick Wainwright was due to deliver the plans to Whitehall, he was found, throat slit, in a seedy basement in a club in Soho. Needless to say, the plans for 'the Guillotine' which everyone assumed were in his satchel were well and truly missing. A search of his hotel room in King's Cross was fruitless too.'

'Yikes. And people – the British government – assumed they had ended up in Germany?'

The Inspector shrugged. 'Nobody knew where they had ended up. Perhaps in Germany or in Russia, maybe. Or in the hands of a spy. Or even with a criminal simply wanting to sell them to the highest bidder. The government is paranoid about spies just now: it thinks they're everywhere. The government were panicking, and hopping mad of course. They had just spent a huge amount of money on hot air and had received nothing in return. The plans for 'the Guillotine' were more precious to them than gold. *Are* more precious than gold.'

'And now you've found them?'

'This is where it gets interesting. The government was contacted a few weeks back by another, third American. Part of Wainwright's original small team. Apparently this third man had been threatened at the same time as Dick Wainwright and the second American who was in their team. But our fella ran and escaped with his life. He got away with the plans and managed to lie low; out of London, and out of the country. He's been biding his time but thought he was just about ready to get the plans back to Britain. He was wary of course; thought he was surrounded on all sides by enemies and people he couldn't trust. Asked for a further sum of money in cash and gold bullion; a fortune, as it happens, for putting his life in danger yet again. And the government, with MI5, agreed to it all. They'd virtually do anything to have those plans finally in their hands.'

'How much?'

'Forty thousand pounds. A fortune to anyone.'

Posie exhaled softly to herself in disbelief.

'So where are they now? The plans and this American chappie?'

The Inspector looked around furtively and came very close to Posie, whispering in her ear:

'The American went to France when Dick Wainwright was killed, and he stayed there. He's now made his way over the English Channel on a fishing boat; sailed single-handed. This was all planned out a few weeks ago, and it was arranged that the handover would take place at Maypole Manor, under cover of a party. It was the ideal spot; couldn't be better. We had word that the American arrived safely last night, fortunately. He's loitering in an old smuggler's cove.'

'Let me guess. The cove is below St Margaret's Bay?'

The Inspector nodded. 'I don't know his real name but when he comes to the party he'll be announced as Edwin Goodman. He'll be pretending to be an American who met Lord Glaysayer once on a safari in Africa.'

'Ah,' said Posie, understanding. 'Your "government" man?'

'The very same.'

Posie thought for a couple of seconds. 'What happened to the second American who was part of the original engineering team, sir?'

The Inspector nodded grimly. 'According to Edwin Goodman the second man scarpered after he got the frighteners put on him; when he saw what had happened to Dick Wainwright. The fella decided to return home to New York. Legged it. Out of the picture.'

'I see. And who is Edwin Goodman handing the plans over to? To you?'

Lovelace shook his head. 'Nope. Not likely. On the stroke of midnight Goodman will present the plans to Bryn

Cardinal, the MI5 chappie. The money is sitting in Robin Glaysayer's safe as we speak; it was put there yesterday by a trusted MI5 courier. So Mr Cardinal will simultaneously take the additional money that the government has promised to Edwin Goodman out of Robin Glaysayer's safe and they will do a direct exchange. I would imagine Mr Cardinal will get those plans speedily up to London tonight faster than you can say "knife".'

Posie frowned. 'So what's your part in all this? General assistance?'

'Essentially, yes. As soon as the plan was firmed up about Edwin Goodman dropping the plans off at Maypole Manor, MI5 requested Scotland Yard's presence on this project. They wanted Assistant Commissioner Scabbes but he's come down with influenza at the last minute so I'm the next best thing. Hence the last-minute nature of my involvement in the plan; I only got told yesterday, like you. So it will be me overseeing the handover at midnight. I'll have Sergeant Binny helping out at Maypole Manor too. You'll see him lurking around incognito, so don't act surprised when you see him.'

'Are we expecting trouble, sir?'

'I don't think so, but never say never. I think MI5 have rather over-egged the pudding; they're on the look-out everywhere for plots and spies just now. They have a huge budget, too. Hence your nice dress and my dapper outfit. But...' and the Inspector paused dramatically, 'this *is* a blueprint with a history of murder behind it. One fella we know about has already lost his life because of it, and another has just risked his life coming across a sea in the middle of winter. The blueprint seems to draw villains to it like a bear to a honey-pot, so it doesn't hurt to be on the look-out for any funny stuff, or anyone acting strangely. But I'll be pleased to get through the party and home again, by Golden Arrow, to Molly tomorrow night. Snow permitting, of course.'

'Mnnn. I see your point about the weather now. It could hinder Mr Cardinal on his way up to London with the plans. That's what you meant, sir?'

'Exactly. We'll want to get those plans safely to the Cabinet War Office and locked up as quickly as possible. Thank goodness the American has already arrived here safe and sound and hasn't been dragged off course or swept away with this wretched weather.'

'Does Mr Cardinal have any helpers with him?'

'I don't know. If he does, I think he'll be posing as a sort of "manservant," like Rainbird is.'

'Is Mr Cardinal here now, on this train?'

'He's driving down, so no. One last thing. I need you to help me by keeping your eyes and ears peeled for any funny business; I know that's what you do best so I'm confident in your abilities. Give me the nod if anything looks fishy. And if my position becomes jeopardised in any way at all there's a Police Constable, name of Cleghorn, who could help you in the next village, at St Margaret's-at-Cliffe. Lives above the Police Station, next to the Post Office. But you won't need to resort to that – there's a telephone at Maypole Manor – old Glaysayer had it installed in his study just earlier this year.'

The Inspector swallowed, a trifle nervously, Posie felt.

'Oh, and Posie. If *everything* goes wrong, if myself and Rainbird and Binny are somehow indisposed or got out of the way or whatever, I want you to contact Inspector Oats. Straightaway.'

'*What?* You've got to be joking, sir?'

Inspector Oats was an old adversary of Posie's; an old-fashioned and bumbling Police Inspector at the Yard who saw Posie as nothing but an interference. And that was putting it mildly.

'Why would I contact *him?*'

'He's the nearest you'll get to Scotland Yard down here in Kent. He's only twenty minutes' drive away. He's spending Christmas and New Year with his wife's relatives in Deal, at the Anchor Pub there; they own it. Probably had enough fish and chips to last him a lifetime by now. I'd imagine he'd be only too pleased to get away from them all. Just bear it in mind, okay?'

Posie mock shivered and then examined her new emerald ring. On second thoughts it wasn't half bad.

'I'm trying to forget you mentioned Inspector Oats already, sir. Too close for comfort and all that. Now, about those chocolates you promised me…'

****

Six

A third of the train passengers disembarked at the domestic side of Dover Marine Station, while the others got off at the next stop, in the Customs Hall, ready with their passports and tickets to catch the ferry to France.

Inspector Lovelace and Posie were first off and they hurried through the huge steel and glass vaulted building which was the Western Docks Reception Hall. The place was echoing and freezing cold, and all the smart booths selling newspapers and sweets were shuttered up for the New Year holiday. Several locomotives were parked up inside the huge building, and, devoid of passengers, they reminded Posie of ghost trains. The giant station clock was tolling two o'clock.

Sergeant Rainbird strode ahead of them purposefully on the platform, wheeling their luggage on a special trolley and pulling a rather reluctant Bikram along on his lead. The Inspector had his arm loosely around Posie and she didn't dare turn her head and look back along the platform to see who else had got off the train with them other than Amory Laine and her artist husband; who else might be going to Maypole Manor. They followed the 'EXIT' and 'TAXI' signs, walking up a curving set of wrought iron staircases which led to a very long glazed pedestrian walkway and the eventual exit.

'Mr Grosvenor, sir. I'll get us a motor cab, sir,' called out Rainbird.

'Fine, Perkins. You do just that. And look lively about it, please.'

When they reached the main exit outside they saw that the hail of the journey had turned into a slow whirl of snowflakes and the grey arc of Dover harbour, docks, pier and sea were blurring away to a gentle nothingness beneath a dancing white blanket. The stunning background of the famous White Cliffs and Dover Castle was absolutely nowhere to be seen; it too had disappeared under the weather, which was closing in quickly. Posie looked up at the louring sky with a sense of real foreboding which she tried to shrug off like a useless, thin coat.

'Ah! Here we are then!' said the Inspector thankfully as a gleaming black Ford motor taxi approached them on the kerb.

Posie jumped up onto the backseat quickly and Bikram followed suit. Inspector Lovelace gave a series of somewhat convoluted directions to the driver and it wasn't until the Inspector was sitting in the car beside her that she realised the whole thing was a clever sham, for a newly-moustached Sergeant Binny was at the wheel.

'Off we go, then!' she heard Binny say, only to look over at the concourse to see Amory Laine standing shivering under a big black umbrella, huddled against a tall man who must surely be her husband, both of them getting soaked by the snow. No-one else was around and there wasn't another motor cab in sight.

'So we *were* the only ones on the train going to Lord Glaysayer's party after all?' said Posie in surprise.

'Looks like it,' said Inspector Lovelace thoughtfully as their cab started to move off.

'Oh, dash it all. Stop! Wait a minute.'

Sergeant Binny brought the borrowed taxi to a standstill once more. The Inspector jumped out and ran over to where the film star was waiting. Posie strained to hear his words:

'Miss Laine? I wondered if you might be going to Robin Glaysayer's place at St Margaret's Bay? We've just enough room in our motor taxi if you want to squeeze in too. If you don't mind our dog, that is?'

'What does he think he's doing?' muttered Posie under her breath.

'Trying to look authentic,' hissed Sergeant Rainbird from the front passenger seat. 'And friendly.'

But the Inspector came hurrying back over, alone, rubbing his hands together for warmth and briskly slammed the door.

'Says she's got too much luggage. But I saw her giving Posie the evil eye. Little fool! You've made a friend for life there, Posie, and no mistake. Right, Maypole Manor here we come! We'll drive through St Margaret's Bay first. See the sea. Let's go.'

* * * *

The journey took twenty minutes and Binny drove, as usual, carefully and calmly, pulling over occasionally by the side of the road in order to wipe away the smears of snow from the windscreen with a bit of chamois leather. This was White Cliffs country, and as they drove further away from Dover, Posie saw how the flat, green landscape of the North Downs dipped and curved ceaselessly; framed magnificently in a big arc by the English Channel, which, between the snow flurries, was a tantalising occasional glimpse of silvery-grey. They zigzagged along the coast-road high up above the sea.

St Margaret's Bay was reached down a windy cobbled

road which ended abruptly at a remote shingle beach. The tide was in and huge grey waves broke over the shingle, making a colossal noise. There was a constant onslaught of seagulls screeching overhead. The place was deserted. The Inspector jumped out enthusiastically.

'Here we are, then! What we can see of it, anyway!'

Posie got out and stared through the snow flurry. The bay consisted of a small beach, about five hundred metres long, surrounded by steep white cliffs. Sharp, craggy, rocky ledges rose up at either end of the bay like a pair of enclosing hands, protecting or perhaps imprisoning you, depending on your mood. A new smart concrete promenade ran along part of the beach, with a fairly nice-looking hotel set back behind it, all shut up for the winter. Big piles of deckchairs and parasols were covered with green tarpaulins emblazoned with the words 'BAY HOTEL'. Despite the cold and snow, the bay was protected from the high winds which were causing such huge waves, and probably causing the boats out in the channel to be rocked around mercilessly.

Posie shivered and rubbed her hands for warmth. Bikram jumped down from the taxi, but, feeling the dropping temperature and a sudden jet of sea-spray, he turned and jumped back up onto the comfortable, warm leather seat. Posie wished she could join him. The two Sergeants sat inside the car, grinning.

'Bracing, isn't it?'

'It is, sir.' Posie tried to look enthusiastic. 'I see what you mean about it being a lonely spot, though.'

'Up there's the village.' Lovelace gestured, indicating far over from where they stood and up on the cliff. 'Took a bit of a battering at the end of the Great War actually. It was the last place bombs were dropped, right at the end of the war. Only just smartened itself up, by all accounts. But the place is a gem, you know. It enjoys a sunny, hot microclimate most of the time, and it's sheltered, with nice warm breezes and plenty of unusual flowers and such like. And this here's the "Bay Hotel". They do a roaring trade over summer, apparently. They can't keep up with demand. Sunbathing, prawning, dancing. A smart little place for the right sort of people.'

'Empty little place for no sort of people, it looks like to me, sir.'

'Mnnn, yes. Well, apparently they always catered for Christmas and New Year before the war, but since then it's been shut for the whole winter. Which suits our purposes nicely, of course. The fewer people around, the better.'

'If you say so, sir.'

'Over there,' the Inspector said, motioning to the clifftop on their left where a few rooftops could just about be discerned and a huge white lighthouse sat proudly atop the chalky summit, 'is St Margaret's-at-Cliffe. Nice little village for the smart set. Panoramic views over to France and lovely clifftop walks on a nice day. Beyond is the South Foreland Lighthouse.'

'Lovely, sir.'

'And over there,' the Inspector swung around and motioned to the cliff nearest Dover, the rising hulk of the thing in all its chalky splendour quite magnificent in a bleak sort of a way, 'is Maypole Manor. Atop that cliff. You can't really see the house from here, it's hidden by pine trees.'

Posie screwed up her eyes against the whiteness of the snowy light. But the Inspector was right; you couldn't see the house, just a flash of what looked like a white chimney pot and a dash of bright red.

'And there, at the very foot of the cliff is the cove.'

Posie glanced quickly at the Inspector and then over at the cove. It was a sheltered spot, dark and dingy and it looked from this distance like a few caves were burrowed around the place, with steep steps cut into the rock here and there. Several boats were tethered together; brightly coloured dinghies tied up with a rowing boat and even a couple of small old fishing boats. There was absolutely no-one about. Obviously Edwin Goodman, the American who had risked his life coming over the channel the day before, was lying low somewhere, perhaps in his boat or in one of the caves.

Posie nodded. She could feel her lips were turning blue. 'That everything, sir?'

'I think so. That covers everything in my notes, anyhow.'

'I thought you must have been here before, sir. You seem very enthusiastic about the place. So you just read about it?'

'That's right.' The Inspector opened the car door for her and gave one last reluctant look back at the English Channel.

'I love the sea and the seaside. Went to Margate every holiday as a child. But I just can't seem to get Molly interested in it. She says it's too cold. Too sandy. Too much fuss. I don't know what she's complaining about.'

Posie tried her best to look sympathetic, but failed. She could see exactly what Mrs Lovelace meant.

* * * *

Maypole Manor was surprising.

Posie didn't know what she had been expecting really. Something like Boynton Hall in the sleepy Cotswolds, the ancestral and ancient home of her boyfriend, Alaric Boynton-Dale. But as they approached Robin Glaysayer's house after having chugged up another steep and snowy cliff road from St Margaret's Bay, and having gone through a small wooded copse of pine trees, the house which appeared before them around a sharp bend looked very different from the usual English crumbling mansion.

For a start the house wasn't old. It looked quite new. It was spectacular in its modernity but somehow unfriendly-looking. It was very large and squat and symmetrical and although it was classically designed it was covered in white wooden cladding, like a house you might find in a book about America. Its doors and windows and roof tiles were all a blazing scarlet.

The house was the epitome of remote. Perched on top of the cliff it meant there were no neighbours at all. Behind the house rose a dark forest, and in front of it was a beautifully manicured lawn, set out in a classical style. Posie saw at once that the lawn ran down to the very edge of the perilous cliff edge, and presumably on a good day the view from the house was spectacular; endless uninterrupted sea. But today in the snow the eye was really drawn to the high red and white maypole in the very centre of the front lawn. Hundreds of glittery red ribbons were attached to the pole and were fluttering around wildly in the wind.

'Bit over the top, isn't it, sir?' said Rainbird amiably. 'I thought they only attached ribbons to those things when they actually used them for dancing; so just at Midsummer?'

'Looks like old Glaysayer has been using the thing as a sort of elaborate Christmas tree,' cut in Sergeant Binny from the driver's seat as he made a smooth job of negotiating the tight turning circle at the front of the house.

'Mnnn,' said Inspector Lovelace. 'Over the top might be a good way of describing our host, too. Now, everyone ready to get into character again? Posie, act up: cling to me; you're supposed to be my adoring wife, for heaven's sake.'

Posie gulped and nodded. She *would* have to act: there was certainly no real attraction on her side for the Inspector, nice man though he was. Apart from the fact that he was very happily married, he was simply too brotherly, too big and burly, too downright *gingery* for her tastes. He was also too secure, too *reliable*. Too steadfast. Posie had always been attracted to men you couldn't pin down, *restless* men.

She had also always aimed well out her league, and often been sore rewarded for it, too.

Why, even Harry Briskow, the handsome, kindly man she had been betrothed to at the time of his death in the Great War, had been a dreamer, given over to a certain amount of wanderlust; a man who longed for other shores, for hotter climes, for more than the quiet and sleepy Norfolk backwater of his solicitors' firm where he had first met Posie.

And then she thought briefly of Alaric, so absolutely *not* like the Inspector at all. The very opposite in fact. With his photogenically fine-boned face, his copper-coloured eyes, and his nonchalant slouch, his dishevelled good-looks sold newspapers whenever he just happened to be on the front page, which was often. Posie loved and loathed in equal parts Alaric's flightiness and itchy feet, his wanderer's soul...

Oh, Alaric. You and I were supposed to be spending New Year's Eve together. And now look at where I am, Posie thought to herself irritably.

But she didn't have time to let her thoughts roam far. She was brought back to earth by the Inspector, cutting in on her daydream:

'And Posie, stay focused, will you? We want this handover at midnight tonight to go as smoothly as possible. Got it?'

* * * *

The two Sergeants both melted away, taking Bikram with them. Bikram had started whimpering furiously at the front door to Maypole Manor and pawing the ground in a strange manner.

'I'll give him a walk and put him upstairs, Mrs Grosvenor,' said Rainbird meekly. 'Probably just been cooped up too long.'

And Posie and the Inspector found themselves stepping into a huge whitewashed hall which obviously served as a reception room for parties.

It was a beautiful space, light and bright and massive. But it was confusing on the senses. Stark white walls were entirely covered with hundreds of African animal heads, stuffed and mounted on great wooden plaques; a lion here, mid-roar; an elephant there, mid-bellow. A bevy of smaller creatures were represented too, and guarding the bottom of the great white wooden staircase which rose from the hallway was a stuffed Indian tiger, one paw raised, as if ready to strike. Taking all this in was hard enough, but mixed in with it, and through it, was a great deal of Scottishness: a blue and scarlet tartan carpet; tartan curtains at the huge windows; an extravagant Christmas tree, twenty foot high tied with matching tartan ribbons.

It was very hot. Glasses clinked and cutlery jangled as somewhere among the throng a Scottish bagpiper was playing. Scents of ocean mixed with Christmas spices, cut through with the unmistakeable scent of mothballs, and a slight edge of decay.

'Welcome, welcome! A good journey, I trust?'

Coming forwards expectantly to greet his newly-arrived guests, Posie recognised Lord Glaysayer from his photos in the newspapers, but he was older and much, much thinner than any picture she had seen him in. Still, to give him his due, he was doing a fine job of pretending to be in control of his own party. He was jollity itself.

He bowed a funny little bow when they introduced themselves:

'How perfectly charming! Come in. Come in, my dears. We are honoured by your presence. So glad you could make it to this little soirée of mine. We're all just having welcome drinkies and then you can retire to your rooms for a bit and rest. The real party starts at six o'clock.'

Lord Glaysayer broke off amid a great hacking cough

which bent him double. *Those rumours about his being ill would have been easily believed*, Posie thought to herself with a stab of shock, for Robin Glaysayer looked like a man with only days left to live.

Famously good-looking as a young man, the vestiges of the easy elegance were still there in the tall, upright man of seventy; in the languid way he moved his limbs, in the boyish grin and the thick shock of grey hair. But the vivid blue eyes which looked out from the dark sockets of a skull of a face were sad and knowing, and the deep creases and mahogany tan of his face caused by years of too much sunshine made him look sicker than if he had been lily-white.

In one hand Lord Glaysayer held a strange wooden pipe shaped like a long, thin face, out of which some horribly noxious smells were coming. He took a deep drag and then coughed and spluttered. Posie's eyes watered at the smell of the tobacco. She clutched at Inspector Lovelace's caped arm for dear life, thinking that she might vomit, which wouldn't have been the best of starts. Lord Glaysayer saw Posie's eyes watching him and a grin split his cadaverous face:

'Medicinal, my dear. Purely medicinal. Bush herbs from Saratonga in Madagascar. None better. Stops the wretched aches and pains. But don't get me started on that, eh? What can I offer you to drink, you gorgeous creature? A Mint Julep to match your lovely green dress? Or a Gin Rickey as sweet as your pretty face? JoJo, be a good girl. Can you do the honours, darling?'

Posie found herself suddenly swept away from the Inspector and being expertly divested of her coat and hat and handbag. Somehow a large and artificial-looking green drink had been fixed in her hand, together with a cigarette in a black ebony holder. Lord Glaysayer was slipping away fluidly among the mass of people in the entrance hall. Posie found herself standing almost right up against the poor stuffed tiger, at the bottom of the staircase, and she turned to whoever was placing things in her hands:

'Oh, but I really don't…'

'A light?' A match was struck from behind somewhere and Posie found her cigarette, a pastel-coloured Sobranie, being expertly lit for her by an unseen hand. She hated smoking but found herself wrong-footed somehow and she took an initial deep drag, then tried not to choke.

'I'm Jocasta Glaysayer. JoJo to my *friends*.' The girl with the light stepped forwards and turned to face Posie with a scornful look. She obviously didn't regard Posie as being worthy enough to become one of her friends; not in a million years.

'I'm Hildegarde Grosvenor,' Posie said, juggling her cigarette and drink and extending her hand, smiling. 'Most people call me Hilda.'

'Yes. I knew *exactly* who you were.' Jocasta nodded in a bored fashion, not bothering to shake hands, her eyes wandering off behind Posie in search of more interesting quarry. Posie kept smiling in a forced manner, inwardly surprised at the girl's rudeness.

She wondered if Jocasta really *did* know who she was, or whether her father had kept his mouth shut about the real identities of some of his guests this New Year's Eve. Hopefully he had done as instructed: the girl looked like a blabbermouth, and worse, a thrill-seeker. Jocasta's roving eyes returned to Posie and Posie noticed how the girl had peculiarly large, dilated pupils. Could her very strange manner be a result of using drugs? It seemed a possibility, in any case.

'There aren't so many of us here today, not like at my father's *normal* parties. Twelve in total. And only five women. You're the oldest of us, by the way. By far.'

Posie stood with her glass half-raised, taken aback, as if she had just received a physical body blow. She wanted to slap the girl hard; at not yet thirty she had not thought of herself as old just yet. And the girl in front of her was, as Inspector Lovelace had intimated, almost the same age. But Posie held her tongue and tried to stay in character: Hilda Grosvenor, that simpering would-be crime writer, would not have behaved so badly. She smiled blandly:

'Oh, right. I see.'

Jocasta Glaysayer was very tall and lean with a creamy skin. She had very long arms and legs and a prominently large roman nose. Her hair was cropped boy-short and dyed a strange bronze-green colour and her wide-spaced green eyes were coated in a sticky-looking gold glitter which didn't suit her. She wasn't pretty, but she looked like she tried hard, regardless. Jocasta wore false eyelashes and a bottle-green tweed suit and the overall impression was of a highly decorative stick-insect. Or perhaps…Perhaps a cat. Posie was reminded suddenly and unaccountably of Mr Minks.

'JoJo, lovey!' she heard Lord Glaysayer call out, between great hacking coughs. 'Can you come over here and welcome our celebrity!'

Jocasta was obviously her father's pet.

Turning in the direction she had just come from, Posie saw that Amory Laine and her husband had arrived at the house, and Jocasta Glaysayer left her side without another word, snaking her way over to where a small commotion now seemed to be erupting at the door.

Relieved, Posie breathed a sigh of relief and was about to put down her glass on a nearby table and stub out the cigarette in a convenient ashtray when a small voice piped up beside her:

'Awful, isn't she? I'm so sorry about her rudeness, Hilda. I heard every word. I'm Jacinta, by the way. Her sister. Well, sister by *adoption*.'

A small, very plump girl in her late twenties came forwards, smiling. Her defining characteristic was that she was all hunched over, disfigured somehow, as if she had spent her life trying to duck under small doorways.

'Let me take that off you. You don't smoke, do you? And I don't think a Mint Julep is quite your thing, somehow. Would you like tea, instead?'

Jacinta's face was freckled and round and plain as a sweet biscuit, with small blue eyes, and she looked like she belonged in the countryside somewhere, or in a cold Cornish fishing village by the sea, like a character from an old, old fairytale. She wore a bright red crushed-velvet cape over a dark black dress and on her head she wore an exotic blue silk scarf with tassels, completely covering her hair. She wore a good deal of bright gold jewellery and smelt strongly of a patchouli perfumed oil. In fact, she was all got up like a gypsy in a fun-fayre and Posie wondered if it was some sort of joke.

'I can't bear celebrities,' said Jacinta Glaysayer matter-of-factly. 'But I love Father dearly, and he adores celebrities, so I humour him at these events. He revels in it all; the fame, the glamour. Although of course this year it's different. Because he's sick, I mean, so we're a reduced number. But you'll see; this film star arriving just now will take ten years off him. Make him feel a darn sight better than that awful stuff he's smoking.'

'Is he very sick?' asked Posie innocently. Although any fool could see it.

'Oh, yes.' Jacinta nodded in her hunched up way, waving at a Butler with a tray of tea to come over. She moved uncomfortably. 'The doctors on Harley Street give Father six months. Brain tumour. But actually he's got six weeks. *If* that. He could even die tonight.'

'Oh?' Posie was shocked. But before she could delve deeper the Butler was upon them and Jacinta was offering Posie tea and taking several biscuits from a tartan-covered tray. Jacinta dismissed the servant with a quick flick of the wrist which caused umpteen tiny golden bracelets on her arm to ring and clatter like a wind-chime and a waft of overpowering patchouli oil to surge outwards into the space they occupied next to the tiger. Posie ate a couple of the shortbread fingers quickly and gratefully. She was warming to the girl at her side; anyone who preferred biscuits over a strong cocktail must be doing something right, even if they did smell a touch whiffy.

'Know anyone else here, do you, Hilda? No? I thought not. Let's put that right, then.'

Jacinta had obviously decided it was her place to give Posie a guided tour of the room and a who's who of the guests assembled there. Between bites of shortbread she indicated around the room with her many-ringed hand.

'You're almost the last to arrive, actually. I think we're just missing our American guest. So, that tiny little chap over there drowning in his fur coat is Duke Luca Del Angelo; barely speaks English but rich as Croesus and owns most of Italy, apparently. Very old family, *apparently*. He's the toast of London right now, everyone who is anyone is trying to get him to invest his money with them. The gorgeous creature at his side is his girlfriend; don't know her name yet to be honest, but JoJo knew her, or *of her*, to be more accurate. The fair chap over by the fireplace with his back to you in the tweed hunting suit is Mr Cardinal, some sort of big shot businessman from London; seems boring enough to my mind. The tall man in the black hat he's talking to is my father's German friend, Rudy Steinhauser. I've never met him before but I think he goes back to Father's days in German-owned Tanzania. Only decided to come down at the last minute; wired us yesterday. I haven't really bothered with him really if I'm honest; seems a bit of a sad case, and sad cases are always hard work, aren't they? You've already met Father, of course and my sister Jocasta. What do you think of her?'

Jacinta smiled strangely. 'Reminds you of a Siamese cat, doesn't she? Cool and aloof, and all chocolate and creamy. But I guess you know a thing or two about Siamese cats, don't you?'

The girl gave a seemingly innocent smile. And Posie almost dropped her tea, but managed a polite shrug. 'I don't know what you mean, Miss Glaysayer. I don't own a Siamese.'

'Oh? Really? My mistake. Sorry.'

How on earth did Jacinta Glaysayer know about Mr Minks?

Had she been told about their true identities by her father and then done some digging of her own? It seemed the most likely thing. Her heart thumping and desperately scanning the room for the Inspector, Posie cursed inwardly: now she was stuck here next to this dratted tiger, having to carry on this stupid charade with her cover blown. But Jacinta carried on regardless:

'JoJo is Father's darling girl, the orphaned baby of a German friend of his who died in Tanzania. Tanzania was all German back then, of course. They adopted her out there. JoJo's never done anything she was successful at, poor soul, for all her heaps of strange friends and parties which she throws here. She tried to run with the Bright Young Things for a while, but it didn't work out: she was too old. Right now she's trying to model at Harrods and Selfridges, but, even with all of Father's connections, she's not doing very well. She's too old for that, too, it turns out. Pushing thirty, so hence her nastiness about your age. She's trying to make herself feel better by comparing herself to anyone who happens to be older. Even in your case just a smidgen older, by just a couple of weeks. You're thirty this coming year, aren't you? This coming October? So you're a Libra…'

'Yes, but how on earth do you know that? I haven't…'

But Posie was interrupted again by Jacinta.

'And she's jealous of your pretty face too. You have a certain "something", don't you? We all saw how every man in here looked at you the minute you arrived, how they couldn't take their eyes off you. Well, JoJo saw that too.

Hates you for it. As does that silly little film star over there. She's flashing you a look of pure dislike even as we speak. It's not your fancy borrowed clothes, either. I suppose the thing is, you're an English rose, and natural, and some women, women like JoJo and Amory Laine, need acres of make-up and hairspray to make them look the part, and still they don't compare. It's very interesting.'

Posie was on her guard now. Almost scared. She had immediately sussed out what sort of a girl Jocasta Glaysayer was, but Jacinta was altogether more complicated. Dangerous, probably. For now she'd play it calmly.

'And what about you, Miss Glaysayer? Were you born out in Africa too?'

'Oh goodness, no. I'm the orphaned baby daughter of a couple of my father's labourers from up on his Highland Estate in Scotland; before he sold it, I mean. The Glaysayers had adopted Jocasta in Africa and then came home to Scotland for a brief visit. Jocasta was just a few months old at the time. It was good timing for me: my real parents had just died in a flu epidemic, and no-one wanted me. My *real* father was a grouse beater who lived in a damp croft, and my mother was apparently involved in magic, some sort of local witch, if you believe in all that stuff. And just look at the state of me! I was born this way, unfortunately, with bad scoliosis. It's got worse over time, too. So you can imagine that no-one wanted to touch me with a barge-pole; the local lot were superstitious and feared I'd give them the evil eye, that my mother's magic was coming out in me somehow, that I'd been cursed as a hunchback. I was destined for the foundlings' hospital in Glasgow, but Robin Glaysayer and my adopted mother saved me and took me away, and brought me up with Jocasta.'

The girl smiled in what seemed a bittersweet fashion.

'They raised us as equals, bless them; twins virtually. Although all that changed when our darling mother died, of course. Then Father couldn't help but show his favouritism to JoJo. He didn't have to hide it anymore.'

'Oh. I'm sorry. That must have been awkward for you.'

Jacinta shrugged good-naturedly and slurped the last of her tea. 'Oh, I don't really mind. *You* of all people must know how very famous men are, don't you? Explorers, adventurers… A law unto themselves. You can't expect them to follow normal rules, can you?'

'I'm sorry?'

How on earth could the girl know about Alaric? Virtually no-one did. Not even their close friends.

Was Jacinta with MI5, too? Spying the Inspector across the room Posie flashed a 'rescue me' look at him. He excused himself and began to weave through the other guests to get to her.

'Besides,' continued Jacinta, 'it's never been a real problem for me, anyhow. I live in London, really, as does JoJo. Neither of us is here that much. I only came back yesterday to help father prepare for this party, but JoJo just breezed in here a few hours ago, which is fairly typical of her. And another key difference between us is that *I* work; I earn my own money, and it's good money, too. Thankfully I don't live off Father's handouts, like JoJo does, as he's virtually broke. He's spent everything and more besides. JoJo often has parties here, and he always foots the bill. But no-one knows the parlous state of his finances except me. I came across some incriminating bank accounts a while back, questioned him and he confessed everything. But he told me to keep it a secret.'

'Golly!' Posie swallowed uncertainly. She didn't ask *why* Jacinta was telling her her family secrets; people often did this and she had got used to it happening.

'And between you and me, even though JoJo is Father's sole heir and is getting this house all for herself under Father's Will, it won't make a blind bit of difference that he hasn't left me anything; he's done me a favour actually. This house is mortgaged up to the hilt and all dear JoJo will be left with is the hassle of selling the place and settling a lot of debts! But she doesn't know that she'll inherit Maypole Manor yet, nor the fact that it's mortgaged, nor how bad Father's finances really are. And Father doesn't realise I know the contents of his Will, either. He'd left that lying around in his study recently, too. I just happened to have a look. A shame for them both, isn't it?'

Jacinta laughed and Posie found herself clutching at the open mouth of the tiger in a wild panic.

'I'd be careful, Hilda, about where you put your fingers, if I were you. Poor Bobbie the Bengal Tiger has had his mouth and teeth impregnated with a good strong dose of arsenic just lately. Father told me yesterday, and told me to tell everyone I spoke to, to keep well away. He said it would be enough to kill a small army…'

'I beg your pardon? I think I may have misheard. Did you say *arsenic?*'

'Mnnn, that's right. He had some horrid wormy infestation. Been blitzed with arsenic by the best restorative taxidermist around these parts; he was up here just a few days ago apparently. It was that or poor Bobbie was going to be put on the bonfire. Careful of your hands. I'd wash them if I was you.'

Was the girl mad? Or was she also employed by the government's intelligence agency and therefore privy to all sorts of secret knowledge?

Inspector Lovelace was suddenly at Posie's elbow holding a Gin Sling in one hand and a cup of strong tea in the other. Posie knew instantly that not a drop of the alcohol would pass Richard Lovelace's lips, but that he was too professional to make it obvious.

'Jimmie, darling!' Posie exclaimed in relief. 'This is Jacinta Glaysayer, Lord Glaysayer's daughter. My husband, James.'

The Inspector smiled, the very essence of charm itself.

Jacinta shook hands. 'Our very own King's Counsel. But you know, I love a man in uniform. Shame you're not in yours today, Mr Grosvenor.'

She smiled innocently. 'Please forgive me, I'd better circulate. As usual, Father thinks Jocasta will be a good hostess, but it's yours truly who needs to go around checking everything is in order. I hope to see you later, when the party really begins.'

Jacinta waddled away on her dumpy little legs, twisted over, leaving an impression of flapping blue silk scarves and a heavy scent of oil trailing behind her.

'She knows who I am!' hissed Posie under her breath at Inspector Lovelace. 'Even knows my star sign and all about my borrowed clothes. Even knew about my cat and about my going out with a famous man! She must know my real identity. And what was all that to you just now about men in *uniform*! She must know you're a policeman!'

The Inspector continued to smile calmly.

'I'm pretty certain she doesn't know your real name and real details, and that's what counts, Posie. Sorry, I should have told you before but to be honest I didn't place much importance on it at the time...'

'What?' hissed Posie. 'Importance on *what*? That she works for MI5 too?'

'Not likely. The woman is a clairvoyant. I think it's Jacinta who uses the Maypole here, decorates it and such like. She has a lucrative little practice for herself on Lamb's Conduit Street in London, too. Quite well known, in fact. I gather she even writes a column for The Associated Press. "Mystic Mirabelle", I think she calls herself. Or something like that.'

'*Mystic Mirabelle's Magical Mondays*? But I know about her! Prudence is always reading out that wretched column! Load of rubbish I always tell her. As for the Horoscopes she writes, well! What a load of nonsense! All made up!'

'Is it, though?' asked the Inspector mildly. 'You seem

pretty spooked by whatever it was that she said to you.'

He started to move Posie gently away from the tiger. 'Let's go and meet some other guests.'

And he led Posie towards the man he had been speaking to, over at the centre of the room by the main fireplace, where a cosy trio of sofas had been set up in a horseshoe shape around the skin of a long-dead zebra.

'Darling, this is Count Luca Del Angelo.'

The man stepped forwards and smiled a cold toothy grin.

'Enchanted to meet you.'

He was in his late thirties, dark and oily and hideously ugly. He barely came up to Posie's shoulder. Posie saw that he was wearing some specially made stacked-heel shoes, and without them he would have been miniscule. He wore a ridiculously out-of-place thick fur coat and his sparse black hair was gelled up in spikes. On his hands he wore several gold rings, heavy with large gemstones. He gave the appearance of some sort of gaudy hedgehog, and the effect would have been comical but for the alert expression which remained on the man's face, and his watchful, deeply set eyes which glittered menacingly, never once leaving Posie's face.

'And this is his girlfriend, Lehni Brandenberger. My wife, Hilda.'

But just then Posie's world felt like it was falling apart. For here in front of her was a girl she knew.

A girl Posie wouldn't have trusted with her life.

But the girl happened to be in disguise too.

* * * *

Seven

Rats.

Would the girl blow Posie's cover and cause the Inspector's plan to come tumbling down around their ears?

For a horribly long minute the two women stared at each other in well-concealed shock.

And then the very tall girl in front of Posie blinked slowly, took the initiative and reached forwards, extending long fingers with navy-tipped fingernails.

'A pleasure. Hilda, did you say your name was?'

She was safe!

Posie nodded dumbly, clutching at Inspector Lovelace's arm, all the while her brain whirring. *Lehni. Lehni Brandenberger.* A German name. Was that her real name or was that as artificial as her appearance just now?

For this was Lenny, a girl she had met earlier in the year out in Luxor, in Egypt. The girl gushed on enthusiastically:

'What a funny house this is, isn't it? And all these African animal heads, too. So strange and exotic. Now there's a place I'd love to visit – Africa! Imagine. But sadly for me I've never left these shores. I'm just *dying* to travel.'

'Oh? Really?'

The girl was lying her head off. As far as Posie knew, Lenny had travelled enough to give Phileas Fogg a run for his money.

Lenny was a professional photographer, and had been part of the British Museum's small team working on a cutting-edge archaeological discovery in Egypt during the summer. Posie had known the man in charge, Harry Redmayne, and she and Alaric had spent time on the dig back in July. One of only a handful of women out in Luxor, Lenny had struck Posie as the ultimate professional. She was talented and charming, but a hard-worker, too; keen to show off her portfolio of pictures to the many world-renowned archaeologists who were gathered in Luxor.

But there was something about Lenny which had made a lasting impression on Posie at the time. It came down to the fact that Lenny couldn't be entirely trusted. She was a girl possessed of a certain ruthlessness, who didn't care how many victims she trampled over in her quest to get exactly what she wanted. Alaric hadn't liked Lenny much either, and had muttered on about how Lenny would most likely 'sell her own grandmother' to get her own way. Indeed, when tragedy had struck out on the dig, Lenny had melted away, unable or unwilling to offer help or assistance, concerned only with her own safety and the preservation of her portfolio of work.

'I was just telling your husband that the Duke and I rode the motorcycle down here from London. We had a good journey but we skidded around a bit on the icy roads, didn't we, Luca? Good job we arrived in time though; the cliff road up here will be pretty impassable in an hour or so if the snow carries on like this.'

Posie nodded. 'It will certainly be cosy, then. Won't it?'

She tried not to stare. The Lenny Posie had known had been blonde and tanned; sportily-dressed and ridiculously healthy-looking. The woman in front of her had translucent lily-white skin, and her hair was dyed a pre-Raphaelite red, shorn short like a boy but with the occasional swirling tendril artfully cut to frame her face. She was edgily beautiful, with a tremulous elegance which someone like JoJo Glaysayer could never hope to achieve.

Her trouser suit was a very dark blue velvet, cut impeccably to skim the body, and Posie spied the tiny, tell-tale 'H' of the House of Harlow, sewn, like her own dress, into the collar. Sapphires flashed at Lenny's earlobes and Posie noticed that the very tall girl had taken to wearing flat blue velvet pumps to complement her tiny companion. These were also sewn with that significant 'H'. So Lenny had money, then; serious money.

Lenny came forwards and fingered the collar of Posie's dress in a way which was instantly too familiar and yet utterly charming.

'Oh! That's too, too funny. We share a designer, don't we? I'm just mad about your collar. It looks like you could hide secrets in there…'

But what was Lenny doing here now, dressed as someone else and on the arm of a tiny, ridiculous Italian Duke? But she was obviously playing along with Posie's disguise, too. So for the moment Posie bluffed it out. Posie turned to the Duke.

'I simply adore Italy. Where is it you hail from, sir? I was just there earlier this year, in July.'

'On 'oliday?' The Duke flashed his toothy grin and chewed on the end of a fat cigar, his words heavily accented, barely distinguishable from each other.

'Sort of. I was in Sicily, mainly.'

'Ah, yees? I expect you ate a lot of cakes, huh? Especially the big cream ones? After all, Sicily is the home of the sfogliatella, huh?'

Posie gulped down her anger at the man's rudeness, blaming his insinuations on the language barrier: after all, she wasn't *that* plump. She focused instead on his error:

'I'm sorry? You mean the cannoli, don't you?' Posie was about to continue when the Duke gesticulated at the Inspector.

'I think your 'usband he stayed at home, no? You look like the sorta couple who 'oliday apart, somehow. So you was all alone there, huh?'

What a funny question, and impertinent too.

Posie had been working actually, on a full-blown assignment. She frowned, then decided to stick as near to the truth as she could. *Strange little man*, she thought to herself. *Tread warily. I feel like he's interrogating me.*

'I met up with some old friends in Sicily. My husband was busy working, weren't you, Jimmie, darling? He couldn't accompany me.'

The Inspector mock-grimaced: 'No rest for the wicked. Or so they say.'

The Duke raised a straggly dark eyebrow in disbelief. 'I thought lawyers 'ad the summer vacation off, Meester Grosvenor? All a' the courts are closed. Even I, an Italian, know this. So why you not go on the 'oliday with your priddy liddle wife 'ere, huh?'

The Inspector guffawed. 'Someone had to watch the Nanny, dear Duke. Otherwise our little daughter Lucy would have run rings around her.'

Posie felt nervous and on edge; was it possible that this strange man knew their real identities, too? The man seemed to listen intently to everything which was said and then to simply throw another question back at them. In fact, so far all he had done was to ask questions. Posie got suddenly angry. The Duke hadn't answered *anything* she had asked him at all. It all seemed highly suspicious.

Was he really a Duke, or was he as fake as the fake Lenny who stood between them, puffing her way nervously through umpteen gaspers? What was going on?

'You didn't tell me, Duke. Where is it you come from exactly?'

'The Veneto. In ze north. That is where my family castle is. My family is very, very old. You ever been?'

'No. And were you ever in Sicily? You didn't say.'

The Duke looked at Posie with his head cocked on one side. He reminded her of a particularly vicious robin. 'No. I was never there. Not enough going on for my tastes. Too 'ot, too dry, too boring. Too many *idiot* tourists.'

'Is that right?'

Posie felt even angrier and was forgetting to be polite. She felt a sharp and well-placed dig in her ribs.

Just then the man from German Tanzania, Mr Steinhauser, approached their group: the twelfth man, whose name had been as unknown to Inspector Lovelace as to Posie on the train ride down. Introductions were made all round.

Mr Steinhauser was probably in his late sixties and the very essence of charm itself. He was very tall with a long arching nose and he stooped over, as if trying to look shorter than he was; less conspicuous. Next to the tiny Duke he looked strangely out of proportion. Up close, his most noticeable features were his very sore, red eyes which seemed to run continuously, as if he had a bad case of conjunctivitis, and Posie decided to herself that this could be the reason the man continued to wear his foreign-looking black felt hat in the house, to hide his affliction.

Mr Steinhauser downed what looked like a Gin Sling in one easy go, and then his watery eyes came to rest curiously on Posie, as if she was the very reason he had come to the party.

She noticed how his large hand with its expensive and shiny wristwatch shook as he held his empty glass.

If I didn't know better, Posie thought to herself with a stab of surprise, *I'd say this man is nervous*. Posie was conscious of Inspector Lovelace goggling at something and she hoped whatever it was would prove interesting. She smiled fixedly.

'I understand you know our host from your days out in Tanzania, Mr Steinhauser. When your country still owned it? That must have been an interesting time for you.'

Posie gestured around the walls, at the stuffed animal heads with their many teeth on display.

'And tell me, did you amass a collection such as this?'

The man laughed. 'I hate to disappoint you, Mrs

Grosvenor, but no; I don't have such a collection. They are not to my taste. Remarkable, for sure, but not for me. Me, I think I would find it difficult to sleep at night, going past so many dead and dusty things up the staircase on my way to bed, reproaching me for killing them. Not to mention I don't think I'd find a maid who would put up with the dusting of all of them in my flat in London.'

When the man spoke it was with the clipped, polite accent of a German who has learnt and spoken English for many years as his main language, the residual accent a mere nuisance.

'I'm going to scrounge a Turkish cigarette. Excuse me, please,' muttered Lenny darkly and she wandered off and plonked herself down on the sofa nearest the fire. Her little Duke followed and out of the corner of her eye Posie watched them help themselves to gaspers from a glass cigarette box on the low coffee table and start to look at a notebook which the Duke had extracted from his coat pocket, ticking things off as they spoke.

Mr Steinhauser looked round the room, fixing his gaze on Jocasta Glaysayer for a couple of seconds and then turning back to Posie again.

'Besides, Mrs Grosvenor, I am afraid that whoever you spoke to about me has done you a disservice. For they were wrong. I *was* in Tanzania, with Glaysayer. That much is true. But I am Swiss, not a German.'

'Oh? Goodness!' Posie's heart had started hammering hard in her chest and she was conscious of clamping the Inspector's arm to her in a vice-like grip.

Swiss.

The man was Swiss!

The only Swiss man Posie had ever met had been earlier that year: an arch-villain who Posie never wanted to have the misfortune of meeting ever again. His name had been Caspian della Rosa. Was it pure coincidence that one of the guests at this strange little dinner party was Swiss, too?

Get a grip, she told herself. *Don't be ridiculous!* There must be a million, perhaps even millions of Swiss people. *Of course there is no connection.*

'You sound surprised at my being Swiss, Mrs Grosvenor?'

'Oh, no. Not really. It's just that I met a Swiss man in February this year, that's all.'

The man smiled his watery smile. 'Ah? You think I might know him? We are a relatively small country; that much is true. But we do like to get about and leave now and again. I left for several years, in fact, to make money abroad. So it's unlikely I know your man. But you never know. What was his name?'

Posie felt the dig in the ribs again.

'Oh. Golly! I'm such an airhead! I can't remember it now. Sorry.'

The Inspector groaned beside her in a good humoured way. 'My wife can never remember *anything*, Mr Steinhauser. Don't mind her!' He pointed chummily at Mr Steinhauser's wrist.

'I should have known you were Swiss. That beauty's a Rolex watch, isn't it? I've never seen such a spectacular thing in all my days. Brand new, isn't it? I've read all about that little company. Ruddy fine business model. Maybe when I'm awarded my Judgeship next year I'll have to make a special trip out to Geneva and treat myself to one. What do you say, Hilda, darling?'

'I say that sounds wonderful, darling.'

Mr Steinhauser had shrugged with embarrassment at the display of enthusiasm over his watch, almost trying to cover it up with his shirtsleeve. He was looking curiously at Posie again, and she had to stop herself from shuddering visibly. It seemed that the guests at this New Year's Eve party were turning out to be more complicated than Posie could ever have imagined.

And just as she opened her mouth to start talking about Africa again with Mr Steinhauser, she caught sight of the man in the hunting suit, the MI5 man, Bryn Cardinal. He was casually weaving his way through the entrance hall, a full glass of green drink held aloft in one hand, a smoke in the other. Mr Cardinal was a tall, fair, bulky figure with a large head and a meaty, florid complexion. He had a piercing gaze and a vivid scar the length of a man's fist running down the length of his left cheek. Altogether he was not at all attractive, but he gave off an impression of sheer physical power, and Posie felt comforted by his presence, somehow.

Mr Cardinal glanced around the room to check no-one was looking and then he winked at the Inspector, tapping his wristwatch and indicating upwards, to their bedrooms. *He wants a meeting.*

Posie felt Lovelace stiffen very slightly beside her and raise his glass just a little in response, but barely perceptibly, so Mr Steinhauser wouldn't notice anything. Mr Cardinal disappeared out of sight around a bend in the staircase.

A clock was striking four from somewhere deep in the house. Suddenly a cacophony of noise started up.

'Everybody! This is the best game! Go grab an animal. The scarier the better! Fight to the kill!'

Turning, they saw that Lord Glaysayer and his daughters were following the strange sight of Amory Laine and her husband who were running amok with a pair of stuffed antelope heads, staging a mock battle with interlocking horns. The couple were obviously already raucously drunk and found their own antics hilarious, but while Lord Glaysayer and Jocasta were looking on in amusement and perhaps admiration, Jacinta's pale face was set as stone, an expression of utter mutiny sketched there.

'Darling,' said the Inspector, smiling. 'I'm not sure I can bear the thought of locking horns with you in such an obvious way. At home over dinner every night is quite enough for me. Shall we retire before we find ourselves partaking in such sport?'

Posie nodded, thankful to disappear and she signalled for a housemaid to show them up to their rooms.

Their bedrooms were on the first floor at the very front of the building. They were each painted a dazzling white with whitewashed timber ceilings. There were flashes of tartan here and there and other than that they were fairly spartan; furnished only with a double bed apiece and a chest of drawers topped with a pitcher of water and basin and a box of Pears antiseptic soap. The rooms were joined together by a small white-painted sitting room suite in between. The interlocking suite also served as a sort of dressing room, and Rainbird had unpacked some of their clothes there, for appearances' sake. He stood mutely folding things as Posie thanked the housemaid and gave her a tip. They all waited a few seconds until after the maid had left, listening to her clear ringing footsteps retreating on the bleached wooden floors of the upstairs landings.

'Better be careful. The trouble with new buildings like this one is that they have thin walls and doors. Speak softly. And remember, walls have ears.'

The Inspector threw himself into a studded leather easy chair, throwing off his spectacles and tugging at his grey-dusted hair. Rainbird put the clothes down in neat piles and came and sat on the chaise longue, notebook at the ready, while Sergeant Binny appeared in the nick of time, holding Bikram's lead.

'Just had time to walk Bikram for a few minutes, Miss Parker. He's not a happy camper, that's for sure. But he's in your room safe and sound now.'

The Inspector looked at them all slowly before taking out the same blue legal notebook he had been using earlier on the train.

'Time for a debrief, folks. Just between ourselves. Let's compare notes before MI5 get here.'

* * * *

Eight

'Why all the secrecy, sir? That chap Cardinal will be along any minute. He called the meeting! And he knows better than us what's happening here.'

'Oh, Posie.' The Inspector smiled wryly at her. 'You know how it is. Have you met a detective yet who likes to be told what to do by someone higher up the food chain?'

Posie smiled. It was true. At the end of the day, just like her, Inspector Lovelace was a lone wolf. It was very hot in the sitting room and she wiped the beads of sweat off her face.

'Besides, these MI5 men always think they know best. I want to get my house in order before I'm told what to do.'

'But you look worried, sir,' said Rainbird, chewing the end of his steel-tipped pencil. 'Anything the matter?'

The Inspector frowned. 'Yep. I don't think this is quite the walk in the park that Assistant Commissioner Scabbes was expecting this to be, or told me it would be. I feel wrong-footed somehow. I think we might be dealing with an *imposter*.'

'You mean the so-called Duke?' asked Binny, stroking his moustaches. Posie was about to break in about knowing Lenny from before, but the Inspector hurried on:

'Yes. I'm concerned as to his motive in being here. I

don't give two hoots if he lives in a make-believe world for the thrill of it and simply fancied a toot down to a country party, as long as he steers well clear of the arrangements we've put in place at midnight. We need to check on his background.'

Lovelace carried on angrily. 'The man's a fraud. I'm sure of it. His accent is just too over-the-top and theatrical to be real. It comes and goes. He's no more a Duke than I'm Fred Astaire. But somehow he's got the whole of London eating out of his hand. Why the blazes didn't MI5 think he was suspicious? They told me they had "cleared" him and that he was legitimate. But I don't believe it for a second! He's a ruthless sort of fellow, for all his ridiculous looks. Cut through Posie like he was interrogating her, refused to answer any questions unless he really had to. And he knew a darn sight more about the British legal system than some mouldy old Italian Duke who never needed to use it. Fishy with a capital "F". And why didn't he take off that wretched fur coat? This house is swelteringly hot. It's my guess he's wearing some sort of holster with a pistol loaded up underneath it, ready to go.'

'A member of this so-called Mafia, living in England, sir?'

'That would be my guess, yes. Question is, is he here for the blueprint, too? Or is he simply enjoying New Year's Eve? My understanding is that he and his partner were members of old Glaysayer's *original* guest list. So what's his game?'

Posie nodded in agreement. 'I think he's a fraud. I'd wager our "Duke" has never been to Italy in his life. I've never yet met an Italian who didn't know that *cannoli* are the typical sweets of Sicily; not *sfogliatella*, as the Duke mentioned, although both are filled with ricotta; so perhaps he just remembered the wrong one, but it's dashed odd. I think he simply didn't know. He's sketchy on the Italian details, hence his panic when I asked him about Sicily and then his subsequent cross-examination of me. I agree, I think he's dangerous. Not to mention exceedingly rude.'

'Shall I telephone the Yard, sir, for further background checks?'

The Inspector nodded. 'Yes, right away, Binny. The "Duke" has such a distinctive appearance that it won't be difficult for them to dredge up the criminal files. Call the Italian Embassy for information, too. Thanks. And good work in there too. You were such a professional Butler that I swear I forgot it was you after a couple of minutes.'

'Binny! You dark old horse! You were serving us drinks?'

'I was, Miss. But I was *observing* mainly. It was useful. I overheard several interesting tit-bits, like how that moth-eaten tiger's mouth has been spiked with arsenic.'

'*WHAT?*'

Posie explained to Rainbird and the Inspector who both looked on in utter disbelief. Binny continued calmly:

'And I also observed that the girlfriend of our little Duke slipped something down your, er, your, erm, your *top*, Miss. You might want to check.'

'I beg your pardon?' Posie was astounded. She turned away from the men and fished down her front in a rather embarrassed fashion, hearing a slight rustle of paper in among the silk and tweed of her dress. She pulled out a fine cigarette paper, folded in half.

She suddenly remembered something Lenny had said to her earlier: '*I'm just mad about your collar. It looks like you could hide secrets in there…*'

Posie unfolded the paper nervously and read what it said.

PLAY NICELY, DARLING.

DON'T BREATHE A WORD.
I WON'T IF YOU DON'T.

'*Rats!*'

She passed the note over to the Inspector and explained who Lenny really was, telling him everything she knew about the girl.

'I was just about to tell you, sir. I promise. It was jolly awkward out there, actually. I swear I have no idea what her game is, sir. Lenny's created a whole new persona for herself. But somehow the stakes must be very high if she's wanting to bluff it out, too; to not reveal my true identity. I was going to suggest you telephone to the British Museum and ask them for more information on her. It seems likely that "Lenny" is another version of "Lehni" but I never knew her surname before, so I can't tell you if the current "Brandenberger" is real or fake. But it's a German name, isn't it?'

The Inspector groaned, his head in his hands. 'This isn't good, Posie. Not good at all. I'll get Binny to telephone the Museum but to be honest I'm not hopeful of our chances in hearing back. It's New Year's Eve, and a Saturday to boot! Even if we reach Kenyon, the Director of the Museum at home he's not going to know off the top of his head the details about one of his itty-bitty photographers who probably only works there very occasionally. What a bally mess! Goodness! Why wasn't this woman vetted properly?'

'Probably just because she was on the *original* guest list, sir,' hazarded Rainbird.

The Inspector was checking his notebook:

'Find out if Lehni Brandenberger has a German connection, Sergeant Binny. Where her interests lie. *If* anyone bothers to respond, that is. I wouldn't normally be so biased based on a name alone, and heaven knows I have nothing against the Germans; why, my best friend, Inspector Rudy Spritz, is German, but our Lehni Brandenberger has proven herself to be dodgy from the outset. Would you say she was capable of being mixed up in some crazy plot to steal the blueprint, Posie?'

Posie puffed out her cheeks. It was so hot. 'Golly. She'd

definitely be capable of being involved in *something* to further her own gains, but I wouldn't like to say if that would include threats to national security.'

Just then an almighty creaking noise erupted from the wall. All four of them stiffened and looked around the room warily. Binny and Rainbird moved along the walls, checking for hidden cupboards, and the Inspector checked the windows and the fish-eye spyhole in the main door.

'Must be the timbers settling into place in this wretched heat. No-one is around. But better safe than sorry.'

The Inspector nodded at Binny and he made as if to move off, glancing over the details in his notes.

Posie cut in quickly, looking at Lovelace. 'Before Binny leaves, can I ask him to check on a couple of others? *Two* other people, actually.'

'Fire away.'

'Talking of Germany, and German-sounding names, I think you'd better check the background of Mr Steinhauser. I don't trust him. Your information was wrong, sir. Lord Glaysayer didn't ask him here as some old friend, desperate for company! It was the other way around. Jacinta told me that Mr Steinhauser got in touch with Lord Glaysayer about coming here for this party. And he only wired them *yesterday*, so his staying here is totally last-minute, and totally suspicious. The man has got a different motive for being here to everyone else, but I'm not sure yet if that involves stealing your bomber plans or not. He's a fake, too, I'm sure of it.'

'So what do you think?'

'Perhaps he's a German spy, not Swiss, as he claims. Jacinta seemed to think he was German, and we wouldn't know the difference, sir, would we? We're not experts on Germanic accents, and we haven't seen his identity papers. The way he looked at me gave me goose bumps all over. Did you see?'

'Mnnn. But maybe he just fancied you, Posie.' The

Inspector raised his eyebrows and laughed. 'It wouldn't be the first time you've attracted attention from an unlooked-for quarter, would it? Besides, you can't go around throwing the book at anyone who happens to be Swiss. It's not a crime. There are more than three million Swiss people, you know. And watch it. You nearly gave yourself away there; you were about to mention Caspian della Rosa's name to a total stranger! Remember, della Rosa is a criminal mastermind and he's out there, at large. You don't want to go advertising your personal connections to all and sundry. Besides, I was told that MI5 had been informed of Steinhauser's presence. All good.'

'Yes, but they don't seem to have been very thorough with the others, do they? There are several dodgy types hanging about. If you don't mind my saying so, sir.'

'Fine, add him to the list of checks at Scotland Yard, Binny. And call the Swiss Embassy to confirm he's a citizen of theirs. Was there someone else?'

'Yes. JoJo Glaysayer. She's a German by birth. Turns out she was born to a German out in Africa. What if she's been "got at" and is sympathetic to Germany's cause? Perhaps she's aiding and abetting someone who will break in and steal the plans? Or maybe she plans to steal them herself? She's certainly foolish enough. And I got the impression she might need the money; she seems to give a lot of parties and leads an extravagant life, mainly on her father's handouts. I think she might be hooked on drugs, too.'

Lovelace huffed and puffed but then waved in acquiescence at Binny, who left the room, telephone-bound.

'Goodness. Next we'll be running checks on Amory Laine. Not that we need to: she's still a cocaine-head if today's little performances are to be believed.'

'*Still* a cocaine-head, sir?'

The loud creaking sound came from the wall again, and all three of them turned in dismay and stared around the place. Through the thin wall Bikram had stared barking crazily in Posie's room, but after a few seconds all was well again.

Inspector Lovelace shrugged.

'There were rumours about her having quit the drugs. But as I said, *rumours*. That's all.'

The door to the sitting room clicked open and shut almost imperceptibly. It was Mr Cardinal, his back against the door and his hat scrunched into his hand.

'*Who* is a cocaine-head?' he whispered in a plummy, educated voice, his eyebrow raised mock-seriously.

Inspector Lovelace smiled and explained, and all the while Posie stared. In a room packed with people, Posie would have realised straightaway that Bryn Cardinal was in charge of proceedings. Power pulsated off him in waves and Posie felt a tingling shiver of – what was it – excitement? attraction? admiration? – running down her spine. She told herself to get a grip. Mr Cardinal seemed familiar, too: had she seen him before?

Was it just possible that he had been the tall man staring at her in Piccadilly earlier today, before she caught her train? Sussing her out? The man was a spy, after all.

'Bryn Cardinal. Pleasure to meet you all. Sorry to be so late. I had something urgent to attend to.'

He turned to Posie and nodded. 'And Miss Parker, might I just say it's a real pleasure to have you on board. Thank you for stepping in at the last minute and sacrificing your own New Year's Eve. I am of course aware of your Detective Agency, and some of your cases have come to my attention this last year; good work all round. So thank you for your time and expertise.'

Posie nodded, the praise warming her and encouraging her. She felt a red flush of pride in her cheeks and hoped that the others would put it down to the heat alone. Mr Cardinal sat down in another studded leather club chair and crossed his legs. He drew out a black leather notebook and a cheapish red fountain pen. He opened the notebook to a particular spot where a neat diagram and accompanying table took up a good two pages.

'So, to keep you updated, our American friend Goodman isn't here yet,' Mr Cardinal said, glancing around, alert. 'But that's not a cause for worry. We agreed on six o'clock as an arrival time and that works perfectly as the guests will be gathering downstairs again for the party to begin.'

'We know he got here okay, though?'

Mr Cardinal nodded, frowning slightly. 'Sent word to us yesterday. He's hiding out at the cove. That should be in your information pack there, Inspector?'

'Oh, it is,' said Lovelace quickly, flushing red. 'I just wondered if you had heard anything from him *today*, that's all?'

'Nope. We have to trust that this boy's a professional and when he says he'll be somewhere, that means he'll be somewhere.'

Not if he's already dead, thought Posie grimly to herself. But she kept it to herself.

A brisk knock at the door was followed almost immediately by Sergeant Binny's hurried entrance. He looked very worried and a heavy frown hung over his normally jovial features.

'Sergeant? Everything okay?'

'No, sir,' said Binny slowly. 'I'm afraid it's not. I went to make the telephone calls, as we discussed, only to find that the telephone is totally out of order. The snow must have brought down the wires. I went to find Lord Glaysayer to see if he knew anything about it, and he didn't. Came as news to him. The man's quite put out about it; seems very nervous.'

'Hell's bells!' cursed Mr Cardinal, and Posie saw his face darken with worry for a brief second. 'That's all we need!'

Posie found herself wondering if this was about as angry as the man got, ever. Inspector Lovelace sighed, almost imperceptibly.

'Well. That's not very handy, I agree. But no point old Glaysayer, or ourselves, getting worked up about it. Perhaps the telephone equipment will work again later? But we need those background checks made. Rainbird, can you get yourself off to the Post Office in the village and send telegrams? Binny will be needed soon to act as Butler again, so he'll have to stay. If they're closed get the Police Constable to open the place up. He lives above the shop, I'm told.'

Sergeant Rainbird pulled aside one of the blue tartan sitting room curtains and watched the snow whirling in the howling wind outside. It was almost totally dark. He nodded and turned to Inspector Lovelace:

'It's a good mile from here so I might be a while. I think I'll walk. Don't want to get stuck out on that road with the car.'

'No, you don't,' said Mr Cardinal archly. 'The connecting road here from the village is perilous even without any snow on it. I was surprised at how treacherous the bends were when we drove down earlier.'

'Fine.' The Inspector nodded. 'You go ahead, Rainbird. Do the best you can. Which reminds me, Mr Cardinal, do your lot have an emergency plan in place in case you can't get your car up to London again tonight, sir? If the snow keeps falling at this pace, or gets worse?'

The MI5 man nodded. 'If the car won't go, we've asked that woman, Lehni Brandenberger, if we can borrow her motorcycle. It will be a bit hairy out on the roads but I have Evans, one of my support staff, down here. He's disguised as a footman, in Glaysayer's pay, and he's an excellent driver of bikes and such like. We'll be fine. If it looks really bad, we'll sit it out here until we can leave. We'll just have to be super cautious. Speaking of cautious, is that what your Sergeant is doing, Inspector, checking on the party guests? I couldn't help but overhear your conversation before I came in.'

Inspector Lovelace coloured red, but then nodded.

'I'm sorry, sir. But a couple of holes in stories have emerged. It's not that we don't trust the information supplied by your lot…just that…'

Mr Cardinal laughed and the sound was light and jolly for such a big man. 'I'm glad to see I have the help of excellent men – and women – who like to do their job properly. I'm sure whatever you find will simply corroborate what we already know, but it never hurts to double-check. Which is what I've just been doing with my man, Evans. Double-checking.'

'Oh?' said Posie.

'We've been around the house double-checking the access points in and out. Just to make one hundred per cent sure no sneaky thief can enter. It's pretty watertight. Did you know the whole house is heated with hot water pipes run from one main boiler? They call it "central heating". Can you believe it? No wonder it's so warm in here. Apparently the fire in the entrance hall is really just for effect. The central heating pipes keep us all toasty. Noisy things, though.'

'No point my having brought this, then,' Posie whispered, picking up Alaric's grey woollen jumper which Rainbird had neatly folded.

'Shall we run over the finer points of the midnight handover one last time, Inspector?' asked Mr Cardinal, crossing one leg over the other and briskly thumbing down another list in his book. 'Just check what we had already agreed on with your Assistant Commissioner Scabbes?'

The Inspector nodded and Posie and Binny found themselves dismissed.

On her way through to her own room to lie down and rest until the party began in earnest, Posie heard the wild antics of the guests continuing on downstairs. But as she closed the interconnecting door from the sitting room and crossed her room to the window she heard something else.

It sounded like muffled shouting.

Bikram growled at her side and she bent to stroke him automatically, to reassure him.

As the Inspector had warned, the walls *must* be very thin. The argument was coming from next door, away from the suite of rooms she shared with the Inspector.

'I WON'T DO IT! YOU CAN'T MAKE ME CHANGE A THING!'

A man was shouting hoarsely, and the voice she could hear sounded distinctly Scottish. Presumably Robin Glaysayer. But even stranger, and clearer, over and above the man's voice she could hear a woman crying, and pleading. The words were indistinguishable and unclear.

It went on and on. Posie stood stock-still in the middle of the whitewashed floor, all her senses razor-sharp and tuned in to whatever was going on next door. Bikram continued to growl. But there was a sudden lull, and then nothing.

And then, loudly:

'JUST TELL THEM TO ALL LEAVE NOW! I FEEL LIKE KILLING YOU MYSELF!'

Sure as bread was bread it was Jacinta Glaysayer. Posie heard a quick slam of a door and then someone's footsteps as they stormed off down the main corridor outside.

What had been happening? What was it that Lord Glaysayer was being asked by his daughter to change? Was it his Will?

Had Jacinta been acting a part earlier? Had she been putting on a brave, unconcerned face when she spoke to Posie about her father's plans for his property after his death? Maybe she didn't earn as much as she made out? Perhaps she really *was* upset that Jocasta, her sister, would become the sole heir of her father's estate; heir to this remote house in this beautiful spot.

It seemed likely that Jacinta *would* care, somehow, for no-one likes to be treated badly, and unfairly. But why bring this up with her father tonight, on the night of a party?

And what was all this talk of killing Lord Glaysayer?

Just what was going on?

* * * *

Nine

Posie stood at the window of her bedroom and looked out. Occasionally the beam of the South Foreland lighthouse seemed to dapple the darkness for a few seconds, lightening the gloom, but there was nothing else to see. She felt sure that under normal circumstances she and the Inspector had probably been granted the best rooms at Maypole Manor, with a splendid view out across the gardens and to the sea beyond, but now she could see next to nothing.

But as she watched, through the swirling snow, she thought she saw something altogether different. A small but distinct bright light was winking out in the endless blackness, from the direction of the cliff edge. It was totally different from the lighthouse beam. Posie squinted.

Yes. There it was again.

FLASH. PAUSE. FLASH-FLASH.

She turned the small lamp off on her bedside table and looked out again from the cover of darkness. Bikram sat whining sadly, longing for Posie to address the issue of whether or not he was going to have another long walk or whether he would continue to stay shut up in such a small room.

'Goodness me! You are out of sorts here, aren't you, old fellow? I don't like it much either, as it happens. Oh, hang on a minute!'

And here it came again. She checked her wristwatch and noted down the time and the sequence of flashes in her notebook and then continued to stare out. But whatever it was had finished and the person had packed up.

'Rats.'

Posie stared on, drawn hypnotically to the whirling snow, and then she saw that much nearer, virtually under her nose, on the manicured lawns below, something was going on.

Two figures, one bent small figure and one tall long figure, in matching hooded cloaks, were walking around the maypole at the centre of the lawn. The larger figure was shovelling snow with a small delicate-looking shovel so that a clear path was visible all the way around the maypole, and the other was bending down awkwardly at regular intervals putting small red tea-lights all around the place. Occasionally the two figures would come together and have what looked like a disagreement. Posie guessed that the figures were Jocasta and Jacinta and that this was the elaborate setting up of some sort of party game for later.

Intrigued, she opened her window a fraction and listened out. It took a couple of minutes to get used to the sound of the howling wind, but then she heard the two girls' voices, carried over to her:

'This is ridiculous! You've gone too far this time, you and your funny witchy ways! You're peculiar; an embarrassment to me and Father. Do you hear me?' That was Jocasta, impatient, dismissive, longing to be out of the cold.

'It's too cold to dance around the maypole tonight. I'd rather be playing bridge or rummy, and so would the guests. And Father won't tolerate your funny magic practices either. What on earth are we doing out here?'

'You're the only one I can ask, as well you know. And I'm paying you, aren't I? Handsomely too, for just ten minutes of your time. And this isn't about dancing. And as for these strange guests, I wish they'd just leave, but Father won't be having any of it. What I'm doing here is trying to make a protective charm, a barrier. I need to protect Father. This is the oldest part of the house, so this is where I'll put the barrier; to catch negative energy, to catch anyone who hurts Father. I told you. I saw it. A premonition. He's going to die tonight!'

'Nonsense. He's tough as old boots. Unfortunately. The man just goes on and on.'

'*Thankfully* he goes on and on, for you. He pays your way, you ungrateful so-and-so. Can you shovel a bit more snow out here? We need to make a sort of shelter right under the maypole.'

'This is ludicrous.'

'No. What is ludicrous is that you, his favourite daughter, treat our father as if he owes you an existence. You treat him so shabbily; in fact, you *use* him.'

'You know nothing about what goes on in this place! You haven't got a clue! You say you're a clairvoyant but I know you're just a big old fraud. And who cares how I treat the old man anyway? He's not our real father anyhow.'

A sharp ironic bark of laugher from Jacinta pealed out. 'You won't be saying that when he's dead. You might as well know now that he's left me nothing in his Will, and that you get everything.'

'WHAT?'

'You heard me. Nothing comes to me; not a dicky-bird. I wasn't going to tell you, but the cat's out of the bag now, isn't it? Well, congratulations. I hope it all makes you very, very happy. You can have as many of your horrible house parties as you like here now, and turn the place into a pleasure playground for all I care.'

The proceedings below were brought to a sudden halt by a banging of an outside door somewhere and Posie guessed that Jocasta had gone back into the house, probably in a state of shock or giddy happiness. That, or she was a very good actress. The small figure which was Jacinta continued to place tea-lights around the maypole and then she, too, was gone. The snow was so heavy now that it resembled a continual white sheet, rippling in the wind.

Turning, still in darkness, Posie heard a click of a door nearby and guessed that Mr Cardinal must have finished with the Inspector in the sitting room. She took her notebook and padded across the bedroom, dragging a reluctant Bikram by his lead. She knocked softly on the interconnecting door. She didn't wait for an answer but slid in quietly with Bikram beside her like a sleepy shadow.

The Inspector was sitting where she had left him in his armchair and he seemed pleased to see her. The clanging, growling noise was coming from the walls again.

'All okay, sir?'

Lovelace nodded, calmer now. 'Bally fine chap, Cardinal. Relaxed, thank goodness. All in hand. I'll be interested to see what news our telegrams bring, but meanwhile, we'll push on regardless.'

Posie nodded in agreement and was just about to tell him what she had seen out of the window when a knock came at the door. The Inspector looked through the fish-eye spyhole and immediately opened the door.

'Come in, my Lord.'

'Grosvenor! Just checking you have everything. I've bought you a bottle of my family's finest Scotch whisky as a wee welcome present. Fifteen years maturing in a smoky barrel on the Isle of Skye; you'll not be disappointed, I promise you.'

As soon as Robin Glaysayer was over the threshold and the door closed his demeanour changed and he seemed to visibly shrink from being the genial host of before to becoming a tiny, worried shell of a man. He perched on the edge of a leather armchair and deposited the whisky bottle on the mahogany writing-desk.

'Does nothing for the nerves, this, Inspector,' he whispered, his blue death's head eyes filled with fear. 'Can't say I'll be sad when this little escapade is over. We don't even have a telephone to connect us with the outside world right now!'

'Nearly over, my Lord. And what a service you'll be doing the country. Just think of that.' The Inspector made more reassuring noises and then explained quietly who Posie really was.

Lord Glaysayer stared at them both a moment too long, and for a second there Posie felt sure that he was about to tell them something vitally important. Was he about to tell them about his argument with Jacinta?

But then his face seemed to harden and glaze over. The moment passed.

'All going to plan, I trust, Inspector?'

'Oh, yes. First class. All going smoothly.'

'And you know the combination to my safe, just in case everything goes wrong?'

'I do, sir. I was told it in my information pack but I saw fit to burn it before I set off this morning. So I memorised it.'

'And? What is it?'

Surprised at the lack of faith, the Inspector bent down and whispered the code in Lord Glaysayer's ear. Satisfied, Robin Glaysayer nodded and got up. Posie remembered what Inspector Lovelace had said about Robin Glaysayer being razor-sharp and not having the wool pulled over his eyes; somehow she was glad that he insisted on these double security measures. They hadn't so much as shown a warrant card or identification paper from Scotland Yard, and the stakes were too high to assume Robin Glaysayer would take everything they did and said on trust at first sight.

Coming closer, Posie heard his whisper:

'Everything's as it should be. Forty thousand has been sitting downstairs in my safe since your man dropped it off yesterday.'

'Good.'

'So I'll see you both later. And just between ourselves, if you have any problems with anything, you ask my daughter Jacinta. She might look like a dog's dinner, but underneath those silk scarves and crooked bones is a first-rate brain.'

When he had left, the Inspector flung himself down again in the recently vacated chair. Bikram, who made no secret of preferring male company to female, settled himself at the Inspector's feet and tried to snooze.

'Glaysayer doesn't seem as unruffled as you thought he would be, sir. Will he be okay?'

'Fine.' Lovelace nodded, ruffling the dog's ears affectionately. 'Don't forget he's getting on in years now, and he's sick, and he's quaffed quite a bit too, rather unwisely. He'll be fine. But go on. You had something to tell me when you came in, didn't you?'

And so Posie told him what she had heard in the corridor, and also what she had just seen out of the bedroom window; the clear lights at the cliff edge and then the odd scene between the Glaysayer girls, culminating in the secret about Jocasta's inheritance which Jacinta had just told her sister.

Inspector Lovelace groaned and rubbed his eyes.

'Murkier and murkier. This place was always ripe for smuggling, I'm told; mainly drugs and black market goods going to and fro between here and France. Let's just hope nothing like that is on the cards for us tonight. We're busy enough. And as for the sisters; well, it's interesting enough but hardly our business, is it? It's up to Robin Glaysayer to whom he leaves this strange house. I'd be hard pressed to choose if I were him: both daughters are funny fish in their own ways.'

Posie nodded, relieved to have shared the burden of her knowledge, and she made to go back to her room. At the door she changed her mind.

'Oh, sir. One thing. Why were you so interested in Steinhauser's watch earlier? You were so convincing, like you really liked it. You think it's stolen or something?'

'The watch? Ah, yes. As I said, what a beauty. I just genuinely liked it. No, I don't think it's stolen. If you steal a watch you don't then wear it to a party where you'll be on public display, do you? Besides, it just highlighted for me that Steinhauser must be seriously, fabulously rich. That watch is one of a clutch of only five made; it's virtually a myth in its own lifetime.'

'And that means, sir?'

'Five thousand pounds, Posie. Too much for a watch. Too much for me.'

'I'd say so, sir. I think your wife might think so, too, if you don't mind my saying so. Come on Bikram, come with me. See you later, *darling.*'

But upon entering her room, now all ablaze with light when she was certain that she had left it in darkness, Posie's optimism and cheeriness deserted her.

She surveyed the scene with dismay, a rising tide of panic threatening to engulf her.

The place had been ransacked in her short absence. Carelessly, too.

Bikram began to bark and then ran around the room, growling and sniffing at everything. Posie's overnight bag had been opened and its contents thrown all over the bed. Her Bally handbag sat open, and it had obviously been rifled through. Her make-up and her one bottle of Parma violet perfume had been thrown with force onto the wooden floorboards, causing the glass bottle to break and her rouge and lipstick to shatter in their packaging.

Posie looked on in despair at her lovely red dress from Harrods. It had been thrown into the pitcher of washing water and it lay, soggy and depressed-looking, like a strange drowned creature from another world. Shoes and a feather boa and her new film magazines were strewn all around the room.

She caught hold of herself and tried to calm down. No point crying over spilt milk, and they were only belongings, after all. *But just what on earth had her visitor been looking for?*

Quickly Posie checked through her things, but nothing seemed to be missing. Fortunately she hadn't brought any 'real' identification with her, and her only personal documentation was the notebook which she had been clutching when she had left the room. She had brought no business cards, no passport. She congratulated herself on that now.

Was it someone desperate to find out her real identity? Or someone looking for something in particular?

Or was it just someone being a nuisance, happy to cause as much chaos and unhappiness as possible. Someone like Jocasta, perhaps, who seemed to genuinely hate Posie? Or could it have been Amory Laine – carrying out her own personal vendetta in the most childish of ways – by ensuring that Posie would have nothing to wear later at the party? Whatever the reason, the person had been stealthily quiet; she hadn't heard anything from next door at all.

Posie retrieved her dress, hung it as best she could and hoped it would dry out in the stifling heat of the room. Certainly not in time for tonight, but perhaps she could rescue it and wear it on some other, future occasion. She sighed. She decided she would ignore the invasion of her room and her privacy and assume it was simply a strange case of jealousy.

She made Bikram a rough and ready bed on the floor with a couple of the tartan pillows and he snuffled down, relieved to be in one set place for a while. She decided to let the Inspector be and not to tell him about the intrusion.

And then she took off her lovely House of Harlow clothes which she would have to put on again for dinner later, hung them carefully and wrapped herself in her old velvet dressing-gown. She got up on the tartan-covered bed, and snoozed.

It had certainly been an unusual afternoon.

* * * *

PART TWO

New Year's Party

Ten

Leaving Bikram, Posie joined the others on the stroke of six o'clock.

She was the only one not dressed up to the nines. She didn't really care; wearing such wonderful clothes, even day clothes, at any time of the day or night was a real treat. Besides, she had added her own lovely cream pearls and she felt a dream. Posie held her head up very high and decided to ignore the raised eyebrows from the women and the quizzical look flashed at her from the Inspector.

Jacinta had transformed herself, and while she still looked like a plump, crooked moorland pony, she had got rid of her many scarves and silk wrappings, swapping them instead for a black sequinned shift dress. As Posie entered the Library on Inspector Lovelace's arm, she saw that Jacinta was locked in what looked like a rapturous conversation with a slim, tall, dark man whom she had never seen before, whose very crispness and smartness seemed to illuminate him. Her sister, by contrast, was drinking steadily from a champagne flute and sitting on the edge of a wicker chair, dull-eyed and bored, listening to Mr Steinhauser and Mr Cardinal, who both looked like they had given up trying to entertain her. There was no doubt that Jocasta Glaysayer was a thoroughly odd sort of

93

girl, and the sparkling green glitter of her evening dress was not matched in any way at all by her general listlessness.

And suddenly, into Posie's mind came a peculiar sensation, a sort of *deja-vu*, as if Posie had met or known Jocasta before somewhere. What was it about the girl that made Posie feel she recognised her?

Jacinta called out to Posie:

'Mrs Grosvenor, I don't think you've met Mr Goodman yet, have you? Can I introduce you?'

So *this* was the American engineer who had risked his life by sailing across the English Channel in the dead of winter with the blueprint.

Posie smiled as he came forwards and bowed a tight little bow, his gloved white hands lithe and expressive. The man would have been matinee-idol handsome, but for an unfortunate resemblance to a horse in the lower face, which was further highlighted by a wide mouth full of big teeth. Posie found the man unattractive, but she could see that the American had a sort of shiny charm. He had such a tan that for a moment Posie thought he must be wearing make-up. When he spoke it was with a top-drawer American accent, polished and clipped.

'I'm sure glad to meet you, Mrs Grosvenor,' he said. 'And what a house! Jacinta sure is one lucky gal! It's so similar to my uncle's in The Hamptons! I feel right at home here already. And what music! I sure love the bagpipes.'

The bagpiper from earlier was over in a corner, bedecked in ruffles of tartan, making what seemed to Posie an infernal racket.

'Oh, good!' Jacinta beamed, and it was the happiest she had looked all day. *She genuinely likes this man*, thought Posie with a wry smile to herself: perhaps it was the first bit of attention the girl had been shown by a more-or-less handsome man in a good long while, Posie reflected sadly.

Excepting a slight sheen of nervousness lurking beneath his healthy tan, and a tiny quiver of the right hand,

Edwin Goodman seemed so much like a genuine house guest that Posie quite forgot that here was a man who had escaped from a dangerous enemy and had been lying low in considerable danger for several months. She had quite forgotten that he was acting out a part too and she started to talk with great interest about New York, the city she had been told he was from, along with the original engineer, Dick Wainwright.

Edwin Goodman was utterly charming and skilfully changed the subject, steering Posie easily onto the subject of Africa, where he had met Lord Glaysayer on a safari. Or that was the cover, anyhow.

After a few minutes, Amory Laine and her husband Julian Carter entered the room, unobtrusively for once. Amory looked subdued in a black velour dress with wide bat-wing sleeves and a long plum-coloured headscarf was wrapped around her shingled hair. She wore almost no make-up and looked pale and wan. But Posie felt the American at her side bristle with barely-concealed excitement.

'Say,' he muttered. 'Ain't that the famous film star, Amory Laine? What's she doin' here?'

'You know of her then?' said Jacinta, coldly, all previous enthusiasm for the American now tightly roped in.

'I'll say.' Edwin Goodman nodded, staring appreciatively in Amory Laine's direction. 'She's quite something, isn't she? Gives off this beautiful sense of danger, like she could stroke your cheek before slitting your throat.'

Jacinta made a strange choking noise.

The American was already moving off. 'Excuse me, I must just…' And he had left them, bowling his way up to the famous film star.

'*He's* not everything he pretends to be,' said Jacinta vindictively, and Posie felt like agreeing sincerely, for Jacinta had hit the nail right on the head, but Posie merely pretended to sip at her drink.

'So what's the plan for tonight?'

Jacinta scowled. 'Oh, just the usual. We'll have drinks, and more drinks, and more drinks. And then we'll play some crazy games my father can ill afford the prizes for, and then we'll eat a dinner worth more than his income for two months, and then we'll have fireworks, come what may. And at some point the clock will strike twelve and we'll all congratulate each other on making it through another year.'

'Golly! I feel like I've hit rather a raw nerve.'

'No, *I'm* the one who's sorry, Mrs Grosvenor, for *you*. I can't help but feeling that something is going to go terribly wrong tonight. For all of us.'

* * * *

The party went on just as Jacinta had described. The bagpipes went on and on and champagne flowed at every turn, and elaborate games of 'pass the parcel' and 'pin-the-tail-on-the St Margaret's Bay cliff edge' ensued. Pound notes were stuffed haphazardly into large white envelopes and chucked around as prizes. Glittering transparent stones in candy-coloured hues were found at the bottom of every champagne flute, which drew gasps and admiring tuts of appreciation all round, but whether these were the real deal, or just paste, Posie could not have said. Whatever they were, they added to the frantic attempts at crazy extravagance.

As one who hated participating in anything resembling a performing art, the evening was a slow torture for Posie. She managed to stumble through a rather wooden performance in 'charades', but Inspector Lovelace won a stay for two at the Ritz in Paris as the main prize, having proven himself a dab hand at singing music hall numbers, in particular Harry Fragson's well-known song from before the Great War: 'Hello! Hello! Who's Your Lady Friend?'

Posie had to act suitably mock-proud from where she was ensconced on one of the Library sofas; the perfect supporting wife, while Inspector Lovelace gave her the gold-edged coupon for the Ritz, telling her to, 'Keep it safe in your bag, darling.'

A small raised mahogany platform took up one entire corner of the Library, and on it was placed a baby grand piano. Lord Glaysayer silenced the bagpiper at long last and invited people up to sing or play, and Posie noticed how all eyes were fixed on Amory Laine: people expected her, as the resident star, to want to perform for them, and to excel. But all she did was sink further down in her chair and wave the air dismissively, smoking at the same time. Posie caught the actress several times just staring strangely over in her direction, but chose to ignore it.

'I bet she can't even sing,' muttered Posie to the Inspector under her breath as she pretended to sip at her champagne.

So instead, others performed. Jacinta recited poetry, and Jocasta revealed herself to have a surprisingly good singing voice. She sang 'I'll Forget You' and Helen Trix's well-known 'Keep Movin'' while Edwin Goodman accompanied her on the piano, himself apparently an excellent pianist. The two launched seamlessly into show tunes, their timing impeccable.

The American then went on to sing the humorous new Novello song, 'And Her Mother Came Too', in a fake British accent, mimicking the famously handsome songster James Buchanan.

Everyone roared with laughter.

Through this and around all of this, Posie watched as the small circle of house servants bustled about, bringing canapés of curried eggs and anchovy pastries on glass trays. She watched as Binny, again playing the Butler, circled neatly with drinks and a cigar box. She tried not to catch his eye.

'Dinner will be served in ten minutes in the Hunting Room!' declared Lord Glaysayer as the clock struck nine o'clock.

He was the very essence of vitality, the perfect host enjoying his own bounty and largesse; a word here and a word there with a favoured servant about some last-minute necessity, a quick nod in the direction of Binny who would come running over with another bottle of something.

But Binny was now speaking to him about something important, Posie noticed. Glaysayer coughed loudly and looked slightly embarrassed as he addressed the room again:

'I must apologise, dear people. Due to the worsening weather conditions I have seen fit to dismiss all of my staff, most of whom live locally, so they can get home safely tonight. Our meal is already cooked, fortunately, and I am releasing my cook and the waiting staff. My Butler here, Binny, and my footman, Evans, will try and cover everything between them. I hope we can all get along just fine. Again, my apologies, but I am sure you can understand. I doubt that anyone's comfort will be greatly affected.'

Posie looked around the room and realised that it was now devoid of the many servants who had been there just minutes before, and even the bagpiper had gone, thank goodness. She suddenly noticed a huge man, all brawn and muscle, squeezed unattractively into the black servants' livery of a footman. He was helping Binny in the corner, loading up dirty glasses onto a small serving-trolley, both men moving with a grace and speed surprising in such big, untrained men.

So that's Bryn Cardinal's right-hand man, she thought to herself reassuringly. *A brute in a suit*. At least he looked capable of dealing with any trouble which might arise. Posie wondered quickly if dismissing the normal household servants was part of the plan cooked up between the Inspector and Mr Cardinal earlier, but there was no way of asking them while they were all still in character.

'Goodness, it looks like we'll be snowed in!' Jacinta announced, standing by the French doors which led out onto the lawns, watching the snow falling.

Posie sat alone on her empty sofa, watching everything unfolding. Inspector Lovelace was smoking a Turkish cigarette with Edwin Goodman, who was cheerfully telling a story with many jokes in it in a very loud voice. Posie watched as Mr Steinhauser and Bryn Cardinal spoke about diamond mining in South Africa on the opposite sofa, nodding their heads together from time to time.

She noticed how Lenny and the Italian Duke prowled up and down the length of the Library, speaking together in low tones about something they obviously found engrossing; Lenny bending down to hang on the Duke's every last word. Posie had done her level best to keep as far away from Lenny as was humanly possible: she didn't want to jeopardise the uneasy tight-rope of an agreement which seemed to hang between them, barely understood by either side.

'You really are a good observer of people, aren't you, Mrs Grosvenor?' came a gentle, soothing voice from the seat next to her which a few seconds earlier had remained unoccupied. 'I suppose it helps in your profession. I know it certainly does in *mine*.'

Julian Carter, Amory Laine's long-suffering husband, the portrait artist, was suddenly sitting next to her, and he held out his hand good-naturedly.

'And might I say, it would be a real pleasure to paint you, Mrs Grosvenor. And *that's* not something I find myself saying very often, you know. It's something about your *eyes*. The light in them. I'd have to focus on them, with very little else going on. You know, no distractions by way of clothing or whatever…'

Posie inclined her head gracefully, genuinely flattered.

'I'll ask my husband Jimmie,' she said, a touch coquettishly. 'Perhaps a birthday present for him? If it's to be *that* sort of a painting?'

Julian Carter laughed easily, a flush of embarrassment lighting up his face.

'Oh, forgive me. I didn't mean a *nude* study…'

Julian Carter was a tall man, fairly undistinguished looking at first sight. He had a pretty but anonymous face and was dressed, like the others, in immaculate white tie. But on a second glance the uniform couldn't quite disguise his uniqueness: the leonine long hair which curled around his ears and at the nape of his neck; the large grey eyes; the way he had tied his cravat with a large, silken bohemian loop. But it was his kind, apologetic manner rather than his appearance which struck Posie most.

She scanned the room quickly for Amory Laine, and then saw that her husband had left her on a third couch, where they had been sitting together earlier; except that now she had fallen asleep in a huddle of silken cushions, her purple velvet headscarf askew. Again, Posie noticed how small the girl was; how like a child she looked. How very fragile. How she *looked* so exactly right for playing a character in a film about innocence.

How deceptive appearances could be!

'You'll have to forgive my wife for her rudeness earlier on that train.' Julian Carter smiled sadly. 'I would say she didn't mean it, but the sad truth is that she *did*. She's vile right now, but it's explainable. But you'll excuse her anyhow because you look like someone who is kind; who understands human nature.'

'Oh! Do I?' Posie made a mock wide-eyed expression, but in truth, she had been told this many, many times before. She frequently had people coming up to her and pouring out their troubles, or their thoughts. Or, and much more usefully in her line of work, confessions.

Mr Carter nodded.

'The thing is, my wife is going through a very rocky little patch just now. In fact, the roughest we've ever experienced. You know she was a drug addict?'

'Er, well, I say…'

'It's fine. The world and his wife know it. You don't need to look embarrassed, bless you, dear Mrs Grosvenor. But that's all behind her now. A thing of the past. As of three weeks ago, she quit the dratted stuff. Swore to me she'd never take it again her whole life. And she's stuck to her promise. And that's why she's like a bear with a sore head. She's missing the drugs and she's doing it the hard way: I think our American friend over there would call it "going cold turkey". She's normally the life and soul of a party. But she's lost all her manners, all her vitality, everything which makes her *her*, including her singing voice, and yes; my goodness can she sing! She'd have knocked JoJo Glaysayer's socks off!'

Posie stared at Amory Laine, then back again at her husband. Why was he telling her this?

'You know, I met her at Wilton's Music Hall in Whitechapel before she was "discovered", before she became a creature owned by the Icon Film Company. Back when she was just plain Brenda Brown. I was painting scenery there for a living and she was belting out numbers like there was no tomorrow. That was before the movies; before she had to change her name and before she became famous. Before she started drinking and taking cocaine, too.'

'Goodness. I had no idea. But she seemed on fire earlier this evening; you both did. I thought there must have been some sort of intoxication or drugs involved… With those animal heads, I mean.'

'Oh!' Mr Carter looked a trifle embarrassed. He smiled.

'Yes. That was my idea, I'm afraid. The thing is, people expect something from you when you have the reputation of being a first-class hell-raiser. In fact, I'm pretty sure that was why Amory was asked to this party in the first place, you know, months back, for a bit of *spice*. I thought we'd act as if we were off our heads on something or other, but the irony is that neither of us have touched a drop of anything, not even the fizz on offer. I told Amory that if she quit I'd stay clean and stone-cold sober with her.'

'So you just pretended to be on drugs earlier?'

'That's right. Keep old Glaysayer feeling like he's got a dash of the glittering London dark-side at his party, even if the event is as dry as a bone. It's so dull, isn't it? This party is an agony for us both. Especially with all the alcohol so temptingly close.'

'Why did you come, then? You must have known it would be difficult to be here.'

Julian Carter nodded. 'Of course I did. But as I said, we were invited to this months ago and when she decided to give up the drugs a few weeks back I looked at our Christmas and New Year's diary and decided to keep to all our arrangements, and, in fact, to fill it up with even more! Not a moment spare to think about things; to be tempted. To cave in. Just keep on going. That's what I thought was best for her.'

'Gracious me. Well, I have to hand it to you, Mr Carter. You've managed so far.' Posie laughed jauntily. 'What did you promise her as a reward?'

Mr Carter smiled sadly. 'A baby, as it happens.'

'Oh!' Posie flushed red. 'I'm so sorry. I didn't mean to pry.'

'That's fine. I've told you everything else, and I'm sure I can rely on your discretion. The thing is, Amory is much, much older than she looks, you know. Pushing thirty-five now. The doctors have said that if she has any chance of having a baby at all, she needs to clean up. And she *does* want a baby. More than anything. Hence the big clean-up. Hence the "cold turkey". But I didn't come across here to tell you all of this; gracious me, no. I had something else to tell you. Something my wife told me earlier just before she fell asleep. It concerns *you*.'

'Oh?'

Just then Binny entered the room and rang a small gold bell. 'Dinner is served, ladies and gentlemen.'

They stood. 'Well, it might be something or nothing. But you know our room is on the same corridor as yours? She told me that earlier, when she went up to her room to get changed, she saw a man coming out of your room. A very tall man, but well muffled up. She said she felt sure you had already left your room, and the man was interfering somehow. He had a guilty stance, apparently, as he came out of the door. Like he was snooping. He was clutching something too; looked like a photo, apparently. Can that be right?'

Posie's pulse quickened. She thought frantically. *A photo*. The only photograph she had brought with her had been a teeny-tiny snapshot of herself standing with Alaric on the steps outside St Bride's Church at a wedding earlier that year. She took it with her for sentimental reasons wherever she went, although sometimes she doubted those sentiments.

She cursed herself for bringing the snap with her. How stupid she had been! Was *that* what the mysterious man had been looking for? The reason her room had been ransacked and her dress thrown aside and ruined? It didn't make sense. She looked over at the sleeping Amory Laine. Just who had she seen?

Suddenly everyone began to move, picking up wraps and bags and jackets from the sofas. Julian Carter stood up, ready to wake his wife.

'Did your wife recognise him at all, this strange tall man coming out of my room?'

Julian shrugged. 'I don't think so, but ask her later about the intruder, perhaps, Mrs Grosvenor. I didn't get that far, I'm afraid. She fell asleep just then.'

Posie looked around and saw that virtually everybody had stopped and was watching them, listening in silence to the last part of their conversation. Sure as bread was bread everyone had heard about the intruder.

'Oh, it must be some silly misunderstanding,' Posie trilled brightly. 'One guest room is much like another here, isn't it?'

The Inspector squeezed her hand insistently and smiled, guiding her along the corridor to the Hunting Room to where dinner was served. They were in the middle of the other guests, moving along as one small crush.

'What on earth was that all about?' he whispered. 'What was Carter going on about? *What* man was in your room?'

But before they had reached the Hunting Room, and before Posie could reply, a sharp trilling sound filled the whole house. Binny took quick control of the situation.

'Please, all of you be seated,' he soothed. 'There are name places set at each seat and it should all be apparent when you get there. Evans will show you if anything is unclear. I'll be back in a second. I'll just get the front door.'

And so they all entered the Hunting Room, a dining hall dressed with more animal heads than was somehow decent, and they all obediently sat down, with Lord Glaysayer at one end of the long dark-wood table and the Italian Duke at the other. Evans was passing around yet another bottle of champagne when Binny returned, looking slightly put out. Someone was following him, close on his heels.

'My Lord.' He bowed in Glaysayer's direction. And then he turned to the rest of the party, and he did his best Butler impression, hand behind his back, head cocked to one side subserviently.

'Ladies and gentlemen. We have another guest. Due to the very inclement weather conditions outside, it seems that Maypole Manor is now virtually isolated. The snow is getting heavier by the minute and it's turning into a blizzard. We may be quite cut off. This gentleman behind me was just passing by on his bicycle and got into difficulties. He's far off course for the village and was in danger of pitching over the cliff. He saw the lights on here and decided to ring for assistance. I'm sure we can oblige, sir, can't we? It is but the work of a minute to set another place at the table and make another room up. It is New Year's Eve, after all.'

Lord Robin Glaysayer looked wrong-footed somehow, and flushed in the face, but he wasn't about to be called a bad host. He nodded and waved at the man who had been standing concealed behind Binny in the doorway to the Hunting Room.

'Please find yourself welcome here, sir. Who are you?'

The man stepped forwards. Everyone turned to look.

He was about thirty, very tall and clean-shaven with ice-blonde colouring. He wore a priest's black cassock with an immaculate white dog-collar. Posie's immediate and entirely inappropriate thought was: *he's too dashed good-looking to be a priest.*

Over the top of his cassock he wore a thick but inadequate hand-knitted Fair Isle cardigan. He smiled nervously all around, taking everybody in with an eagle eye. Just then the doorbell rang yet again, and excusing himself, Binny darted out of the room.

'Good evening all. I'm Father Moriarty. My parish is over at River, past Dover.'

When the man spoke his voice was low, melodious, calming, and underneath it, pinched in like a little ghost from the past, was a trace of a German accent. 'I'm so sorry to intrude, but thank you for your kind invitation. And good job you're not superstitious, too, my Lord. Many would not oblige me in this manner.'

'What *are* you talking about, my man?' asked Lord Glaysayer, his senses blurred by all the champagne he had been quaffing.

'He means that he's the thirteenth guest,' said Jacinta

105

in a low, measured voice which everyone could hear, that everyone was *designed* to hear.

'And that's *always* unlucky.'

* * * *

Eleven

'*No-one* is called Moriarty. And a *priest* to boot! Who on earth *is* he?' whispered Bryn Cardinal to Inspector Lovelace in a low, measured undertone. 'He must have made it up on the spur of the moment; said the first thing that came into his mind. I'm surprised he didn't call himself Sherlock and be done with it.'

Posie's thoughts were decidedly elsewhere: she was thinking that Mr Cardinal had certainly scrubbed up well in his white tie tonight. At least he owned a set of decent evening clothes, which was more than could be said for Alaric…

They were standing upstairs in the little sitting room again, and Posie and Sergeants Rainbird and Binny were grouped around nervously, with Evans on the periphery, arms crossed across his wide body. It was half-past ten and they had all excused themselves temporarily from the party below. Bryn Cardinal rapped his knuckles swiftly on the mahogany desk.

'And the man's a German, too. I'm sure of it.'

The Inspector nodded but kept his cool. 'I know I sound like a stuck gramophone record, but being German has never been a crime in my book, Mr Cardinal. And there's nothing we can do about it, anyhow. We can't very well ask the priest to go on his way in this weather, can we? It was the only decent thing to do, to take the man in. Besides, who's to say the fellow's not telling the truth; that he's really just a priest on a bike, far from his parish?'

But the Inspector looked his own sort of doubtful as to the real identity and purpose of the newly-arrived thirteenth guest at the house party.

'Evans, why don't you keep a close eye on the priest? Anything suspicious just shout. And Rainbird, can you try the telephone in Lord Glaysayer's study again? See if it's working now? If so, call Scotland Yard and ask them for an identity check on the priest. You got the details?'

The brute in a suit nodded and departed, surprisingly quietly for such a large man. Rainbird followed.

'I'd better get downstairs again, too. They'll be missing the champagne going around,' said Binny pulling at an imaginary forelock and doing a complicated little servants' bow. 'Although I think they're onto absinthe shots now, so maybe they won't even notice that I'm gone.'

He fished in his inside waistcoat pocket.

'By the way, sir, the second bell you probably heard was the boy from the village Post Office, the policeman's son. He brought you three telegrams, which must have arrived at different points throughout the evening. Rainbird had obviously promised him a very, very juicy tip if he could see his way to delivering them, whatever the weather, and the bright lad improvised with a couple of what looked like old lead drainpipes. Used them as skis to get on over here. We might be seeing him again later with more, sir. I promised him even more money if he came again. But there's nothing on our mysterious Mr Steinhauser as yet. I've read them all, by the way.'

Binny passed the telegrams over and disappeared.

Posie stood all agog, while Mr Cardinal obviously had no intention of letting anything slip past his attention, either. Inspector Lovelace read quickly and then passed the telegrams over to Posie and Bryn Cardinal.

The first telegram read:

To: POST OFFICE, ST MARGARET'S-AT-CLIFFE. 017 From: NEW SCOTLAND YARD, THAMES EMBANKMENT, LONDON

TELEGRAM 1 OF 2.

DEAR INSPECTOR LOVELACE,

SERGEANT NOAKES HERE, REPORTING FOR DUTY. SENDING THIS BY TELEGRAM AS YOUR TELEPHONE EXCHANGE NOT WORKING. HAVE BEEN ASKED TO CHECK ON THE FOLLOWING PERSONS:

DUKE LUCA DEL ANGELO - NO CRIMINAL RECORDS HERE. ITALIAN EMBASSY WILL CONTACT YOU DIRECTLY.

JOCASTA GLAYSAYER - NO CRIMINAL RECORDS HERE. RECORDED AS BEING A BRITISH CITIZEN. NO FURTHER INFORMATION HELD.

RUDY STEINHAUSER - NO CRIMINAL RECORDS HERE. GERMAN EMBASSY CONFIRMS HE IS NOT ONE OF THEIRS. HAVE CONTACTED SWISS EMBASSY AND THEY WILL CONTACT YOU DIRECTLY.

WILL TELEGRAM LATER ABOUT LENNY BRANDENBERGER - AM CURRENTLY AWAITING INFORMATION.

HOPE THIS HELPS.

YOURS,

SGT. L. NOAKES.

The second telegram read:

To: POST OFFICE, ST MARGARET'S-AT-CLIFFE. 017 From: NEW SCOTLAND YARD, THAMES EMBANKMENT, LONDON

TELEGRAM 2 OF 2.

DEAR INSPECTOR LOVELACE,

SERGEANT NOAKES HERE AGAIN. TASKED TO FIND OUT ABOUT ONE LEHNI OR 'LENNY' BRANDENBERGER.

OUR RECORDS OFFICE CONFIRM THAT LEHNI BRANDENBERGER (REAL NAME) IS GERMAN. BORN HERE OF ARISTOCRATIC GERMAN PARENTS. BOTH DEAD.

I SENT ONE OF MY BEST CONSTABLES TONIGHT TO THE BRITISH MUSEUM BUT, AS EXPECTED, ALL WAS SHUT UP. HE THEN WENT NEXT DOOR TO THE HOME OF SIR FREDERICK KENYON, DIRECTOR OF THE BRITISH MUSEUM.

KENYON COULD ONLY CONFIRM THAT THE GIRL WAS WORKING AT THE MUSEUM UNTIL SEPTEMBER. SHE WAS KNOWN AS 'LENNY BROWN'.

BUT IT WAS LITTLE KATHLEEN KENYON, HIS DAUGHTER, AGED 12, WHO KNEW THE MOST.

LITTLE KATHLEEN IS A KEEN PHOTOGRAPHER AND WOULD-BE ARCHAEOLOGIST AND SEEMS TO HAVE IDOLISED LENNY BROWN AND FOLLOWED HER AROUND A GOOD DEAL AS SOME SORT OF ROLE MODEL.

SHE TOLD MY CONSTABLE THAT LENNY BROWN 'CHANGED' OVERNIGHT THIS AUTUMN, WHEN SHE RESIGNED AS AN OFFICIAL PHOTOGRAPHER AT THE MUSEUM AND APPARENTLY SOLD ALL OF HER PHOTOGRAPHY EQUIPMENT TO A CAMERA SHOP ON BEDFORD AVENUE, ROUND THE CORNER.

WHEN ASKED BY THE LITTLE GIRL WHY SHE WAS SELLING UP, LENNY BROWN LAUGHED WILDLY AND REPLIED THAT SHE 'NEEDED THE MONEY URGENTLY' AS SHE WAS 'STONY BROKE'.

LITTLE KATHLEEN WAS APPARENTLY QUITE HURT AT MISS BROWN'S DEPARTURE AND HASN'T SEEN HER SINCE.

HOPE THIS HELPS.

YOURS,

SGT. L. NOAKES.

And the final telegram read:

To: POST OFFICE, ST MARGARET'S-AT-CLIFFE. 017 From: ITALIAN EMBASSY, 14 DAVIES STREET, MAYFAIR, LONDON, W1

DEAR INSPECTOR LOVELACE,

WE CONFIRM THAT LUCA DEL ANGELO IS OF ITALIAN NATIONALITY, BORN AND RAISED ON THE ISLAND OF SICILY. HE HAS LIVED IN ENGLAND FOR THREE YEARS AND SEEMS TO WANT TO STAY HERE, DESPITE THE TERRIBLE WEATHER.

HE HAS NO CRIMINAL RECORD AND NEITHER DOES HIS FAMILY.

IN FACT, THEY ARE EXEMPLARY CITIZENS, RUNNING A HUGE TOMATO EMPIRE WHICH STRETCHES ALL OVER ITALY, MAINLY CANNING A TOMATO SAUCE KNOWN AS 'SUGO'. THEY ARE THE SECOND WEALTHIEST FAMILY IN ITALY. THEY GIVE A GREAT DEAL TO THE POOR AND ALSO TO THE GOVERNMENT BY WAY OF DONATIONS. IN FACT, DUE TO

THE EXTREMELY VAST SUMS DONATED, HIS FAMILY WERE AWARDED A NEW 'DUKEDOM' JUST THREE YEARS AGO BY WAY OF REWARD.

THE DUKE GOES OUT OF HIS WAY TO DISASSOCIATE HIMSELF WITH THE SO-CALLED MAFIA, SOME OF WHOM HAVE APPARENTLY COME TO LONDON AND SETTLED IN CLERKENWELL.

A FURTHER POINT IS THAT THE DUKE IS A SICK MAN; FOLLOWING A FALL FROM A HORSE AS A SMALL CHILD HE HAS SEVERAL DISFIGURING DISABILITIES, AND FEELS THE COLD IN ENGLAND LIKE NO OTHER.

WE DO NOT MIND GIVING YOU THIS IMFORMATION BUT WOULD STRESS IT HAS ALREADY BEEN SUPPLIED TO YOUR GOVERNMENT'S INTELLIGENCE AGENCY.

WITH ALL BEST WISHES,

B.ZAGLIONI (ACTING OFFICER AT THE ITALIAN EMBASSY, LONDON)

'Well, I could have told you all that about the Duke, without bothering the Italian Embassy,' said Mr Cardinal coolly, but not without a trace of humour.

'Talk about mistrust! I agree he *looks* suspicious, but looks aren't always everything, are they? Take our Mr Edwin Goodman for instance: the man's just sailed himself over a dangerous and unknown seaway in wintertime; the fella must be nervous as hell but he's as cool as a cucumber and the life and soul of the party downstairs. Some might say that looks suspicious. You just can't tell.'

Posie chewed her lip. 'I feel awful,' she said quickly. 'You're right; I *did* judge the Duke on his appearance, his silly fur coat. But why deny the link to Sicily so clumsily with that silly thing about the *cannoli*? It makes no sense.'

The Inspector grimaced. 'As the Embassy say, I think our Duke doesn't want any personal connection with Sicily becoming common knowledge, for that's where a good deal of these so-called Mafia men are coming from now. I suppose he doesn't want to advertise the fact that his "Dukedom" is a brand new "bought" thing, either; that he's really just the heir to a tomato-factory empire. You have to feel for the man, I suppose. But we still don't know *why* he's here tonight, or why he's so desperate to cover up his past.'

'And Lenny is even more complicated than we first thought,' said Posie worriedly. 'She's abandoned a profession she loved; that she excelled at. She was proud of what she did. And she's definitely not "stony broke". Did you see her clothes and jewels? All real. I still don't know what on earth her game is. It makes no sense.'

'I don't much care,' said Mr Cardinal, checking his wristwatch. 'As long as we keep a tight ship, keep people in their rightful places and move things along with no problems, as far as I'm concerned people can pretend to be whoever the blazes they want to be. I'll keep an eye out for Miss Brandenberger. Shall we get back down to the party? I'll go separately from you; we don't want anyone to think we all know each other.'

Feeling very much like they were being marshalled by a very efficient school prefect, Posie and the Inspector found themselves following Bryn Cardinal along the landing, but a few paces behind. They waited a bit until he had gone down the staircase.

Posie sighed. She wasn't that keen to re-join the party. The dinner earlier, with its endless varieties of alcohol which she and the Inspector had skilfully dodged at every turn, had dragged on forever, despite the fact that, as Bryn Cardinal had mentioned, Edwin Goodman had proved to be highly entertaining company; singing, doing impressions in American and English and French accents, making people laugh.

'Let's go. And Posie, you still need to tell me why you didn't change for dinner. Dashed odd of you.'

Arm in arm Posie and the Inspector descended, and Posie was about to explain everything, but before she could, they saw that someone was lurking at the bottom of the staircase waiting for them.

It was Amory Laine, looking like death warmed up. She stood next to Bobbie the Bengal tiger, leaning one arm along his flank, as if for support. In the other hand she clutched a water glass, half full.

'I say, Mrs Grosvenor,' she said in a small voice.

'Can we talk? I fink I've got somethin' to tell you.'

* * * *

Twelve

No-one else was around. Laughter could be heard coming from the Library. The large grandfather clock in the corner began to strike the hour. Eleven o'clock.

'I'll be quick. Apparently there are fireworks in a minute on the terrace. But I can't see why they're botherin', what with this blizzard raging.'

The film star played with her purple headscarf nervously. Posie tried to forget about earlier and the horrible remarks which had been aimed at her, and she nodded at Amory Laine encouragingly.

'Anything you say to me you can tell me in front of my husband. He's the soul of discretion, I assure you.'

'Not like *mine* then, is he?' Amory's voice was bitter and the words were spoken harshly. 'Tellin' you all about me and what I'm goin' through right now. And all about the blimmin' baby too, I expect?'

Inspector Lovelace's eyes boggled, but only for a split-second, and then he resumed his smiling, benign air of reassurance.

'I assure you that whatever your husband told me will go no further.'

'Pah! You *would* say that! But you're a crime novelist! A collector of characters for your stories! That's what I wanted to talk to you about. Don't you dare put me in one of your little books, will you? Swear to me you won't.'

Posie shivered slightly, and looked around for a draught, but could see no doors or windows open.

'I swear upon my life.'

Amory Laine stared hard at Posie, then nodded, seemingly satisfied at the given answer. She swilled the remnants of the drink in the beaker, pulling a face as she did so.

'The water's filthy here. All I can taste is blimmin' chalk. Tastes like bicarbonate, actually.'

'This *is* White Cliffs country, Miss Laine,' the Inspector murmured good-naturedly.

'You wanted to tell me something, Miss Laine, or was it just to warn me off using you as source material?'

The girl looked up at Posie strangely. She had put her glass of water down on the broad span of Bobbie the Bengal tiger's nose, and then started to play absent-mindedly with the whiskers and the teeth of the creature with one hand.

'That's a very strange feelin', for inside a tiger's mouth. Somethin' sharp. Why, it almost feels like…'

'NO! NO! DON'T TOUCH THAT!'

Amory Laine was staring at Posie as if she were quite mad. Posie explained about the arsenic and the worm infestation and the taxidermist.

'So you'd better go and wash your hands carefully, Miss Laine.'

'Blimey! What a house of horrors. I can't wait to leave tomorrow, get back up to London. Thanks for the tip-off.'

The laughter from the Library suddenly got louder, amid sounds of people chattering, coming their way.

'So was there something else? Only I think we'll have company any second now.'

Amory Laine's voice became suddenly urgent as she whispered:

'Julian told you that I'd seen a fella coming out of your room earlier, holding a photograph?'

'Yes. Did you recognise him at all?'

Amory shook her head. The Inspector was looking at both of them in disbelief.

'What on earth? *What* man? *What* photograph? Is this what Carter was talking to you about in the Library earlier, when everyone was listening? No, never mind: tell me later, my darling. Miss Laine, what was this intruder into my wife's room wearing?'

'All black. He had a homburg hat pulled down over his face and a scarf up over the lower half of his face.'

'I don't know what this is all about,' said the Inspector, frowning, 'but your description of the intruder could apply to any one of the men here tonight, save for the Duke, of course. Or it could even be a third party, someone in hiding somewhere.'

Posie chewed her lip. Sure as bread was bread it sounded much like the man who had been eyeing her at Green Park Station earlier that afternoon, outside the Ritz. But she hadn't told the Inspector about that yet, of course.

'Anything else which seemed peculiar to you?'

The film star nodded, nervously. 'I *did* see somethin' strange, but it's unbelievable. You'll think I'm cream crackers.'

'Go on.'

'After I'd seen that fella I went into my own room very quickly. But I thought it was downright odd, and so I came out into the corridor again, pretended I'd dropped a pin or somethin'. But what I saw next didn't make any sense at all.'

'Try me.'

'I saw the tall fella in black keep walkin' on down the corridor, to the very end, past where all the rooms had ended. And then he knocked on the wall at the end. The blank wall! And do you know what happened? A tiny, miniscule hidden doorway opened, just for a flash, and the man disappeared through it!'

The Inspector was looking ashen in the face, but continuing to smile fixedly. Posie was troubled. *What could it mean?*

'And you know somethin' else?' Amory said, bemused. 'Now I come to think of it, I'm sure there was someone standin' in the hidden doorway, meeting the tall fella. Like he was waitin' for him. A really small man, I think. Tiny.'

Posie and the Inspector looked at each other, dumbfounded, but before they could discuss it further, Lord Glaysayer waved over at the three of them cheerily. 'Time for fireworks, everyone! Just quickly outside the front door. On the terrace.'

'This is ridiculous!' muttered the Inspector under his breath. 'We'll never see anything out there in the driving snow! Thank you for the information, Miss Laine. It certainly sounds like it may prove useful.'

Father Moriarty was bending over near the fire in the big central hearth, lighting sparklers and handing them around, keen to help out. The fire was still burning, but only just, sending cosy flickers of an orange glow across the zebra-skin hearth-rug, illuminating all the guests in their gorgeous clothing.

Posie hugged her glittery tweed jacket to herself a little tighter. Someone *must* have left a door open somewhere: she felt decidedly chilly, which came as a shock after the furnace-like temperatures she had got used to inside Maypole Manor so far. For a second there, she wished she was still wearing her lumpy tweed suit jacket; at least it was warm, if not particularly elegant.

Amory Laine sighed and retrieved her half-full glass from the tiger, gathering her coat up around her. 'I'm sure this party would seem much better if I was drinkin' somethin' with a bit of pep to it.'

The Inspector tried not to roll his eyes in exasperation.

They reached the front door, where everyone was gathered on the threshold, waiting. Amory Laine swilled her near-empty glass towards Posie:

'Do you know what, Mrs Grosvenor? I *do* have something for a plot in one of your books, as it happens. I think I'm beginnin' to hallucinate as part of my withdrawal symptoms: why, do you know, tonight I thought for a second that I saw a man I used to perform with, back in my music hall days? But it couldn't be; it wasn't possible. It was absolutely impossible, in fact. Do you remember, Julian, darling? That strange little affair in Whitechapel...'

Julian Carter was at his wife's side, and the whole party stepped outside into the freezing snow, the white blur enveloping them, Amory Laine's words trailing off. Sergeant Binny could just be observed, lighting a Catherine Wheel on a quickly-erected post. Nearby, the circle of red tea-lights which Jacinta had set up underneath the maypole glittered on, winking through the snow. Amory sighed extravagantly:

'Jeepers. I'm so blimmin' thirsty tonight. What's wrong with me? My throat is like sandpaper. Has anyone got a flask of water or a lime soda out here?'

A chain of hands automatically passed a glass decanter of water down to her and Julian Carter re-filled his wife's glass. A pointless rocket went off, smoke belching everywhere, its noise obliterated by the snowstorm. It was absolutely freezing and Posie was shivering violently. So much so that the Inspector put his arm around her and held her very close for real. Amory continued to talk very loudly in Posie's direction:

'And you know another strange thing, Mrs Grosvenor? I keep thinkin' I'm hearin' noises in my room; like pipes or creakin' windows or somethin'. But what if it's not that, Mrs Grosvenor? What if there are *people* creepin' up and down, inside the walls? So the walls literally have ears? Like I said, I'm going to be pleased to leave this place tomorrow.'

* * * *

It was eleven-thirty and people had been more than willing to come back into the house again, to gather by the embers of the fire in the entrance hall. For some reason the house was much, much cooler now, and the fire seemed the only real heat, so it had become a focal-point for the house party.

Sergeant Rainbird had managed to convey by a subtle shake of the head across the room that he had not managed to get through to Scotland Yard by telephone to ask about the priest, and Posie saw Inspector Lovelace blow out his cheeks in a slightly exasperated manner. The Inspector kept checking his watch and licking his lips slightly nervously every couple of minutes. Minutes were ticking by and yet midnight felt a long time coming...

It was odd to hold the Inspector's hand, but Posie squeezed it now in what she hoped was a reassuring gesture. Bryn Cardinal poured himself a whisky from the decanter on the side-table and sat, ready and waiting for midnight. Lord Glaysayer was nowhere to be seen.

A group had gathered by the fireside.

Jacinta Glaysayer was relaying the history of the house, and she was a surprisingly good storyteller. Lenny was standing riveted, the Duke beside her, his head cocked to one side, his notebook at the ready.

'So there's always been a house here, on this land, since the invasion of England in 1066. It's been called Maypole Manor since the medieval times, too. There's been a maypole dance here every summer for five hundred years, or so I'm told. The house may be new and state-of-the-art, but the maypole itself on the lawn has never been changed.'

'But what happens if you changed the name of the house?' Lenny asked, taking a deep drag on her gasper, and blowing out a perfect smoke ring. 'Or if you got rid of the maypole?'

'Oh! We couldn't do that!' trilled Jacinta, as if she had been physically hurt. 'Maypoles were put up in magic places; places where important events took place. They are supposed to protect, to *contain*. To take away a maypole would be to rob the place of its protection. It would be a disaster.'

Just then Julian Carter clattered through the entrance hall, coming to an abrupt stop by the sofas. He looked utterly dishevelled and wild-eyed, his longish hair flopping all over the place, his sleeves rolled up to his elbows and his bow-tie undone. His stance was of one in panic.

'I say, old chap, everything okay?' Bryn Cardinal was alert, on the edge of his seat, eyes scanning Julian Carter's face.

'No,' the artist breathed wheezily, bent over, his hands resting on his knees, as if he had just completed a big race. 'It's *not* okay. I can't find my wife. Anywhere. And no joking please. I've spent the last ten minutes going backwards and forwards searching for her in this dratted great house, and I'm no nearer to finding her than when I began.'

Bryn Cardinal got up. 'On the sauce, was she, old chap? Could have collapsed down drunk somewhere, I suppose?'

'No, she was not drunk. And I won't have you insult my wife in that manner!' Julian Carter had bunched his fists up, and looked all set to start a fight with Mr Cardinal.

The Inspector was on his feet instantly, taking Julian Carter's arm and steering him gently away.

'Where did you last see her, Mr Carter?'

'On the terrace, watching those darned foolish fireworks, as it happens. I came back inside quickly for my lighter, and when I went out again she had gone. But the fireworks had ended, and most people were coming back inside anyway, so I didn't think anything of it.'

'Let's search the house again before we panic, shall we?

Chances are she's fallen asleep somewhere. Out of genuine tiredness, I mean.'

A search was instigated, and everyone took part, Edwin Goodman more fervently than most, Posie felt.

Ten minutes later everyone had re-grouped in the entrance hall beside the dying fire. A quick glance out of the window was enough to deter most people from making a search of the garden.

'It's unlikely she'd have stayed out there, Mr Carter. But let's just make sure.' The Inspector checked his watch for the umpteenth time.

'Anyone coming with me and Carter?'

The Inspector glanced about him but several people had melted away already, unwilling to be drilled into going outside again.

'I'll come with you, sir,' said Binny, in his guise as Butler, bowing low, and taking a packet of matches from an inside pocket.

'Me too, darling.' Posie nodded, privately dreading the cold.

'I'll come,' said the priest calmly. 'The more of us search, the quicker we find her. No?'

The five of them went outside, with Binny in the lead, carrying an old storm-lantern ahead of them. The night was even wilder now and Posie could barely see where they were going. She felt the snow seep through her green pumps, soaking her feet instantly in their thin nylons. Her beautiful tweed jacket was no match for the elements, and for the second time that night she found herself wishing for her lumpy brown tweed, so carelessly cast off.

'Let's stay together!' called out Binny authoritatively. 'Keep looking out. Miss Laine was wearing black, so she'll be easy to see. *Not* that we hope to find her out here of course!'

They traipsed up and down the paved terrace, all along the front of the house. There was nothing to see, apart from the long yellow oblongs of light thrown out from the windows, cast out as reflections over the snow. The salty air was suffocatingly close, and Posie imagined she could hear the sea crashing beyond the clifftop garden.

'Not here! She'd never have wandered off here! It's too dark.' They had reached the edge of the house, near the pine woods, and Carter was standing nervously next to Binny, watching the storm-lantern's light carry uselessly through the still falling snow.

BANG.

A sudden strange piercing sound seemed to cut through the fuggy night air. It was hard to tell but it had seemed to come from the house. From the very heart of Maypole Manor.

'What the blazes was that?' asked Carter, turning, wild-eyed.

'I'm sure it was nothing, Mr Carter. Let's get back inside. There's nothing to see here. No cause for concern.'

The Inspector dragged Posie back towards the house. *He's nervous*, she thought to herself uneasily as they all reached the front door again. *And what on earth was that noise just now?*

'Wait a moment!'

A slight fluttering, jangling sound could be heard behind them; rather like rigging on a ship – the wind blowing through it on a stormy night. The many red ribbons of the maypole were rippling wildly, noisily in the wind.

'The maypole!'

The priest had made a sudden dash towards where just a few of the little red tea-lights from earlier were still burning.

'Over here! Over here! Come quickly! She's over here.'

* * * *

Thirteen

Amory Laine was lying with her back to them within the circle of the red tea-lights, under the maypole itself. Her purple scarf was pooled around her head like a dark, plum-coloured pool of blood.

The ribbons from the maypole fluttered around in the wild wind uselessly, brushing against her. The film star was lying in a slight hollow of snow, a bit like an ice bed, protected from general view. Posie suddenly remembered watching Jacinta and Jocasta digging this very ice bed earlier in the evening; arguing, fractious. A couple of the tea-lights winked through the darkness, then flickered, then died out completely.

'Darling?' Julian Carter was calling, huddled over on his knees, wildly digging into the snow, pulling at his wife, his body trembling.

'I wouldn't do that, sir, if I was you.' Sergeant Binny was attempting to restrain the man. 'Wait a minute, sir. She might be hurt, or needing special attention.'

But Inspector Lovelace and the priest were already there, turning Amory Laine gently over.

And Posie saw at once that there was no special attention in the world which could help the woman now, for she was dead. Julian Carter saw this too, and started screaming.

Posie gasped in horror and dropped to her knees at Inspector Lovelace's side, snow and ice seeping through the House of Harlow dress which was now ruined forever. The hollow which Jacinta had created hours earlier provided a bit of protection against the snow and howling wind.

She whispered to Lovelace urgently:

'Has she frozen to death, sir? Got caught out here unawares? What a tragedy. But she's been out here less than fifteen minutes, surely? That was very quick.'

Before the Inspector could speak, the priest looked up at them both and pointed down, authoritatively, all the while supporting Amory Laine's lolling head. 'No. She hasn't frozen to death. She's died from drug ingestion.'

'I'm sorry?' The Inspector was looking at the priest incredulously.

Posie gasped and felt sick in the pit of her stomach. She remembered Bobbie the Bengal tiger and the arsenic in his mouth, and her warning to Amory. Had the girl somehow and unwittingly poisoned herself by not washing her hands?

'Was it arsenic?' she found herself saying aloud with a horrible sense of dread.

'No. Certainly not,' said the priest with conviction. 'Look at the lips. Around the mouth is a frosting of chalky white, completely unnatural. I'd say it's cocaine. And what's this?'

The priest bent down, picked up Amory's hand which was still clutching her water glass and smelt the contents. He licked his finger, dabbed it inside the glass and then tasted it quickly. Julian Carter, crying and howling, was pawing at his wife's icy cold face, rubbing at her arms as if to bring back the warmth.

'As I thought.' The priest nodded. 'Cocaine. She's drunk cocaine mixed in with water. Unusual, granted. A huge overdose. I'd say she's suffered a huge respiratory attack as a result. Was she a drug user, do you know?'

Julian Carter pawed at his face, rubbing away the tears.

'She *was*,' he said, defiantly highlighting the use of the past tense, turning to Inspector Lovelace and the priest, his eyes pleading with them for a bit of understanding.

'But that was in the past. She'd given it all up. There's no way she'd have drunk cocaine mixed in with water; that's just crazy! Amory had never done that before. No-one does that, it's virtually suicide. And she wasn't suicidal! I swear it. She had everything to live for. We were going to have a baby! I swear to goodness, someone put that drug in her drink tonight. It's foul play. My wife's been murdered.'

And Posie felt chilled to the bone, and it was nothing to do with the weather. She couldn't help but agree with the artist that his wife had been murdered. The very doggedness and bad temper of the girl earlier were surely proof enough that she was, with a great deal of difficulty, steering well clear of drugs.

She remembered the silence in the Library earlier, when Julian Carter had told her that his wife had spotted an intruder in Posie's room. She also remembered Amory Laine out on the terrace, trilling lightly on about how the walls had ears.

The walls have ears.

How many times tonight had Posie heard that expression?

The question was: had the intruder or his accomplice been one of the people to hear these snippets of conversation tonight? And had they then decided that Amory would have to die because of it?

And was this all to do with stealing the plans for 'the Guillotine'? Or was there something else going on, as yet completely unknown?

* * * *

126

The Inspector rapped out instructions.

'Binny, take Mr Carter straight to his room, please. And bring him a stiff drink: poor fella's had the devil of a shock here tonight. I don't want either of you breathing a word about what has happened to Miss Laine to the other house guests when you walk past them, understand? And Mr Carter, I'd be grateful if you'd stay in your room until I fetch you in a minute. Got it?'

The two men nodded and left, Mr Carter stumbling and holding onto Binny for support.

The Inspector took off his jacket and covered Amory Laine's face with it. The priest said nothing, and then walked slowly back with them in silence.

Posie was thinking about Amory on the terrace with the fireworks.

She remembered the girl's sudden thirst, and the flask of water which had been supplied so readily; the many hands who had passed it along. But *who* exactly had had the water with them outside in the first place? Had *they* laced it with a deadly dose of cocaine?

Outside the front door, the Inspector turned and looked quizzically at the priest.

'You certainly know a lot about drugs and death, for a priest.'

The priest smiled. 'And you lot work so well together that I'd be surprised if you weren't an undercover police team; that knowledgeable Butler included.'

He extended a hand. 'I was a doctor, up to and including serving in the Great War. In fact, I was trained in poisons and drugs, and dealing with their effects. Doctor Matthias Brenner, at your service, sir. Obviously, I'm a German.'

'Obviously. And not a Father Moriarty in sight, eh?'

But before the German doctor could answer, the front door was pulled open and Sergeant Binny looked out at them, squinting into the snow-filled darkness. The chimes of the grandfather clock could be heard in the background, striking midnight.

'Dash and blast,' exclaimed the Inspector, dragging Posie by the arm. 'Let's get to Glaysayer's study quickly and deal with this handover. That's our priority; make sure it goes off all right. We'll have to sort Amory Laine's death out in a minute. For the moment we say nothing about it.'

But Binny stopped them and spoke in a low tone, a hushed whisper. He sounded unusually nervous:

'Just so you know, sir. There's a problem.'

'What the blazes is it now?'

'I think that the handover can go ahead as you planned, sir, if you wish, and Mr Cardinal and that chap Edwin Goodman are already in the study. But something terrible has happened: there's been an *incident*. None of the house guests know about it as yet. They're all drinking whisky like there's no tomorrow, and I think a good few of them are already blotto.'

'Get to the point, man.'

'Lord Glaysayer is dead, sir. Just now. In his study. That was the shot we heard when we were outside on the terrace looking for Miss Laine. It seems fairly clear-cut, sir. The fellow has put a bullet to his brain.'

* * * *

PART THREE

Murder at Midnight

Fourteen

'I don't think Miss Parker should go in with you, sir,' said Binny in a muted whisper. 'It's not pretty in there.'

'Oh, rot,' said the Inspector gruffly. 'Now isn't the time for playing nicey-nicey, Sergeant. And Miss Parker is used to a dead body or two. She's from the school of hard knocks. Aren't you, Posie?'

'I am, Binny.' Posie nodded. 'Don't worry about me.' But really she was filled with a horrible sense of trepidation and hoped her fear didn't show. After all, Inspector Lovelace wouldn't want a quivering little flower of a girl on his arm just now; he needed real help, and nerves of steel.

A look of pain passed over Binny's face and his new moustaches quivered. 'Very well, sir. You know best. I'll show you along now.'

Robin Glaysayer's study was at the front of the house, like Posie and the Inspector's bedrooms, and it was a large room, dominated by an oak desk sitting on a raised wooden platform. The room was fairly dark, lit only by a green-glassed reading lamp which sat next to a telephone on the desk.

It was the work of a split-second to take all the details in. The great desk faced the visitor, and Posie saw, with dread, that Lord Glaysayer was slumped across it, face down, sitting in his chair. The desk had a horrible-looking grey leather inlay of what looked like elephant skin on top of it. A pool of blood was gathering on the elephant skin and trickling down onto the platform below. In his right hand Lord Glaysayer held a small shiny automatic pistol. Despite the fact that her heart was juddering, Posie tried to summon up all her professional reserves and look as if she was cool as a cucumber.

The room was very cold. The Inspector winced and cursed under his breath:

'What a bally mess.'

He turned to his Sergeant. 'Binny, make sure to guard the door from the outside.'

Posie heard Binny close the door quietly behind them.

Like some horrible tableau, Edwin Goodman stood to the left of the desk, visibly shaking and looking on the point of hysterical tears, and Bryn Cardinal, as was to be expected in one who had been covered in silverware in the last war, stood on the right, steadfast. His thin mouth was set in a grim line, undeterred.

Just then Posie suddenly became aware of an overpowering stink filling her nostrils over and above the iron-y smell of the blood, and for a second she couldn't place it. And then it came to her in a confusing and sudden realisation...*patchouli oil*. Masses of the stuff.

Jacinta!

Had Jacinta been in here recently?

Posie bit her lip anxiously and tried to keep a clear, open mind. She had a good look around the room for anything else which seemed strange or unusual while the Inspector went and examined the body, his black leather policeman's notebook in hand.

The walls were devoid of any books, but, instead, huge wall maps of parts of Africa were the main decoration. One rather clumsy oil painting was hung in pride of place behind Lord Glaysayer's desk. A fire in the grate to Posie's left had long since gone out. She noted how the huge bay window which was behind her, which by day would flood the whole room with light, had no curtains at all and that the window frames were becoming clogged up outside with a thin layer of drifting icy snow. A magnificent and professional silver telescope sat perched in the middle of the bay window on a big A-frame, trained on some point out there in the snowy blackness.

The Inspector nodded to himself and then headed back to Posie's side and stood in front of the platform. He cleared his throat:

'This is some mess on our hands, chaps. Either of you got a clue what happened here tonight?'

Edwin Goodman pulled himself together with an effort, his American brightness seeming to recover just a little despite the horror of standing next to Lord Glaysayer's body, but he still seemed close to tears.

'No, I swear on my mother's life that I know nothing. We came in here at a quarter-to midnight, and this is what we found. As you see it now. It goes without saying that I wish things were different.'

'Get yourself together, man,' said Bryn Cardinal matter-of-factly, his voice resonant in the room. 'Things *aren't* different. They are as they are. So get a grip.'

The American nodded, chastised. But his cheeks still shook flabbily. The Inspector folded his arms in annoyance.

'You were both here early. How come? I thought we agreed to come in here all together. At midnight. That was the pre-arranged plan, wasn't it, Cardinal?'

Bryn Cardinal nodded his big head.

'It *was*, Inspector. It was. But plans can change. As we both know. You had dashed off outside to try and locate that actress woman, and meanwhile I was getting the wind up me, as Glaysayer seemed to have disappeared into thin air. It seemed dashed odd, him being the host of the party and everything. I wanted to check on him, make sure he was okay; the man had been putting it away a bit all night. You must have noticed? I was worried he'd had a collapse somewhere.'

Bryn Cardinal looked down at the corpse in front of him with some distaste. 'As it happened, on our way here along the corridor we heard what we thought was a shot and we were right; we came in here and found this. Poor old fellow's seen fit to end it all – the coward's way out, of course.' He frowned and crossed his arms, but not before checking his wristwatch.

'And I'll mind if you don't use that accusatory tone with us, Inspector. We're here to help *you*, remember; not to be grilled like common suspects. Remember, we're supposed to have completed a highly dangerous and top-secret assignation by now. Dash it all, Inspector; who knows who could be lurking around about to put paid to all this? Let's get on, man. We're already ten minutes late!'

Inspector Lovelace glowered at the harsh words.

'That's as maybe, Mr Cardinal. But you'll appreciate I have to find out what happened here with Lord Glaysayer, and that's my job, too: dead bodies, and the manner in which people die. I agree it looks fairly open-and-shut in this case, but I *do* have to ask questions, especially when it concerns the first people to find a body, which happens to be you two. The first few minutes are crucial. And no, I won't apologise for that.'

The Inspector clicked his tongue in irritation.

'Right. Let's get this over with, fellows. As you say, Cardinal, we're running late, and I'll thank you that I need no reminding that this assignation should already be completed. It will be a relief to us all to get it over with, I daresay. I'll deal with Glaysayer afterwards. First, Goodman, you have the blueprint?'

The American nodded, a slightly pained look settling across his horse-face. He fished inside his immaculate dress-shirt and withdrew a slim, long envelope made of fine blue oilcloth. He waved it in the air.

'Here, sir. And mighty glad to get rid of them. I can explain them if you want, sir, just say the word. You wanna inspect them first, sir?'

'Yes,' said the Inspector. 'I've been told what to check for, how many pages and such like. There's a special number on them, too, isn't there? Bring them down here, away from all that blood. Can you come here too, Cardinal, and check that these are what you're after? What the country is paying all this money for?'

There followed an inspection of the plans for the bomber, which turned out, surprisingly perhaps, to only be a mere three pages long; codes in black ink on waxy architects paper. From where she was standing Posie could see that two pages were entirely taken up with diagrams, and a third page was covered almost completely in black rows of figures and letters, so tightly-hewn that the colour of the paper beneath was almost totally obliterated. The plans were replaced in their special envelope and then the Inspector and Mr Cardinal concurred that all seemed to be in order. Inspector Lovelace held onto the plans tightly.

'Now for the money.'

Posie stayed where she was. She had looked for the safe when she had first entered the study, but it wasn't visible.

She had guessed, correctly, as it turned out, that the safe was located behind the desk, in the wall, hidden behind the rather badly-executed oil painting in burning oranges and reds of Lord Glaysayer sitting atop an elephant; his eyes shielded against a scorching African sun, forever scanning the horizon for something or other which would now remain a mystery.

Between them the men managed to get the great painting down without touching the body which was very close by, and there was a small ruckus as they manhandled the picture further along the platform, avoiding the pools of blood.

'Do you want to do the honours?' asked the Inspector,

bowing with what looked like mock-reverence to Mr Cardinal.

'No. You be my guest.'

The Inspector paused, shrugged and then opened the safe. After a combination of four numbers was entered, a loud clicking sound could be heard and the safe door sprung open smoothly.

The Inspector reached inside and brought out a brown cardboard box, roughly the size of two shoeboxes joined together. He lifted it out with a visible effort, and managed to stagger with it to the side of the desk, where he dumped it on the floor at Mr Cardinal's feet. Posie came over, keen to see what forty thousand pounds looked like. She held her breath as the Inspector counted it all out on the floor. There were ten rich gold bars, shining lustrously in the light of the dim desk lamp. One thousand per bar.

'Ten thousand pounds,' counted the Inspector calmly, putting them aside.

And then, slowly and methodically, he counted out neat piles of stiff white pound notes, packed into bundles of one thousand pounds each.

'Thirty thousand,' he said at last, quiet satisfaction in his voice. 'So forty thousand in all. You agree that all is in order, Cardinal?'

'I do.' The big man nodded. 'Look here, we need some sort of receipt from you, Goodman, to show everything's as it should be. We'll need your name, signature and contact address here.'

Mr Cardinal leaned over the dead body and pulled a sheet of paper from a jotter on Lord Glaysayer's desk. While Inspector Lovelace re-packed the money, Mr Cardinal took out his own fountain pen and wrote quickly. He showed it to the American, who nodded in agreement.

'Sign here, if you're happy. This shows you have no further claim on the British government once you take this money. Understand?'

The American signed where indicated and seemed to breathe a huge sigh of relief. Mr Cardinal added his signature and then passed the note to the Inspector to counter-sign.

Cardinal looked at the American shrewdly. 'On a more practical note, Goodman, how are you going to transport this little lot? And where are you going now?'

'I'm going to New York, sir. And blow me if I'm never leaving it again. I'll get the first berth I can out from Liverpool. I think there's a Cunard steamer leaving from there to New York in three days' time. I'll hate the crossing but it's only for six days. And as to *how* I'll carry it, sir, I have this with me.'

He darted to his left and picked up a tough-looking leather carrier bag, the sort used by mail boats and trains when transporting heavy post.

Inspector Lovelace shrugged.

'If you think it's up to the job, Goodman, that's your look-out, apparently. Better come here and we'll load it up.'

The three men packed the bag, and then Mr Cardinal took the blueprint from Inspector Lovelace and pocketed the receipt from Mr Goodman at the same time. They all stepped away from the platform with some relief, Mr Goodman dragging the heavy bag along the floor. They gravitated to where Posie was still standing at the window. She shivered. How cold the room was, even without the knowledge of the dead body behind them. She rubbed at her arms through the thin tweed jacket which refused to dry; the wet cloth limp and useless.

'I don't suppose either of you will be going anywhere in a hurry in this weather,' the Inspector said, gesturing at the window.

'I'd like to leave as soon as possible, sir,' said the American. 'That was the plan. But you're right, I'll have to sit tight for now.'

'I'd wanted to get straight up to London, too,' said Mr

Cardinal, peering out into the snowy darkness. 'But I think I'll have to sit out the night here and leave at the crack of dawn. It's not at all ideal but there's no way my motor car, even driven by the amazing Evans, will make it in this. And neither will Miss Brandenberger's motorcycle; that wouldn't work at all. The only thing I can think of that would make it in this would be a plane; a robust sort of plane, like an Avro. I flew one in the war in weather just like this. Got through the snow just fine. But I don't have one handy. More's the pity.'

Posie stared at the man in surprise, but why was she surprised? He was apparently a war hero. She found herself on the brink of blabbing proudly about Alaric; about how he too had flown planes in the last war, and had been one of the country's top flying aces – perhaps they had known each other? – when they were all distracted by the sight of a very bright light flashing from what looked like the cliff edge, cutting through the darkness. It was the same light she had seen earlier from her bedroom.

FLASH. PAUSE. FLASH-FLASH.

And then it came again.

FLASH. PAUSE. FLASH-FLASH.

They all watched, fascinated. The Inspector bent down and looked through the telescope. But the lights had stopped. The clock struck half-past the hour.

'Can't see a dashed thing,' he muttered. 'But it's trained on exactly the right spot. Maybe Glaysayer was suspicious; knew there were rum goings-on in his back yard. But you'd think the smugglers would be giving it a break on New Year's Eve, especially in this weather!'

Bryn Cardinal nodded. 'Seems our Customs and Excise boys need to sharpen up their act. Looks like a full-scale operation to me.'

'Rather them than me.' The Inspector turned back into the room, sighed and crossed his arms. Mr Cardinal followed his gaze.

'What will you do now, Inspector? About old Glaysayer here, I mean. I'm assuming all police procedure is thrown out of the window when there's no outward lines of communication in place, no professional experts on hand?'

'That's right, Cardinal. We go into emergency mode; do what we can, contain everything until help arrives. I'll get what help I can, where I can, but I suppose it will be dawn for me too before I can contact the Yard and get our forensics boys down here.'

The thought of his esteemed place of employment seemed to shake the Inspector up; galvanise him into action, give him direction.

'Right. So now for Glaysayer. We'd better get the daughters in here, sharpish.'

'Is that wise, sir?' asked Posie. 'They might collapse. They don't know he's dead yet, let alone bring them in here and expose them to *this*.'

'Why not? At some point they'll need to identify their father's body and they might as well do it now. Besides, they might be able to shed some valuable light on this scene – why the chap chose to shoot himself and so on.'

He paused, looking over at the desk, drumming his fingers against the windowpane. 'Something isn't right here. But I'm not sure what, *yet*.'

'You want us to stay or go?' asked the American, obviously longing to get as far away from the body as possible.

'Stay, please. As I said, the first people to find a body are always important.'

The Inspector opened the door of the study cautiously, and within seconds Sergeant Binny entered the room. The Inspector murmured a command and Binny nodded, and then he muttered something in Lovelace's ear and passed him what looked like a sealed telegram.

For just a second the Inspector's face betrayed a look almost akin to panic, but then he recovered himself quickly.

'Tell the Cleghorn boy to get on home as quickly as he can then, and to bring his father and any other support he has available. Thanks. You go and get the daughters. Now, please.'

Inspector Lovelace turned to the window again and looked out, his mind elsewhere.

'Sir?'

Posie didn't like the awful turn the evening was taking. A premonition of being utterly stranded and alone here in the midst of some terrible danger reared its ugly head.

The Inspector spun around and addressed the three of them, a weary look of resignation in his eyes behind their fake gold spectacles.

'You should all know that we just had a visit from the boy from the Post Office, the policeman's son. Unbelievably, really, in this weather. Seems he was driven on by my Sergeant's promise of an even bigger tip than last time. The boy brought a telegram which arrived much earlier in the evening for me. But he wanted to tell me that no more telegrams will be getting through for the rest of the night; the blizzard has caused the electricity and telephone lines to go down in the whole village. The whole area of St Margaret's is unreachable; totally cut off.'

'Can this get any worse, sir?' Posie looked at the Inspector aghast. But he silenced her with an upturned hand.

'It will all be fine. Nothing to worry about. I've asked the local bobby to come, if he can make it through the snow; with whatever support he can muster.'

Bryn Cardinal emitted a puffing sound, almost amused.

'A lone country bobby on the beat? I wouldn't have thought that would help us much, Inspector. Are you envisaging problems ahead?'

'No, of course not. We just need to wait it out until morning. It's not as if we're in danger of anything, is it? Poor old Glaysayer up there won't be giving us any trouble, will he? But I always say any help is better than nothing, so I won't be turning our country bobby on the beat away, I can assure you; *if* he makes it here, that is.'

Inspector Lovelace opened up the telegram and read it, his characteristic 'v' mark of worry deepening between his eyebrows. Three pairs of eyes regarded him closely.

'As I said, there's nothing to worry about. Mr Cardinal and Mr Goodman, can you stand to one side, please? I'd like to give the Glaysayer girls room to view.'

They did as instructed and Posie was vaguely aware of a commotion in the corridor outside, of the Inspector going out and speaking to Jacinta and Jocasta in calm, soothing tones. But before he had left the room, he had given Posie the telegram, almost as a sleight of hand. She turned to the window and read it quickly.

It was very short.

To: POST OFFICE, ST MARGARET'S-AT-CLIFFE. 017 From: SWISS EMBASSY, 16/18 MONTAGUE PLACE, MAYFAIR, LONDON, W1

DEAR INSPECTOR LOVELACE,

YOU ASKED FOR INFORMATION ON ONE RUDOLPH 'RUDY' STEINHAUSER.

WE CONFIRM HE WAS A SWISS CITIZEN.

BUT OUR RECORDS SHOW THAT THE ONLY SWISS CITIZEN OF THAT NAME DIED IN A FREAK ACCIDENT IN A DIAMOND MINE OUT IN TANZANIA, AFRICA, IN 1892.

I HOPE THIS HELPS IN YOUR INVESTIGATIONS.

WITH ALL BEST WISHES,

R.NOSER (ACTING OFFICER AT THE SWISS EMBASSY, LONDON)

Posie's mind was racing. *Yet another fake!*

Who on earth was the man pretending to be Mr Steinhauser? The man who could talk so knowledgeably about Africa? And what was he really doing here?

Posie skimmed the telegram again, and a mass of uncomfortable thoughts crowded into her head. Something about the telegram gave her the jitters, and not just the news of the stolen identity. But before she could ponder it more, Jacinta and Jocasta, no longer willing to be cajoled and contained in the passageway outside, burst into the study.

* * * *

Fifteen

The two girls stood in front of the platform and stared at their father's prone body slumped on the desk. They remained speechless.

For just a heartbeat.

Then an almighty wail started up, desperate and helpless. Posie stared at the two girls uncomfortably. It was Jacinta doing all the noisy crying, uncontrollable sobs wracking her small, twisted body. She looked in danger of falling over, and Edwin Goodman evidently thought so too, for a chair was found out of nowhere and she collapsed into it.

Jocasta was an altogether different creature, but Posie watched as a slow-dawning fear and horror gripped her, a dark shadow of despair crossing her face. She stood, ram-rod straight in her glittering green sheath. She refused the offer of a chair and stood as far away as she could from Bryn Cardinal and Edwin Goodman, smoking a black cigarillo. After a few minutes, she turned and stared rudely at Posie. Then she looked at the Inspector and snarled at him.

'I don't understand why *she's* here. In fact, I don't understand why *any* of you are here, before us.'

'I'll explain everything, Miss Glaysayer, if you give me a moment. But won't you sit down? You've just had a nasty shock.'

Jocasta refused the offer, and so the Inspector quickly explained who he was, and who Posie really was, and who Mr Cardinal was.

He didn't explain who Edwin Goodman was, or explain about the bomber plans; just that they were all engaged here on 'government business' which was secret, but which Lord Glaysayer had known about, and had approved of.

For a couple of seconds the two girls just stared at them all in apparent disbelief. And then Jacinta spoke up from her chair:

'I *knew* this was all a strange set-up. That something funny was going on. I kept getting these vibes.'

She turned to Posie. 'For example, I *knew* you weren't meant to be with this very dull man who was apparently your husband. I was getting strange signals. I could see that you were meant to be with a man who flies planes. A famous man…A man who travels and smells of cardamom and lemon and the trade winds…I'm right aren't I? I just thought that perhaps you had married the wrong man, and were having an affair with the man with the plane or something. And the cat. Do tell me you have a cat? A Siamese cat? It was a very strong signal.'

'Er…well, I do happen to have…'

'Oh for goodness' sake!' cut in Jocasta. 'You and your stupid hunches. You're no more a clairvoyant than I am! You make yourself ridiculous; that's all you do. Our father is dead up there on that desk, and all you can talk about is cats! Good grief! Have you no shame?'

Jacinta flushed with embarrassment but then she regained her composure a little and stood up. She faced her sister across the room, her poise one of righteous indignation.

'I told you he'd be dead tonight, didn't I? I had a premonition. I told him too. I read his palm, like I did often. I knew his death would be linked to this house party tonight and I begged him to cancel it; told him he'd die otherwise.'

'Well, maybe it was *you* who gave him the idea to shoot himself, then? By keeping going on and on about it. Poor devil only had a bit of time left anyway, but you obviously convinced him to make that even shorter!'

'How can you say such things?' screamed Jacinta hoarsely. 'As if you cared when he died! And as to me convincing him to shoot himself – what rot! Our father was one of the bravest men I knew. It's totally out of character. He'd never have done such a thing. Besides, he loved you too much. He would have wanted to live right until the bitter end just to see more of you and your ugly face. Don't you realise that?'

Jacinta launched herself towards her sister.

'Ladies, please!' Inspector Lovelace came between the women, calmly splaying his hands. But Jacinta carried on regardless:

'And I didn't have a premonition about him killing himself, as well you know. I saw that he was *murdered*. By someone at this house party.'

The room went very still.

Posie exhaled silently, watchful. *If* what Jacinta was saying was true, then the conversation she had overheard earlier between the girl and her father upstairs was starting to make sense: Jacinta had begged him to cancel the party, to get the guests to leave; Lord Glaysayer had said he wouldn't do it, that he wouldn't change a thing.

'Ladies, can you just come and look closely at your father's body. It will only take a second, I promise you. Tell me if you see anything suspicious or odd about it. Posie, can you come here too and make notes?'

Posie nodded, darting forwards, pleased to be doing something useful at last. What the Inspector meant was that he wanted her to study how the girls behaved when they were confronted with the dead body, and then report back to him later.

The two Glaysayer girls stepped up onto the platform

and stared down at their father. Both walked around a little, gulping nervously, trying to avoid the blood.

'Anything, ladies?'

Jacinta nodded, her small eyes set as flinty blue stones.

'Yes, Inspector. I do see something odd. It's as I thought. I didn't *see* this scene in my premonition, but it's the same result, regardless. *Murder.*'

Posie felt the Inspector tense at her side. Was Jacinta just raging and ranting wildly in her grief? Throwing mad accusations around?

'And why do you think this is a case of murder, might I ask, Miss Glaysayer?'

'Look at the pistol. It's a classic schoolboy error. That pistol *did* belong to our father, I'll give you that: he kept it in the top drawer of his desk. But our father was left-handed. Just look! The pistol is clutched in his right hand! And he's shot himself in the right temple! There's no way he could have done that. No way!'

Jacinta moved stealthily around, and went to the pen-holder at the front of the desk, near the telephone. She pulled out the sleek black and silver pen which was resting there.

'Anyone who knew my father can vouch for the fact he was left-handed. He couldn't write right-handed for toffee: he even had a special pen. See, here it is. Cost a fortune and was one of my father's most valued possessions. And go and check his golf clubs; they're all for a left-handed player, too. Ask his Golf Club at Sandwich; they'll have him down as left-handed. And look at that picture which someone has just dumped down there on the floor. I painted that one summer when I was about twelve. I wanted to get it just right; our father always stood like that, shielding his eyes with his left hand. You believe me now?'

Jacinta's voice had got higher and higher and Posie realised she was on the verge of giddy tears again. She turned to her sister imploringly:

'Tell him, JoJo. Tell him our father was left-handed.'

And Jocasta nodded grimly, reluctantly.

'My sister is correct, Inspector. You can ask anyone who knew him. They'll all tell you the same thing.'

She bent her head, as if in quiet acceptance of a truth. 'My father does seem to have been murdered. And by an ill-informed fool, or a first-class idiot. So my sister *would* seem to have a point, Inspector. With or without her premonitions. Which you can take or leave, as you wish.'

The Inspector nodded, his face set in an unreadable mask. He shepherded the girls off the platform, guiding them from the room.

'Thank you for your time, ladies. Obviously tonight we won't be able to get to the bottom of this, and we'll need our specialist forensic teams here to take away the evidence and check details, just as soon as the road becomes passable again. But thank you for giving me a steer. Please don't mention your father's death to anyone else just yet; I'll come and address everyone together. Would you like to return to the entrance hall for now? It seems to be the only warm place in the house for some reason. Why is that? It was hot as Hades earlier, and now it's freezing. Unreliable central heating, is it? New-fangled stuff!'

Jacinta shook her head, dabbing her eyes.

'I don't know, sir. It's never failed before. The house is always unbearably hot. I've never known it so cold. It's most peculiar. What can have happened? I don't know if my father even bothers to keep firewood, it's so uncalled-for. The fire in the entrance hall was only lit tonight for the appearance of the thing.'

But Jocasta had turned and was staring wide-eyed behind her again. Posie followed her gaze but she saw that the girl was not looking at Lord Glaysayer, but rather at the safe which was still open, the door hanging wide, inviting. Before anyone could stop her she had made a bolt for the safe.

'I say!' shouted the Inspector, and Posie watched uselessly as Jocasta got to the safe and rifled around in it. She drew out one large cream piece of paper, tied with a pink ribbon and sealed with a small red globule of wax. It was obviously a last Will and Testament.

'Why is the safe open?' she spoke angrily to the room at large. 'And why is it empty except for this? Where are our mother's jewels? Have you devils taken them? Is this all part of the payment of taxes which he apparently owes?'

'Oh, JoJo!' wailed her sister. 'Can't this wait? Now come with me. Hand that to the Inspector and I'll get you a brandy.'

But Jocasta had pushed her sister away and stopped in her tracks. She tore open the paper, the pink ribbon and shattered wax dropping like sad rags to the floor. She read the document, and a brief smile lit up her features, illuminating her strange widely-dilated eyes. She licked her lips and Posie was reminded more than ever of a cat. A greedy cat. She looked directly at her sister with gleeful surprise.

'You were right, then. At least our killer has done me a favour. I'm Lady of the Manor now, a bit earlier than I would have been. So I can do as I choose here!'

But Jocasta sounded fragile, as if she were on the verge of tears, at last. Handing the opened Will reluctantly to the Inspector, she allowed herself to be taken out of the room by her sister.

Inspector Lovelace read the Will quickly and folded it, putting it back into the safe and locking it again.

He nodded. 'She's right: the old fellow left everything he owned to Jocasta. Apart from something called Bobbie, apparently. *That* goes to Jacinta.'

'The tiger,' murmured Posie. 'Bobbie the Bengal tiger.'

'Ah. I see.'

'I say, sir, can we leave now and get back to the entrance hall? It sure is darn cold in here.'

The Inspector swung around and saw Edwin Goodman, weighted down by his mail bag with its precious contents, leaning against the wall. Bryn Cardinal was playing with the telescope in the window. He was holding a packet of matches in one hand, flicking one after another carelessly.

'I'm *so* sorry, gentlemen. I should have sent you there earlier. But it was important for the Glaysayer women to know what this was about; roughly, you know. Go, but please don't say anything about what's happened here. Not yet. I'll come and speak to the house guests together.'

The two men made to leave the study at once, Goodman dragging his heavy bag, but the Inspector called out again, and Posie could hear the fear in his voice all too plainly.

'Tell me you *have* got that blueprint on you safely, Cardinal; that no-one will be able to take it from you during the course of the night? We all know that it's entirely possible that we have got a first-rate maniac among us tonight; either that or a calculating schemer.'

The Inspector smiled weakly.

'And call me an old wind-bag but at present we have no idea if old Glaysayer here was killed as part of the attempt to get the blueprint for the plane – perhaps the murderer thought Glaysayer was holding onto the plans personally – we can't rule it out. It was one thing you getting the plans up to London double-quick, but I have to confess I'm worried about you sitting around here all night with a killer in our midst. And I can't even tell you who to steer clear of; there are simply too many fishy characters for my liking.'

Bryn Cardinal came up very close to Posie and Lovelace. Edwin Goodman eyed the three of them a tad cautiously from his position near the door.

'Rest assured, Inspector,' Cardinal whispered in a low tone. 'Everything is in hand.'

And then Posie nearly fell off her wet green velvet shoes in surprise as Bryn Cardinal pulled up his shirt to reveal a surprisingly buffed torso for so large a man, the muscles clearly defined and rippling in the light of the dim desk lamp. She was so busy appreciating the man's chest that she almost didn't register the strange black bandages, criss-crossing over Cardinal's body like a harness and enclosing both the blueprint and a gun.

A gun!

Posie heard the Inspector catch his breath next to her.

A sleek black pistol was nuzzled up close to the blueprint against Cardinal's chest. It looked like a Luger to Posie, though she was no firearms expert, but she had seen one before. On second thoughts Posie wasn't at all surprised that a man such as Cardinal carried a gun. The man was a spy, after all. Why, even her business partner Len Irving still carried his old war revolver around with him everywhere, and he wasn't involved in anything like the important issues of national security which Mr Cardinal found himself in.

'See?' hissed Mr Cardinal. 'You have to be prepared for just about anything in my position. And I am. So don't worry about me. Or 'the Guillotine'. She's safe as houses with me. No-one will take her off me. Okay?'

Inspector Lovelace paused for a second and then nodded curtly.

'Fine. I wasn't told you would be armed, but it's just as well, bearing in mind the circumstances we're finding ourselves in here. Even though you didn't ask me to bring it, I have my own Webley with me, just in case, but I was hoping not to have to use it. My Sergeants are both unarmed, of course, in line with regulation police procedure. Fine, both of you go and get warm. We'll be along in a tick.'

Without looking back the American and the MI5 Agent left the room and the Inspector sunk into the chair recently vacated by Jacinta.

He whispered softly:

'I don't like this, Posie. I don't like it one bit. I knew something wasn't right the minute I saw it; the whole set-up up there looked staged to me and what with this new knowledge about Glaysayer being left-handed, I can't help but agree with the strange daughters that we've got a murder on our hands.'

Posie tutted.

'*Two* murders on our hands, sir. You're forgetting about Amory Laine. We both know it's possible she was killed for what she saw tonight – witnessing that strange intruder coming out of my room – and it could be linked to Lord Glaysayer's death somehow.'

'Mnnn. Could be. Might not be.'

The Inspector groaned and put his head in his hands. His white tie was all dishevelled and he looked in need of a stiff drink. Posie felt for him, she really did. He flung down the fake spectacles and rubbed the grey powder from his hair.

'That stuff itches like mad! So what did you think about the way the daughters reacted to the death of Glaysayer? Funny lot, aren't they?'

'I'll say so, sir. I thought Jacinta might be a suspect, sir, initially. Can you smell that very strong perfume of hers in here? It lingers horribly. Why is that? I thought initially that she might have been the killer; you know, jealous of the way her father treated her in comparison to her sister.'

'Pah! It would have to be a pretty big case of the old green-eyed monster to want to kill your own father. Besides, Jacinta's the very one who's just helpfully told us about her father being left-handed, about how he couldn't have killed himself like that. I'm not ruling her out; I'm not ruling anybody out, but in my mind she's not a prime suspect.'

'I agree with you, sir. And while Jacinta knew her father was going to give everything to Jocasta, she also knew it was a worthless gift. She was privy to a knowledge which no-one else had.'

'How so?'

'Debts, sir. Apparently Lord Glaysayer doesn't even own the gravel on his own driveway here at Maypole Manor. The whole lot will have to be sold. Jocasta is apparently totally unaware of it.'

'I see. Interesting stuff. And Jocasta? What do you make of her? She'd have had a motive for killing her father if she wanted to get her hands on this place quickly; if she believed it would come to her with no ties or debts attached.'

Posie shrugged. 'I don't like the girl, sir. I think she's wild, and unstable. I think she's taking drugs, too. But that's it. I don't think she's a murderer. She's all sham. Besides, I think she was very shaken up about the death tonight, for all her cool, calm posturing. I thought she looked almost frightened when she first saw her father lying there.'

The Inspector stood up, sighing.

'Quite. We'd better go and inform the others about what's happened here, and tell them about Amory Laine, too – I managed to keep our American friend and old Cardinal in the dark about that during the big exchange – did you notice? I didn't want any distractions. Dash it all! Two murders in one night! *Someone* here knows something about these deaths. This whole thing stinks: all these people here who say they're one thing and it turns out they're another. Who knows just *who* exactly is in cahoots with who?'

'I know, sir. It's a very rum do.'

The Inspector started to tuck away his policeman's notebook in his jacket pocket.

'The exchange with the blueprint seems to be just the tip of some almighty iceberg. Hopefully the local policeman will arrive soon; I'd certainly appreciate a bit more back-up during the night. The sooner those plans for 'the Guillotine' are off to London the better. I don't mind admitting to you, Posie, that I'm not enjoying this house party one bit.'

'Nor me, sir.' She eyed the notebook greedily. 'I say, sir. Was there anything else odd which you noticed up there at Lord Glaysayer's desk which you've jotted down, or kept for yourself? I'd like to help, sir, if I can. Two heads better than one and all that old guff...'

The Inspector almost grinned.

'The Posie Parker School of Detection never rests, does it, Posie? Even during a crisis?'

'Well...'

'Go up and have a close look at Glaysayer yourself, then. You didn't get a chance before, really, did you? Then come here and tell me what you think.'

Posie marched up to the desk and had a good old look at the body there. Swallowing down her squeamishness and pulling out a clean hankie from her pocket she managed to tug something out from under the dead man's head, and then hunted around the environs of the desk, and under Lord Glaysayer's chair, all the while the Inspector watching her.

Her heart was thudding like mad. If truth were told she still wasn't that good with corpses, despite having seen hundreds and hundreds out on the front line of battle in the Great War when she was a Red Cross Ambulance Driver. The sight of just one corpse, alone, but known personally to her, was altogether different somehow. Especially when there seemed to be a strong whiff of murder hanging heavy in the air.

She marched back to Inspector Lovelace, who was eyeing her half-warily, half-appreciatively.

'And?'

'Three things to report, sir.'

'Yep?'

'Glaysayer's watch, sir. It's smashed, presumably by the force of his head hitting his hand as he fell against the desk. It stopped at exactly quarter-to midnight.'

The Inspector waved his notebook.

'I have that here myself. Noted. Next point?'

'There are teeny, tiny slivers of what seem to be glass mixed in with a pool of blood under the desk. I can't tell, and I promise I didn't touch, but the scent of patchouli oil is especially strong there. There's also what looks like a very slight oil-like residue in the pool of blood under the desk. I'd hazard a guess that the glass is from a perfume bottle; a tiny vial filled with patchouli oil, and that it was crushed underfoot somehow to let off its scent.'

'Why?'

'To frame Jacinta, I think, sir. The old red herring routine, sir. Perhaps a touch obvious, though?'

'Or desperate? Or someone stalling for time? Throwing us off the scent, perhaps…' The Inspector grinned at his own pun, and then looked contrite.

'Hmnn, sorry about that. Tasteless under the circumstances of course.'

Inspector Lovelace waved his police notebook again. 'I noted that too. Third point?'

Posie frowned, perplexed. 'It's an odd one, sir. I'm sure you have it written down there, though. The photo. I didn't touch it with my bare hands, I promise; I used a handkerchief.'

'Photo?'

'Yes. The small silver-framed photo which Lord Glaysayer is lying on up there, which he must have collapsed on when he died. It looks very old; taken at the turn of the century, most likely. It shows a beautiful woman, I suppose his wife, in full Highland Dress, but wearing a big glittery tiara and a big necklace, with a little girl of about ten at her side, also in a kilt. I'm pretty certain it's Jacinta in the photo.'

The Inspector frowned, piqued.

'Why's that strange?'

'It's *Jocasta* who's supposed to be the favourite. Why is she missing from the photo? Seems odd.'

The Inspector shrugged. 'I'll admit I didn't see the photograph, but it sounds a mare's nest to me. Probably some old sentimental thing. Or are you thinking that that, too, has been "placed", like Jacinta's perfume?'

Posie scrunched up her mouth and chewed at her lip. She couldn't tell the Inspector that somehow the photograph was important, that she just *knew* it was important. She would be beginning to sound like Jacinta herself with her strange visions and premonitions, and that would never do. She could see that the Inspector wanted to move on, to impose as much order on the evening as he was capable of.

'Probably nothing, sir. You're right. Can I ask what your current thoughts are, sir? Whom do you most suspect?'

The Inspector nodded briefly.

'As I said, I can't rule anyone out. But we know Glaysayer died at a quarter-to midnight, and at that exact time you, me, Binny and the dodgy priest were all out with Julian Carter looking for and then finding his wife's dead body. So that leaves your pal Lenny, her Sicilian Duke, JoJo Glaysayer, Jacinta Glaysayer and this impersonator of a dead Swiss mining man, Steinhauser, all unaccounted for. All of whom, to my mind, are in the frame for Glaysayer's murder.'

Posie nodded. 'It's a line-up filled with possibilities, sir. So who's your favourite?'

They were at the door and neither of them were sad to leave the horrible, freezing room.

The Inspector sighed. 'If I were a betting man, I'd put my money on Steinhauser being the man seen coming out of your room. And the small man in the hidden doorway helping him or showing him where to go must have been the Duke. He's the only one here who fits Amory Laine's description of a small man. And for all his goody-two-shoes behaviour as reported by the Italian Embassy, I'd wager the man's as bent as can be, in with the best of the Italian Mafiosi: drugs; smuggling; the lot. He'll be the mastermind behind whatever the blazes is going on around here with these flashing lights we've seen. Why else would a man like that be down here on New Year's Eve of all places?'

They were out in the corridor now, and the Inspector's voice came as a carefully-controlled and barely-audible whisper in Posie's ear:

'And as for Steinhauser, we don't know the man from Adam. He could be *anyone*. Sure as bread is bread he knows the Duke from somewhere or other and the two of them are thick as thieves. They're just pretending not to know each other, of course. We'll have to keep a careful watch on them through the night. They'll be in on this as a team, sharing a shady past, I'll warrant. Perhaps with your pal Lenny.'

'She's not my pal, sir. But why murder Lord Glaysayer, sir? It doesn't figure. What had the poor old chap done to deserve that? He had only weeks to live, apparently.'

'No idea, Posie. Not yet. Happy New Year, by the way. We missed it in all the chaos.'

'A fine way to spend it, too, sir. We're stuck here with no telephone, cut off from everything. And we have a murderer among us.' Posie gulped. 'Golly, can it get any worse?'

The Inspector patted Posie's arm in a brotherly fashion.

'No, it can't get any worse. Thing is, not to panic. It's only for one night. Local help will come soon, and *real* help will come in the morning. You'll see.'

And as they came out into the big white expanse of the entrance hall, Posie bit her lip and hoped against hope that the Inspector was right. She repeated his words in her head as a kind of mantra: *it can't get any worse.*

But how could she stay calm when there was a killer in their midst?

Posie told herself to get a grip and act like the professional she was, not like Hilda Grosvenor, a great woolly sheep of a crime writer who wouldn't say boo to a goose and clung to her husband for all she was worth. *That* pretence, at least, was all over. Thank goodness. She could be herself again.

And she tried to focus on staying grateful for small mercies.

* * * *

PART FOUR

The Long, Long Night

Sixteen

'Two terrible things have happened here tonight,' Inspector Lovelace announced sombrely, looking around, gauging reactions.

The Inspector stood, hands behind his back, in front of the almost-dead fire, and addressed the guests. The horrible animal heads stared down, eyes glittering reproachfully. Everyone was assembled on and around the trio of sofas in the entrance hall which was brightly, garishly lit up. Mr Carter had been fetched down from his room at last and he sat, whisky-soaked and snivelling, on an otherwise empty sofa. People stared at him, unapologetically fascinated.

'Two deaths.'

Everyone sat up, riveted. Posie perched on an arm of a chair next to Mr Cardinal. She noticed that up close he smelt faintly of vetiver, promising of warmer, duskier climes. She toyed with the idea that it was not entirely unattractive.

Sergeants Binny and Rainbird were at the front door, leaning mock-casually against it but clearly acting as wardens. Evans, Cardinal's man, had gone for firewood earlier and was hunting for it in the outhouses and sheds near the pine forest. The Inspector, satisfied he had everyone's attention, pressed his point:

'I am sorry to say that Amory Laine, the film star, is dead. And so too is Lord Glaysayer. Further, it pains me to tell you this but there are suspicions of foul play – murder – in each case. And given the inhospitable weather conditions suffered here tonight, it is therefore highly likely, almost certain, that the murderer or *murderers* of both of these victims is sitting among us now. So, in short, you are all suspects.'

And then, among all the gasps and exclamations of horror, and the crying noises which came from Julian Carter's direction on the sofa, the Inspector explained who he really was, and who Posie was, and who Mr Cardinal really was. And who his Sergeants were, and who Evans was. As with the Glaysayer girls, everything else was left hanging in the air, unexplained.

Everyone stared at each other on the couches, speechless. Surprisingly, it was the Duke who broke the silence.

'How do we really know you is who you say you is, *Inspector*? You cudda be anyone! You know, you cudda be masquerading as someone else. An imposter! A fake!'

Posie turned to the Duke, surprised. *The cheek of the man!* The Inspector evidently thought so too, as he glowered angrily but took out from an inner pocket his Scotland Yard gold badge sewn onto a leather fob, with all of his identity details secured to the back of it. He passed it over to the Duke and kept his hard, polite voice trained on him:

'A fair point, Duke. A fair point, well made. You can pass that around among you if you like, if it sets your minds at ease. And if you'd like my Sergeants to do the same, I'm sure they'd be only too willing. No? Fine. Let's crack on.'

No-one else having taken Inspector Lovelace up on the offer of inspecting his identity card, the Inspector reclaimed it tetchily and turned to the room, more riled than before. He patted a back pocket smartly.

'Oh, and perhaps it would be a good thing for you to all know that I'm armed, so no funny business please; I don't want to have to use my firearm.'

He was met by silence. Inspector Lovelace turned to the Duke, who was, unsurprisingly, nestled next to Lenny, still in his thick fur coat.

'You speak of false identities, Duke Del Angelo; of people masquerading as others. And I have to say I find that surprising, given what I know about you, sir. For it seems that nothing is quite as it seems here at this party tonight. Why, I know of at least two people who are masquerading as others, sitting here in this very room. And one of you is even pretending to be someone who is actually dead, but to what end I know not why, *yet*. Others of you surely have murky secrets and identity issues, even if you are here under your supposedly real names.'

Posie looked carefully around her, first at the Duke, and then at Mr Steinhauser, still in his hat, who she now saw was staring across at the Glaysayer girls with a strange look in his poor weeping eyes. He was smoking a cigarillo, long legs crossed, wrapped in his black wool cape, seemingly oblivious to what the Inspector was alluding to. Into Posie's mind came a sudden remembrance, of who the man was, but then it went again. Maddeningly.

The Inspector's ringing voice, now full of menace, blocked her own scattered thoughts, and recalled her back to herself.

'Every single person in this room is keeping something from me. You are all hiding secrets. Some big, some small. Some deadly. I want to know who you are, and why you are *really* here tonight, and what you were all doing at a quarter-to midnight. And I tell you this. If you do not volunteer your secrets, I will automatically designate you as prime suspects for both murders, and have my men, when they arrive in the morning, cart you off double-quick to the cells at Scotland Yard in London. And I can assure you of this, the cells are certainly *not* the Ritz Hotel, and no, you won't be afforded any special treatment by me there.'

Posie looked around and noticed that most people on

the sofas were sitting with their eyes fixed at a point on the floor or on one of the ghastly stuffed heads; anywhere other than on the Inspector.

'So this is what will happen here,' the Inspector continued briskly.

'We have the whole night to sit here, and sit here we will, together, fortified perhaps by some coffee and whatever else the kitchen has to offer up, until the morning comes and help – proper help – arrives. In a minute you will be allowed up to your rooms to gather whatever necessities are needed for the night, and you will be accompanied by one of my Sergeants. At the same time one of my men will search both you and your room, to check for any incriminating evidence and anything like arms or weaponry you may have with you. You will then surrender the key to your room to my men. Afterwards, as I have said, we will all sit the night out here, together. Understand?'

'So what you're actually telling us is that we're under some sort of arrest, Inspector?' This spat scathingly from a sarcastic-sounding Jocasta, one carefully-drawn eyebrow raised indignantly. 'In *my* house?'

'Yes, Miss Glaysayer. That's right. House arrest in your house. I must contain you, but I must protect you too. You are all, to an extent, prisoners. After all, it galls me to emphasise this but emphasise it I must, we have a killer among us. I must try to ensure your safety.'

No-one said a word.

'If you need to visit the bathroom at any point, one of my Sergeants will accompany you. You will not go anywhere alone. During this time, should you wish to tell me anything which will add to my knowledge about the dead actress and the dead adventurer, please do so. If you wish to tell me anything which will clear yourselves of the victims' deaths, or to explain your presence here, you will be most welcome to. You can also tell my associate here, Miss Posie Parker, should you find that a more agreeable prospect.'

Posie blushed with a barely-concealed pride to be described as an *associate*. She was aware of many eyes upon her. But the Inspector was concluding:

'Oh, and did I mention that we should have some local help arriving during the night? The local policeman, Cleghorn. It will just add to our security here. Everyone understand? Good. Now, who needs to get things first?'

* * * *

It was a quarter-past one in the morning, and Posie sat on the sofa huddled in her brown lumpy Peter Jones tweed skirt, her thankfully dry shoes and Alaric's huge grey fisherman's jumper. She wore her own cream pearls atop this unlikely combination. She had worked her thumbs through the big holes in the wrists of the jumper and sat pulling at the loose threads. She had been up to her room, accompanied by Sergeant Binny, changed, and brought down a few things for the night.

She had also brought down Bikram, who had trotted quietly over to Mr Cardinal, settled at his feet and hadn't moved since. The fire was now totally out, and Evans, having come in and explained that he had found no firewood of any sort, had gone out again to desperately cut some up in a far-off woodshed.

Everyone had now been up to their rooms. Inspector Lovelace had instructed Posie to accompany Sergeant Binny to search the three women, and all had accepted the invasion of their privacies with a sort of sullen but resigned ill grace. To the best of Posie's knowledge, nothing of any interest had been found at all, in anybody's rooms, or on anybody's person. Certainly not on the women.

Now Posie sat wedged in between Mr Cardinal and

Julian Carter on a sofa, the latter seeming almost paralysed by his grief and unable to move or speak.

Posie was very aware of Bryn Cardinal pressed up against her. He was very close; so close that Posie fancied she could feel the Luger and the precious papers cradled against his chest through his shirt and waistcoat. His warm arm in his rolled-up shirtsleeves was trailing the back of the sofa, almost right up against her bare shingled neck. She could smell the strong nicotine tang of his breath and the vetiver coming off him like waves of shimmering heat in a desert, and there was something else, too: something familiar and slightly intoxicating. She tried not to look at him, at the jagged scar on the side of his face which was nearest her, at his clean-shaven neatness broken only by a tiny smudge on his cheek. His arm came closer and closer and for a second Posie fancied she might close her eyes and pretend to snooze, and accidentally loll her head against that capable arm, and move in against that broad, armoured chest and see what it felt like.

But her afternoon nap combined with a sharp sense of duty towards Inspector Lovelace forbade her from doing any such thing. Oh, and then there was *Alaric*, of course. Far, far away from here…

Fortunately just then the doorbell rang.

Inspector Lovelace answered it and found Cleghorn, the local Police Constable, a fat, bullish sort of a man enswathed in a snow-dusted policeman's navy cape and hat, marshalled together with two other men on the doorstep.

'Cleghorn, 'ere, sir. Reporting for duty, sir.' The man presented the Inspector with his leather identity fob, and, satisfied, Lovelace returned it with a nod.

'My wee lad said there was trouble across 'ere and you needed 'elp. So 'ere we three are. I ain't got no other policemen to help you out, but I've brought across the two best local men from St Margaret's-at-Cliffe that I could muster, sir. This 'ere is the local Headmaster, Protheroe.'

And here Cleghorn motioned towards at a very short, squat ginger man muffled up in snow-encrusted tweeds. He then gestured towards a nervy-looking man in thick spectacles with round wet eyes.

'And this 'ere is the local butcher, Ellacott. Both are first-class men; served in the last war, for what that's worth. And I've told them discretion might be everything. I hope I was right to bring them, sir? Between us we've brought a police baton, a cricket bat and a meat cleaver. I ain't got no real weapon in my Constable's kit, sir, as you well know, which is unfortunate in my opinion. I hope I did right to bring what I did, sir?'

The Inspector nodded and the three men entered the vast room, dazed by the bright lights. Cleghorn continued, desperate to introduce some normality to the strange situation he found himself in:

'For what it's worth, sir, the blizzard has almost blown itself out, thank goodness. It's just steady snow now, petering out. And as you know, the snow has brought down all the telephone wires in the area, which is a nuisance. It will be morning until they can be fixed, and until anyone else can get 'ere to Maypole Manor, sir. The roads are quite impassable.'

The Inspector could be heard briefly outlining the current situation. He tried to sound as matter of fact as possible; as if such murders and parties happened to him on a daily basis, and that dead film stars regularly figured in his line of work. Regardless, the three local men looked with a good deal of fascinated horror at the assembled guests on the sofas, much like you would stare at an exotic caged animal in a zoo.

Mr Cardinal rose from his place at Posie's side and introduced himself to the newcomers in his usual rather authoritative manner. Bikram trotted after him. Posie watched, intrigued, as between them, Inspector Lovelace and Mr Cardinal neatly arranged for Mr Ellacott to stand guard outside Glaysayer's study, for Mr Protheroe to man the back door to the house, and for Constable Cleghorn to join the rest of them at the fireside in the entrance hall. It was agreed without further argument that it was simply too cold for anyone to be dispatched to watch over Amory Laine's body outside under the maypole.

When Cleghorn and Cardinal re-joined the party at the fireside the silence seemed even more weighty and unbearable.

'So how did you fellas get here exactly, then?' asked Cardinal conversationally. 'It must have been dashed difficult.'

'It were! But it were all my wee lad's bright idea,' said Constable Cleghorn, proudly, relieved to speak again. 'We followed his example and used lead piping, sir, and strapped our feet to the piping with our belts. Never skied before in my life, and I can't say I will again, but it was all downhill from the village up on the other cliff, so we got 'ere in the end, even though old four-eyes Ellacott kept falling over every couple of yards. It were raging something terrible, the blizzard, but soon as I 'eard Lord Glaysayer was in trouble, there was never a moment's 'esitation in my mind, sir. Terrible news. Terrible! A suicide. On New Year's Eve. Terrible.'

Bryn Cardinal seemed on the verge of disabusing Constable Cleghorn of the suicide idea but obviously thought better of it and changed the subject swiftly.

'By jove, I could do with some hot coffee. It's freezing in here now without any heating on. Will you help me in the kitchen, Cleghorn? Is that okay with you, Inspector?'

Lovelace, who was locked in conversation with Father Moriarty in what sounded like surprisingly good German, looked over and nodded briefly.

'We could all do with some, I think, Mr Cardinal. Thank you. Hands up for coffee, anyone?'

Several people including Posie put up their hands

and the two men left, kitchen-bound, Cardinal obviously relieved to stretch his legs for a bit and to kill some time. The others sat on and waited in the ghastly silence. Edwin Goodman sat alone at one end of an empty sofa, his coat and heavy-duty postman's bag with its precious swag secured tightly under his legs. His expression was of one who desperately wished he could be anywhere but here and he moved his passport restlessly through long, restless fingers. He attempted a weak sort of smile when Posie caught his eye, as if he thought it was expected of him.

'Say,' he announced warily, 'I don't know about you fellas but we could have some sort of a sing-song if you fancy? We don't need a piano; I've got perfect pitch. Or else, we could have a round of cards? Rummy, perhaps?'

The Inspector was now standing at a window facing over the front lawn, alone. He turned and gave Goodman a fairly withering look. 'Thank you, Mr Goodman, but I think we'll pass. This is no place for music or games tonight. Miss Parker, could you come here a minute?'

As she got up from her sofa, Posie was horribly aware of Jocasta scowling at her and of Jacinta staring disconcertingly into mid-air, a puzzled expression on her face. She heard the clock striking half-past one. She reached out for Bikram but found he had disappeared.

'What is it, sir?' Posie asked quietly, joining the Inspector at the tartan-curtained window and trying her best not to scan the room for the dog in a kind of mad panic.

She saw that Constable Cleghorn had been right; the snow had stopped at last. A glance out revealed a clear and beautiful silver landscape, the lawn stretching away to the cliff tops in pristine white layers like Christmas-cake icing, with a moon riding high above broken black clouds. Posie tried not to look at the maypole, or at the dark shape which was visible beneath it.

And then the small flashing light came again from what looked like the end of the lawn, at the edge of the cliff. Exactly the same as earlier.

'See?' hissed the Inspector.

'Mnnn. I'll admit it's dashed odd, sir.'

And then Jacinta was at their side. She looked out too and caught the tail end of the sequence. She nodded in a resigned, unexcited fashion.

'Oh, *those*, Inspector. I wouldn't worry about those, if I were you. They're pretty frequent around here.' She returned to her seat wearily and Posie followed her, the Inspector darting towards the fireplace again. All eyes were on Jacinta.

'You sound as if those lights are familiar to you, Miss Glaysayer?'

'They are, Inspector. Regular as anything; going back at least two or three years, to the best of my memory. You know this whole area is a smuggler's haunt, don't you? I imagine that's one of the reasons you police people are here tonight, although you won't admit it, will you?'

The Inspector maintained a total silence in the face of her almost-question, so Jacinta carried on in a resigned fashion.

'I don't know anything about the smuggling, but I *do* know it's been going on in St Margaret's Bay forever, and Maypole Manor used to be the nerve-centre for it, too. Certainly every time I stay here there's something afoot outside. Did you know this very house is connected to a warren of tunnels in the chalky cliff? That they go from under the house all through the cliffs and down to the beach? And probably further afield, inland, too. They were used in the old days, but they were bricked up sometime at the end of the last century when the previous owner bought Maypole Manor. The place has always had a chequered history to it; that's why the maypole has to stay up, to safeguard it. And when Father bought the house himself a few years ago he kept those tunnels bricked up, but he was always fascinated in its smuggling past.'

The Inspector looked thoughtful, but the 'v' of worry

was there too. 'What sort of goods are you talking about, Miss Glaysayer?'

'Oh, everything, I suppose. Silks, tea, coffee, drugs, stolen valuables…you name it. But this was yonks ago.'

'Mnnn. I see. And you're quite sure that these tunnels *were* bricked up, Miss Glaysayer?'

'Oh yes. I was with Father when he came around with the Land Agent who sold him the place; we both were, weren't we JoJo? It was during the last war. We saw where the tunnels started and we went down to the beach to see where they ended up, too. In a sort of cave above a cove. Entrances all bricked up at both ends. It was fascinating stuff.'

'But are they *still* bricked up, Miss Glaysayer?'

'I wouldn't know, Inspector. I'm not here that often and I haven't had reason to look since the time he bought the place. I'd imagine they are as Father found them, untouched.' She turned to her sister, who was puffing disdainfully on a cigarette.

'Do you know anything about those tunnels, JoJo?'

'How the very devil would I?' snapped Jocasta irritably, clutching at herself tightly. 'I have better things to do than poking about in old, forgotten tunnels. Besides, they sound bally dangerous to me.' Her nostrils flared and she seemed very angry.

Jacinta spoke again in a reflective, sad way; even more hunched up than usual.

'Our father wanted to make the house "modern". He had to have the place gutted and re-fashioned fairly extensively to make it work. That included an all-new central heating system, supposedly one of the best in the land, which runs right through the house. It *usually* works a treat. He fitted it for JoJo: she begged him for it, she's always so cold. I suppose it's possible that the old tunnels were disturbed, or investigated at the time of the redevelopment.'

'When was that?' Posie asked.

'End of the war. In 1918 it must have been.'

The Inspector was tapping his finger anxiously with his pen. 'And your father never spoke to you again about those tunnels, Miss Glaysayer? Or about a use he or some friends might be making of those tunnels?'

He lowered the pen and looked at Jacinta mildly but sharply. Suddenly the girl lost her temper.

'If you are trying to imply that our father was somehow implicated in smuggling, Inspector, or in black market goods, then frankly I'm appalled. He was an honest man who always did things in accordance with the law. He wasn't a swindler or a crook, whatever else he was. He believed in doing things the right way; the *honest* way.'

For a second, Posie thought about the apparently vast amount of unpaid taxes and duties which lingered, unaccounted for on the Customs men's ledgers, and how Jacinta's picture of her deceased father must be skewed somehow, for he couldn't have been entirely honest to have got himself into a mess like that in the first place, or to have run up such big debts, unless he was just confoundedly unlucky. But her thoughts were interrupted by a sharp, loud bark of laughter which shocked everybody.

Posie turned, surprised. It was Mr Steinhauser, sitting near the fire next to the Duke and Lenny.

He had bent so sharply backwards with incredulous laughter that his black hat with the feather had fallen quite off. He hurriedly replaced it. But not before Posie had seen something important.

Her flash of intuition came to her clear as a bell, as a certainty.

She knew who he was now.

'Forgive me,' said Mr Steinhauser, wiping a tear from his infected eyes and addressing Jacinta in the main. 'But I've never heard such rot in my life. Your father wasn't an honest man, and he never did *anything* in accordance with the law. Quite the opposite, in fact.'

Jacinta struggled to her feet. 'I'm sorry, and I don't know you from Adam, but I thought you were meant to be my father's *friend*. And now you say terrible unwarranted things like this? If I could I'd get you to leave right now.'

Mr Steinhauser was on his feet too, all gangly six foot five of him. Posie noted how the Inspector had carefully reached for his gun, but was moving slowly, in measured paces.

'I *was* his friend,' Mr Steinhauser said carefully in his neat, measured tones. 'But that was thirty years ago now. Robin Glaysayer revealed himself in his true colours to me back then, and he obviously didn't change a bit. He was up to his old tricks to the very end, no doubt.'

'*What?*' Jacinta snapped. 'What *are* you talking about? And who the blazes are you exactly? And why had our father never spoken of you before? But here you are anyway, swanning in for New Year like you were best buddies. What's your game?'

Jacinta seemed about to throw the full force of her small body towards the man, and Posie found herself jumping towards the woman, arms outstretched.

'I'll tell you then, shall I?' came Steinhauser's measured tones.

But then, as if in slow motion, several things seemed to happen at once.

Evans came through the front door, balancing a great pile of firewood in his arms. Simultaneously Mr Cardinal entered the room, accompanied by Constable Cleghorn, both men carrying trays laden down with coffee things, Bikram was at the big man's heels. And then Mr Cardinal was shouting something and dropping the coffee things and running all at once:

'She's fainting! Someone catch her!'

Turning, Posie saw Jacinta Glaysayer collapsing dramatically right in front of Mr Steinhauser. She went down like a rag doll onto the zebra-skin rug, all wobbly.

She was foaming at the mouth and twitching among her shawls, writhing around and shouting and flailing her arms about.

Suddenly it seemed that coffee was flying everywhere; people darted downwards in a big scrum, trying to help, even Mr Steinhauser. It was chaos. Even Edwin Goodman with his big unwieldy bag was bobbing about all over the place, everywhere at once. Bikram started barking wildly and Father Moriarty abandoned his priest's disguise and automatically snapped into doctor's mode, clearing a way among the people on the floor.

'Move please. She's having some sort of fit,' he said calmly, feeling Jacinta's pulse. 'Anyone got any smelling salts on them?'

No-one had. The Inspector darted towards the drinks-trolley with its many cut-glass decanters, which had been hidden away earlier.

'What about a strong whisky?' The Inspector waved a flask of whisky under Jacinta's nose.

'I wouldn't bother,' said Jocasta unfeelingly from her position on the couch, curled up and taking another drag of her cigarette. Mr Steinhauser stared at Jocasta in what looked like utter disbelief.

'She's just having one of her *premonitions*, that's what she calls them. Heaven help us all. Best not to listen too closely to whatever it is she says. Likely it's all just put on. Made-up nonsense.'

And then, perhaps because of the alcohol fumes, Jacinta suddenly sat up and seemed to recover. But then her eyes rolled back again and she was lost to whatever darkness had subsumed her in the first place.

And then she began to shout.

* * * *

Seventeen

'Many have tried to protect this place,' came Jacinta's voice from Jacinta's body, although she seemed totally unconscious and oblivious to all earthly comforts, her body collapsed as if she were fast asleep.

'But all have failed. *I* have failed. The power here is too strong.'

Everyone except Jocasta was staring in fascinated horror at Jacinta. Julian Carter looked like he might start to weep again, and Constable Cleghorn shuffled from foot to foot in sheer embarrassment. He started to mop up the hot mess of coffee from the rug and floorboards, trying to ignore the odd voice which went droning on and on.

'This place is rotten; rotten to the core like a big bad apple. There are maggots everywhere, digging tunnels. Walls have ears. And the tunnels are full of precious cargo too. Do you know what this is? Snow! Snow everywhere. And heaven help you if you get caught up in the snow. It suffocates you. You'll never breathe again. Not even the power of the maypole can protect against it. Everyone is in disguise. It's all over. *Over.*'

The last word was screamed aloud, and the effort of it seemed to force the girl to come out of her trance and sit up, suddenly wide awake. Jacinta blinked and looked confused.

Posie saw that Jocasta had now deigned to stand up, and was looking down at her sister furiously, but there was fear in her face, too. Posie was sure of it.

'What a load of nonsense! I always said you were a big old fraud and now you've disgraced yourself in front of all these people, including the police, with your mumbo-jumbo. Pah! I'm ashamed of you. You're mad! Quite mad!'

Father Moriarty was helping Jacinta up, while Inspector Lovelace darted around to Posie's side.

'What do you make of that little show, sir?'

'Not a lot. I've got enough *real* problems to deal with tonight, so for once I'm inclined to agree with the delightful Jocasta Glaysayer: our Mystic Mirabelle is just an attention-seeker. That's all. Now, can you do something for me while this hullabaloo is going on?'

'Of course. But there's something I need to tell you; something I've just realised.'

'It will have to wait, Posie. Now under cover of this commotion I want you to slip away. Take Sergeant Binny and go upstairs. Take Cardinal too; you hear me, Cardinal? Binny has the keys to everyone's rooms. I want you all to search in the Duke's room, and Steinhauser's room too. Oh, and make that three rooms. Search in your pal Lenny's room, too. They're my key suspects.'

'What am I looking for, sir? Those rooms have already been searched. What are you looking for that hasn't been found already, I mean?'

'Anything odd. No-one is forthcoming with anything just yet. There must be *something* to be found. Be quick.'

Posie nodded and did as she was told, although she didn't like the sound of poking around in people's rooms at all. She glanced quickly in Mr Steinhauser's direction but saw that he had sat down again, his attempts at whatever confrontation he had been planning quite scuppered. Posie followed Sergeant Binny past Bobbie the Bengal tiger and up the stairs, aware of Mr Cardinal a few steps behind her,

Bikram loping along at their heels. On the corridor upstairs they turned into the left-hand portion of the house, away from Posie's room, and Posie saw that this stretch of rooms was the exact mirror-image of where she herself was staying. Binny had come to a standstill and he fumbled in an envelope among the many keys he had collected.

'Rum show, downstairs, what?' said Mr Cardinal from a pool of shadows, leaning against the wall in a rare space where the bright landing lights didn't quite reach, looking down at Posie intensely. Bikram sat at Mr Cardinal's feet obediently.

'I know,' replied Posie sagely, trying to sound sympathetic. 'I hope the poor girl is going to be all right. It must have been something to do with her father's death which drove her to act like that, shouting out all that gobbledegook.'

'I didn't mean *that* little performance. I meant that now we know what Steinhauser is doing here. You saw it too, when he took off his hat; I saw the look on your face.'

Posie stared sharply up at Cardinal. She held her breath; normally she kept her own counsel, but then she nodded.

'I *did* think I had seen something, yes. And it incriminates him, unless he can explain it away.'

'Sharp little thing, aren't you?' whispered Cardinal, his eyes never wavering from Posie's own. He moved closer to Posie so he was right up against her. She stood utterly still. For the first time Posie found herself wondering about the man himself: whereabouts did he live in London? What did he do when he wasn't working, or did he always work? What was his secretary like? Surely not someone like Prudence Smythe – who was frighteningly efficient, but as unglamorous as a kipper for your breakfast – he probably employed someone the very opposite, in fact.

Oh, and was he married?

Mr Cardinal smoothed the rope of lustrous cream pearls at Posie's neck. 'No-one else noticed what you and

I did, downstairs just now. Lovelace is a lucky boy, having you on his team. I don't know how he can resist you…'

She felt a finger teasingly run up her back, beneath Alaric's old jumper. It felt quite nice.

'I say…I…'

'The thing is, you and I are cut from the same cloth, Miss Parker. Both of us sharp as razor-wire. We don't trust anyone. *Everyone* is suspicious in our worlds.'

Cardinal moved closer, and his chest was now flat up against Posie, tight up. She found herself pinned against the wall, held in an expert clinch. And there it was again, that smell: nicotine and vetiver and – what was it? – it reminded her suddenly and unaccountably of Dolly Price, now Lady Cardigeon. *How bizarre.*

Posie saw his head coming down lower, noticed his mouth with their almost blue-tinged teeth, felt his stubble. There was a tense thrill of anticipation, of crackling, tingling energy like static electricity passing between them. She reached out for Cardinal and they moved together as one, fluidly, their arms entwining, anticipating the kiss which was now a certainty…

But something was wrong; something felt wrong.

Alaric.

Cardamom and lemon and the trade winds.

Oh, Alaric…

Posie couldn't do it; she couldn't kiss the man. She jerked her head away at the very last moment, pulled sharply away.

'I say, here we are,' called out Binny from up ahead. 'The Brandenberger girl's room is open now. Are you coming? I say, Miss Parker, is all quite well?'

'Of course, Sergeant. Mr Cardinal was just looking for an earring I had lost. We found it, too.'

Skirting around Mr Cardinal, and bustling on ahead, flushed with embarrassment and something else – guilt, perhaps – Posie charged into Lenny's room at full pelt. Mr Cardinal swung in neatly behind her, quietly amused.

It was exactly the same as Posie's own room, and obviously linked in the same way by a small sitting room to the Duke's accommodation. But, unlike Posie's room, there were no personal objects on display at all. No travel candles or photos; no perfume; no shoes thrown round about, no magazines. One minuscule brown leather suitcase sat packed ready on the bed, and the cupboards and dresser were bare. A suit of soft leather Belstaff motorcycle clothes, identical to Alaric's, who had recently taken up the sport and had an eye to buying a Triumph of his own, hung from the peg on the back of the door. A search of the wooden bedside table revealed absolutely nothing, as did a search under the bed.

Lenny was obviously used to travelling light, even to parties which demanded several changes of clothing. Posie assumed you *had* to travel light when you rode a motorcycle and your sidecar was taken up entirely with a squat little Duke in a bulky fur coat.

The suitcase, obviously expensive, contained only a pair of red silk pyjamas, a small purse of Maybelline make-up and a single change of clothes; the blue House of Harlow clothes from before. Posie remembered that Lenny was still wearing her ball dress downstairs, but she had wrapped a white fox-fur stole around herself for added warmth.

Posie searched the silk lining of the suitcase for any hidden pockets or compartments but there was nothing to be found.

'We need to hurry, Miss. The Inspector said we had to make it snappy. We don't have permission to do this, you know.'

Binny was fingering his moustaches nervously, and Cardinal was already leaving the room. Sighing, Posie followed them, almost pulling the door to.

Suddenly she remembered the leather motorcycle clothes. She backtracked swiftly. Feeling like a horrid little thief, she took down the soft nappa Belstaff jacket, which would be miles too big for the slender Lenny, and fished inside the front left-hand side, where she knew there was a small, hidden, rubberised pocket, meant for storing money or documents, ensuring whatever was put inside would stay dry and protected in the event of very wet weather.

She knew this because Alaric, rarely given to praising anything very much, had gone on and on about the practicality of this feature; so much so that he had taken to wearing the jacket on the rare occasions when he still flew, and whenever he travelled anywhere cold or wet, regardless or not of whether he was riding a motorcycle.

Posie slipped her fingers inside. Sure enough, the rubberised pocket was full. Heart racing, she drew out a fistful of white pound notes which had been crammed in, willy-nilly. She tried not to act surprised, as if holding such a great deal of money happened to her every day. And then she felt again. There was something else inside, something round, the size of her palm; perhaps a travelling mirror or a compact of powder. Posie drew out the round object and looked at it in total surprise: it was the screw-on silver-coloured lens protector from a Leica camera. Turning it over in her hands, Posie saw that the other side had been fitted with a piece of cardboard, cut neatly and inserted as a type of lid so that the effect was of a small, round box. Posie shook it and it rattled dully.

What was inside? Drugs?

'Miss Parker? You coming?'

There was nothing for it but to take the Leica lid-box with her. Outside in the corridor, Binny was loitering nervily, Cardinal having already entered the sitting room which the couple shared, searching it efficiently. Posie opened the Leica lid carefully and under the light of a corridor-lamp she pulled out two things, almost losing one in the process, it was so small.

The first was a photograph, an original. It was a very good photograph, as it happened. And Posie recognised it immediately. It had been taken that year, in 1921, at high summer in Luxor, Egypt, and it had been taken by the skilfully talented Lenny.

The photo was of a sphinx, and was one of a set of sphinxes which had lined the road in ancient Thebes, right next to a dig the British Museum had commissioned; a dig which Posie and Alaric had been out working on. Lenny had been the official photographer for the British Museum, and this particular photograph had been used by the Museum again and again since the dig, advertising the Museum's wares and the Egyptian exhibits especially.

The photo could be seen all over London adorning flags and banners, covering the bill-boards and posters which rippled across pillar-box-red buses and the many, many Underground Stations. It had also been used for the cover of many books, too. Posie hoped that Lenny had been paid well for her image. But why carry this here?

Posie turned to the second, last item. It was very small, almost ridiculously so: it was the size of four or five postage stamps stuck together, and made from very thin, very glossy paper. Posie recognised it as being a cut-out advertisement from an upmarket women's magazine.

She squinted in the light and read it:

COMPANION/ WIFE SOUGHT FOR
VERY WEALTHY DUKE

1. ARISTOCRATIC AND CHARMING FOREIGN
   GENTLEMAN (OF LONG LINEAGE) SEEKS LONG-
   TERM COMPANION WITH A VIEW TO MARRIAGE.

2. APPLICANTS MUST BE BEAUTIFUL, BELOW
   THIRTY, HAVE RED HAIR, HAVE A CLEAN
   DRIVING LICENCE, HAVE ABSOLUTELY NO
   DESIRE TO WORK AND NO PAST HISTORY OF
   ANY GAINFUL EMPLOYMENT OR EXTENSIVE
   TRAVEL EXPERIENCE WHATSOEVER.

3. APPLICANTS MUST SHARE A DESIRE TO LIVE THE HIGH-LIFE, AND WILL RECEIVE GENEROUS ALLOWANCES TO COVER EVERY EVENTUALITY AND EVERY POSSIBLE DESIRE.

4. NATIONALITY UNIMPORTANT, BUT A WILLINGNESS TO REMAIN IN ENGLAND AND ENJOY A COUNTRY LIFESTYLE IN AN ENGLISH STATELY HOME IS ESSENTIAL.

5. IF INTERESTED PLEASE REPLY TO BOX NO. 456, *THE LADY*, 39, BEDFORD STREET, LONDON WC2.

'Nothing doing here,' said Mr Cardinal, and they all processed along from the sitting room to the Duke's room, Posie trotting along too.

But Posie's mind was miles away, on the advert. So much now made sense. She exhaled heavily.

So Lenny had sold out.

But *why* exactly was unclear.

But something, somehow had gone so badly wrong that Lenny had turned her back on a dazzling, if perhaps not very well-paid, career in photography and become the paid companion to a snivelling, jumped-up little man who fancied he would 'keep' a woman just because he could; a naïve, inexperienced, old-fashioned type of beautiful woman at that. Posie felt almost overcome with rage at the man, not to mention the fact that he was a first-rate liar ('of long lineage'!) but then she remembered that the many changes and deceptions which Lenny had put herself through to become the chosen companion of the Duke Del Angelo were all her own choice, too.

No-one had forced her to answer that advert, or to carry it through when she was chosen as being successful. Sure as bread was bread it took two to engineer such a ridiculous arrangement.

And no wonder Lenny had looked worried when Posie had shown up at Maypole Manor; the naïve little woman Lenny was pretending to be could so easily have come tumbling down around her. Posie betted that all of Lenny's previous acquaintances and friendships had been severed overnight when she took up with the Duke; she had never been someone with many friends, anyhow, and the transformation from working girl to kept It-girl, no better than a mistress really, would have been fairly easy to pull off.

Now flushing with embarrassment for the girl that she had found herself in so low and awful a position that she had had to answer the advert in the first place, Posie replaced the papers into the Leica lid-box carefully, almost reverently.

Posie realised that here, in one tiny place, was a reminder to Lenny about who she was; or who she had *been*. The Leica lid itself was surely from her own, beloved camera which, for some reason or other Lenny had been forced to sell; the photograph was a reminder of what she was capable of; the personal advert was a reminder of who she was *now* and what she had had to stoop to in order to survive.

But how could she bear to endure that man? Surely there could have been some other way? *Be* some other way?

'Here we are, then, folks,' said Binny, opening up the Duke's room, and they all trooped in.

Like Lenny's room, there was nothing much in the way of personal items lying around. One small Louis Vuitton suitcase lay open on the valise-holder, and all three of them searched through it, reassuring themselves as to its banal, unsurprising contents: an Italian passport; a tub of hair putty; foreign aftershave; a large velvet jewellery roll containing a bright gold watch and cufflinks and the largest solitaire diamond Posie had seen in a good long while. But tonight was not the night to get excited about jewels.

Some prescription medicine sat on the dresser, the gluey-looking bottle was half-empty.

Binny was leafing through a set of high-class magazines, provided by the host, no doubt, and ranged around on the bedside cabinet next to a jug of dried flowers, when Posie heard him exclaim aloud:

'Would you look at that!'

'What is it, Sergeant?'

'This magazine here, this purple one on top, that's Maypole Manor on the front cover, isn't it? Lawks! It must be famous to appear on the cover of magazines!'

'Mnnn.' Posie was looking over Binny's shoulder. But then she saw the title of the magazine and she gave a start.

'That's not a magazine, Sergeant! That's a Sales Particulars from an Estate Agent! Look at the title – *Hander & Glover, Estate Agents and Land Agents* – but it does look at first glance like a normal magazine, you're right. Can I?'

Posie grabbed the thin purple brochure and stared. Then she started flicking through the brochure quickly, revealing one smart photograph after another. The Land Agent had gone to quite a lot of trouble to try and sell Maypole Manor as a would-be hotel, what with the ample rooms and suites and the location. At the back was a map of the location of the house in relation to the seaside, and another map showing the exact layout of the rooms. There was even a diagram of where the old tunnels were, linking the house down to the beach below.

She whistled in surprise: 'This house is up for sale! Jacinta didn't know *that*, I'll warrant, for all her being a clairvoyant. And neither did her sister!'

Binny nodded thoughtfully. 'Their father must have been desperately trying to settle his debts in his lifetime; pay off the mortgage now, rather than let his daughters have to sort it all out after he had gone, don't you think, Miss?'

'Mnnn.'

Posie flicked through the brochure and saw how tiny,

cramped notes in Italian covered many of the pages. The descriptions about St Margaret's Bay having a 'microclimate' and the up to date central heating system had been circled copiously and exclamation marks dotted the pages.

'Flipping central heating system,' Posie muttered irritably, aware of her cold nose and fingers and toes. 'I'm fed up of hearing about it, it's not that important! If only the bally thing would actually work!'

She saw that at the front of the brochure a smart pocket had been made with a slice of glossy card, and that some typed correspondence was tucked inside. Pulling out the letter inside and handing over the brochure to Mr Cardinal simultaneously, she skim-read the letter quickly.

Mr Cardinal was sat on the bed, which creaked beneath his large frame, and he was scanning the brochure with a surprised look on his face.

'Hell's bells!' he exclaimed. 'This is quite something! Puts a whole new spin on things, doesn't it? I never thought the Italian was a suspect before, but this just goes to show I was wrong. You think he had got hold of this diagram of the tunnels somehow and was trying to blackmail old Lord Glaysayer about it? That he wanted to route his dirty drugs smuggling operation through the place and old Glaysayer would have none of it?'

'Er, no, sir. I don't think that.'

'Or you think it's simpler? That the Duke actually wanted to *buy* Maypole Manor from the old Scot for his smuggling, and that he was trying to drive a hard bargain and lost his cool and shot the fella? I notice there's no mention of the price here: just says "price on application", which, as we all know, means if you *have* to ask, you can't afford it. But it surprises me: I thought the Duke was loaded with money.'

Posie was thinking furiously into the silence.

'I suppose we'd better get downstairs and report this to your Inspector, Sergeant,' Cardinal said, standing up.

'This certainly casts a different light on things, and not a particularly good one for the Italian, either.'

'Agreed, sir, but we've been tasked with checking Mr Steinhauser's room too, sir. We'd better do that, otherwise the Inspector will have my guts for garters.'

Cardinal chuckled: 'We can't have that, can we? Lead on, man.'

But Steinhauser's room was virtually empty, save for a pair of slippers and a dressing-gown. There was no bag, no change of clothes, no paperwork, nothing.

'This is bizarre,' said Mr Cardinal. 'Unless the fella is storing his kit somewhere else, he must be a ghost or something. I'm yet to meet a man who can travel in just his coat and hat, without an overnight bag. Besides, where is his outfit from earlier? He's in white tie now.'

At a total loss as to understanding the lack of clothing or bags in Steinhauser's room, the three returned the way they had come, back along the corridor and down the stairway, and out into the entrance hall. Just as she was stepping off the last step, Posie felt Mr Cardinal's hand lightly on her back again, that tingle down the spine.

Turning, she saw that he was looking over at the party ranged around the fire, which was, thankfully, now roaring away again. *He's an expert at making love to girls like this*, thought Posie to herself, not without a flicker of amusement. And she was flattered, too, if truth be told.

But then she focused intently on the scene unfolding in front of her. The two Glaysayer girls were shouting and screaming at each other, Sergeant Rainbird holding Jocasta back. What on earth was happening?

But when Posie looked properly at Jocasta's face she saw that it was full of absolute hatred.

And worse, she had turned her gaze directly on Posie and the hatred had intensified yet more.

What exactly had Posie done to so anger the girl?

* * * *

Eighteen

Posie sidled up to the Inspector. She hated to admit it but she was mighty glad of the Sergeants' presence and of the additional local back-up, and thankful too for Mr Cardinal. Inspector Lovelace looked on the verge of losing control; something she thought she'd never see. She felt horribly sorry for him. His clothes were unusually dishevelled and his hair-paint was now half-off, giving him a wild, theatrical look.

Father Moriarty was trying to calm Jacinta down and Jocasta was sitting in a sulk on a chair next to Edwin Goodman, who was pretending she wasn't there.

'Anything doing?' Inspector Lovelace whispered.

'Yes. For Lenny and the Duke, anyhow.'

The Inspector nodded happily. 'Good. I was beginning to think it could have been one of these girls who killed Glaysayer; they're slightly unhinged, especially Jocasta. Did you say you thought she was on drugs?'

'I'm almost certain of it, sir. And what was all *that* about?'

'Storm in a tea-cup. Something about their mother's jewels: gone apparently. Sold up. Although Jocasta seems not to have known about it until now. Very tetchy, she was. So, we've got evidence against the Duke now, have we? Is that it there? What it is? Let me have a look.'

But their private conversation had suddenly become the centre-piece of the house party, and everyone was looking over.

'Sir, I don't think…'

But the Duke had already seen the purple brochure in the Inspector's hand and had risen from the couch in a frenzy.

'Wadda ya think you is a-doin'? You in my room? Goin' through my things? Without my permission?'

He hurled himself at the Inspector, who stepped neatly aside. He tried to hurl himself again, and Mr Cardinal caught him and pinned him down in a rugby tackle.

'Oh, no, you don't, you smarmy little fellow. It's all up! We know your game! We know what you've done.'

Lenny was standing now, the fox fur slipping from her lovely shoulders, her face pale beneath her make-up, a picture of total dismay.

'*What's* he done?' she demanded anxiously. Everyone looked at the Inspector, who was staring at the brochure in a panic.

'Erm, it would seem that…it would seem…'

'That everything is quite in order,' cut in Posie quickly, speaking calmly to the room at large and avoiding looking at Mr Cardinal or the Inspector for too long.

'It would seem that Lord Glaysayer had put Maypole Manor on the market a couple of months ago, with a London firm of Estate Agents called Hander & Glover. He put it up for sale due to his, er, money troubles.' She tried not to look over at Jocasta Glaysayer's face, but she heard the thunderous howl of surprise.

'And it would seem that in the Duke here he had found a willing buyer. A good, decent buyer, who was after a country stately home where he could bring his new wife and enjoy life. The Duke was attracted to the idea of the area having a warmer temperature than most, and had probably been advised that the sea air would do him good.

188

He also liked the fact that the place was modern and had good central heating, and was only a couple of hours away from London. I'm right so far, aren't I, Duke Del Angelo?'

The man stared up at Posie from between Bryn Cardinal's vice-like grip and nodded, his face sweaty and pale.

'Yes. The house was perfect for me; for us. *Is* perfect.'

The Inspector cut in, incredulous: 'You just wanted to *buy* this place, that's all? Fair and square?'

The Duke nodded, and Posie continued, waving the letter she had taken out of the flap in the brochure.

'It was very fair. And in fact, you had agreed a price and were going to make everything final in a few days' time, weren't you? It was a condition of sale that you buy the contents of the house, too, wasn't it? With two exceptions. I'm correct so far?'

'That's right. He wouldn't sell the paintin' of himself in his study, and he wouldn't sell the old mouldy tiger over there. Suited me fine, anyhow. A lot of the stuff I didn't want anyhow, but it was part of the deal. He just needed extra money.'

'Exactly. This letter confirms all of that.'

'So why attend this house party, Duke Del Angelo?' cut in the Inspector, bemused. 'If you knew the house was perfect for you?'

The Duke shrugged his shoulders in his big coat.

'At the beginnin' of all of the legal proceedings Lord Glaysayer issued us with an invite for his famous New Year's party. He said it would be good for us to see the house at full capacity, with a lodda people in it: better by far than seeing it always empty. He said the house would sell itself. And also, Lord Glaysayer was a kind man, a good host. He liked to invite people to share in his generosity; like the Italians. It's a tradition I wanna keep goin'. Parties here. But not like *your* parties, Miss Glaysayer. Which I've 'eard all about.' He flashed a malevolent look at Jocasta, whose dilated pupils were now so large that her eyes looked all black. She sat speechless, suffused with anger.

The Inspector stared hard at the Duke, and then turned to Lenny.

'Miss Brandenberger. I suppose you are about to corroborate this whole story, are you?'

Lenny nodded, scared under all the sudden attention.

'Of course I confirm it. Luca had already decided to buy the place. Had already wired the money across to his lawyers. You can check if you like: it's Pring and Proudfoot on Bedford Row, London. But we thought we might as well come down anyway: as well as being fun, we wanted to look at the place and see what we wanted to change; you know, carpets and curtains and the like. We were talking about it together all the time since we got here; how we wanted to make the place our own. All the tartan has to go, of course. And the horrid heads. And the maypole. *Especially* the maypole, after what's happened here tonight. Magic or no magic. We'll change the name of the place, too. Perhaps to something Italian.'

Posie didn't look at Jacinta, for privately she agreed with Lenny about the need for changes, and she was remembering the couple's total self-absorption earlier in the evening in what had seemed like nothing at the time: their pacing around rooms, locked in conversation with each other; their frenzied questions to Jacinta about the history of the place.

'Fine,' said the Inspector, trying not to let the disappointment show in his voice, for his prime suspect was slipping through his fingers right in front of him, but Inspector Lovelace was a fair man, and chased the truth whenever possible.

'Cardinal, please let Duke Del Angelo go free. I can't see what he would gain by murdering Glaysayer. In fact, his death only complicates things for them. But what I don't understand, Duke Del Angelo, is why be so furtive about the whole thing? Why not tell people you were going to be buying the place?'

The Duke had wriggled from the big man's grip and stood as tall as his five foot nothing would allow him.

'That was another condition: I was told not to mention it. Lord Glaysayer phoned me a few days ago and begged for my silence, for my co-operation. Said he hadn't yet told his girls; was waitin' for the right moment. He had jus' booked himself into a smart London hospital from next week onwards; said he would tell them just before he moved and took up residence there.'

The Duke shrugged. 'I don't think he wanted big arguments; and I can see why, after tonight and the way these two carry on. I don't think he expected to live much longer.'

Posie didn't look at the Glaysayer girls, but saw that Lenny was continuing to look over at her, in a half-challenging, half-pleading way.

She thinks I'm about to give away her secret.

It's all right, Posie tried to nod. *I'm not going to say anything. Much though I wish I could.*

'Anything else you want to add, Posie?' asked the Inspector quietly, covering his mouth with his hand. He spoke half-eagerly, half-bitterly. 'You're doing a dashed good job of clearing my key suspects of the crime. You sure about this? What about the fact that your pal Lenny is a German. Nothing doing there?'

Posie whispered back. 'No, sir. I can't tell you the whole story right now, sir, but I'm pretty certain Lenny's not guilty of anything at all. She's just a girl down on her luck, trying her best at reinventing herself. A bit of a silly girl, perhaps, but one with an eye to the future, which isn't a crime, as far as I know.'

Evans moved forwards.

'Sir, requesting your permission to cut more firewood, sir. We're getting through it like nobody's business, and I didn't get enough before. I'll be ten minutes. I know where to search now.'

The Inspector nodded curtly, and Posie tugged at his arm. 'But I wanted to tell you something earlier, sir, and it's got to come out *now*. It's Steinhauser, sir. *He's* your key suspect.'

'You sure?'

'Not certain, sir, but almost. Guard him well.'

The Inspector stared at her, then motioned for Sergeant Rainbird to come closer. Posie caught sight of his policeman's baton and a pair of glittering handcuffs being taken quickly from a pocket. Sergeant Binny seemed to have disappeared.

Turning to the room at large the Inspector said:

'I think it's jolly high time that the dead man among us spoke and told us who he really is.'

Silence greeted his words. Posie looked at Steinhauser, sitting wrapped up near the fire.

'Mr Steinhauser?' she said lightly, a note of cajoling in her voice. 'You were interrupted before by Miss Glaysayer's unfortunate attack of nerves. I think that you were about to tell us what brings you here to Maypole Manor. Weren't you?'

* * * *

Posie was certain of pretty much everything when it came to Steinhauser. The only thing she *wasn't* sure of was whether he was the man who had rifled through the belongings in her room earlier, stealing her photo. The man Amory Laine had seen. She remembered telling the Inspector earlier in the evening that she thought Steinhauser had a different motive from everyone else for being at the party, and she felt a quiet thrill of satisfaction at having been right. Posie hated being wrong, about anything much.

As the tall man got to his feet, she wasn't surprised that he didn't address himself to her or to the Inspector, but that he faced the Glaysayer girls directly, apologetically.

He took off his hat, and there it was again. *How could she not have seen it earlier? How could anyone have missed it?*

The arching, prominent nose; the green cat eyes, even hidden by the eye infection; the height. The strong resemblance that had nagged at her all along. The feeling of *deja-vu* which had made Jocasta seem familiar to Posie.

He pointed at Jocasta, as Posie had known he would. Said the words she had known he would say.

'I am your father, Jocasta. Your *real* father.'

There was a collective gasp from around the fireside.

'Don't be absurd!' spat Jocasta, but she could see it too, for she had put her hands up to her face, covering her eyes in something like horror and disbelief. Steinhauser continued to stare at Jocasta, willing her to look at him.

Posie chastised herself: she had been arrogant enough to think that Mr Steinhauser had been staring at *her* on occasion but now it made more sense that he had had his eyes glued on his daughter the whole time.

'Did you kill my father tonight, sir?' asked Jacinta from the sofa, in a very quiet, very scared tone. 'So you could get JoJo back, all for yourself?'

Steinhauser barked with laughter. 'Of course not! That's absolutely ridiculous! I didn't like your father, but I certainly didn't kill him.'

'I think you'd better explain yourself, sir,' said the Inspector, warily, not knowing what truths or lies were about to be told, and what light it would shed on Lord Glaysayer's murder.

'And let me remind you, sir, that this new information doesn't look good for you. Not good at all. So you'd better think about that as you speak. And try and convince me that you *didn't* murder Lord Glaysayer here tonight.'

Posie cocked her head, interested. She too had simply no idea what sort of a story Steinhauser might tell, although she could guess at the bare bones of the thing. Steinhauser rubbed at his eyes, which looked worse than ever, again only choosing to address the Glaysayer girls.

'I worked with your father out in Tanzania, in 1891. We were south of Mwanza. It was Glaysayer's first time out in Africa, but I had been there a while, with another Swiss fellow, Stefan; a man I had judged sound enough at the beginning, but he was a drinker as it turned out. I had my wife, Gretchen, out there with me and we'd been through some really good times, and then some really hard times. Our baby, Caroline, had just been born. It was no place to raise a child, but we got on with it as best we could. The Swiss man, Stefan, and myself had found a rich seam of diamonds, and we quickly set up a working mine. We got a load of local men in to dig it out. And then we met Robin Glaysayer, a Scotsman abroad; an aristocrat, rich, curious, hardworking. He also had his wife out in Tanzania with him, a charming woman who was the life and soul of any social gathering. Her only sadness was that she couldn't have children of her own, and she came every day to play with our little baby daughter. We quickly all became partners on the new mine. It looked like it would be fantastically successful. We would all become wildly rich.'

He sighed.

'But out in the colonies it's a different way of life. Things are done differently. Lives are held cheap and guns are fired often. Things can go wrong just as quickly as they can go right. And that's what happened to me; to *us*. Late one afternoon I returned to our house on the camp to find Gretchen, my wife, missing and the nursemaid holding an inconsolable Caroline. I asked where my wife had got to, and the nursemaid said the last she had seen of her was when Stefan, the other Swiss, had come up to the veranda an hour previously and told Gretchen to come quickly; something dreadful had happened.'

Steinhauser fumbled for a handkerchief for his eyes. Father Moriarty darted forwards with a fresh one.

'Naturally I felt something terrible had happened, too. So I summoned some of the men from the mine and we searched for both Stefan and Gretchen. It didn't take long to find them. Their bodies were behind a little hillock, in some scrubland. Gretchen had been shot several times, and there was blood everywhere. Stefan had been shot once, at point-blank range. The murder weapon was lying on the scrubland between them, and it was *my* pistol which had been used to kill them both.'

'A smoking gun,' muttered the Inspector uncertainly. 'Incriminating stuff.'

'Quite.' Steinhauser nodded. 'Although I didn't see it like that at the time. I was beside myself with grief, wailing and shouting. The men I had taken with me ran and fetched Glaysayer, together with all the other men from the mine. It was dark by now and they all came back with burning torches. The local men were very afraid of spirits and black magic and such like. I remember they wouldn't look at the two bodies at all, and wouldn't help carry them back to the house, either. It was just Glaysayer and myself, carting first Gretchen, and then Stefan back over the rough ground until we had reached my house. I remember the baby was still wailing, and the crickets and mosquitoes were making an almighty din. Much like any other night, but my world was falling apart. I had yet to realise quite how much *more* it would fall apart.'

Steinhauser had come to a stop, and was staring into nothingness, immersed in memories from thirty years before.

'What happened next, sir?' asked Lenny, fascinated no doubt by another life which had had terrible pitfalls of its own.

Steinhauser refocused his rheumy eyes, attempted a smile. 'Ah, this is where it all fell apart. Glaysayer asked me straight up what had happened: I told him I had no idea, but Stefan, our partner, had been trying it on with Gretchen for months, even when she was pregnant. And she had always told him to stuff it and leave her be. I said that I supposed the same thing had happened tonight, and Stefan, who was always a great drinker, had had enough of the rejection and seen fit to kill both Gretchen and himself, perhaps wanting to implicate me if at all possible.'

'But we only have your word for this, Steinhauser,' said Mr Cardinal, quite coldly, Posie felt. 'You could have killed them both. Perhaps they were having an affair under your very nose and it was *you* who had had enough of it all?'

Steinhauser sighed and nodded. 'You have my word for it that that is *not* what happened, as did Glaysayer at the time. But what Mr Cardinal has just alluded to, my murdering the two of them, is exactly what Glaysayer came up with. He saw his chance and he took it. He took *everything* from me.'

'How so?' asked Mr Cardinal, his eyebrows knitted together.

'He said he knew I was jealous of Stefan and Gretchen, of the love they had found together. He said he knew I had murdered them both in a fit of jealousy. He said that he had witnesses who could prove they had both seen and heard me confronting the couple earlier in the evening, and he even had a witness who had seen me approach the clearing where they were making love. Apparently I was armed with my pistol. Glaysayer said that he would make sure I was found guilty in whatever court of law I ended up in, whether that was back at home or out in Africa. He said that it would be best if I went away and shot myself. Either that, or disappeared. Made it look as if I had died naturally in a disaster at the mine. He would register my death and take my baby daughter and raise her as his own, and he would take over the mine.'

'I don't believe you!' said Jacinta, wide-eyed. 'If you *weren't* guilty you could have proved it! You should have stayed on and defended your innocence, if that was what it was. Running away was surely an admission of guilt?'

'Running away was all I *could* do in the circumstances, Miss Glaysayer.' Steinhauser bowed his head sheepishly.

'I am afraid I was too much of a coward to shoot myself. I've always been a coward, a poor excuse for a man, but I've never been a murderer; I swear it. And as I've already tried to explain, things are different out there: I couldn't have defended an innocence which wasn't backed up by any evidence. There was, quite simply, no evidence to help me out. Glaysayer had bribed the lot of the remaining "witnesses" with cash; probably the equivalent of a year's salary or more. Those men and even the nursemaid would have sworn to my guilt with no hesitation. Glaysayer had pots of money, and he had his eye on making more. The only thing I could do was run.'

Steinhauser looked at Jocasta and a vain flicker of hope crossed his face as she turned to him at last. 'And I am so, so sorry. That's what I meant about Glaysayer not being an honest man; not doing anything in accordance with the law.'

'Where have you been all these years, then?' Jocasta hissed. 'Why didn't you come for me before?'

Mr Steinhauser nodded.

'I've been on the run; I've been working for other men, other rich men, making them money. Making myself money, too. Mining, mostly. I've lived thirty years under a collection of false passports and false identities. I tried to put the events of thirty years ago behind me; they were too painful to dwell on. And I was powerless to do anything. Glaysayer had got you, and I knew he could give you a good quality of life, if nothing else. The thing that made it all bearable was that he had a good wife. I could imagine her raising you well. I didn't come for you because I lived in fear that Glaysayer would expose me, even now, even thirty years later. He held all the cards, and I had none. I never kept track of where he lived, of what he did, because it was just too painful.'

The Inspector stared at the Swiss man hard. 'You had good motive for wishing Glaysayer dead, though. Admit it, sir. A long-held grudge; a gross wrong committed against you; the loss of your shares in the mine, and the loss of your daughter. A first-class motive, I'd say.'

'Perhaps. But that wasn't my motive in being here for this New Year's party. Again, I'm a poor excuse for a man, but I'm no murderer. *My* revenge was simply turning up for this party; watching old Glaysayer's face as he had to play the perfect host towards me. I knew when I saw how ill he was that he wouldn't start accusing me of an ancient crime. Besides, he probably thought it was good timing; I was wealthy enough to step up to the plate and take care of Jocasta when he died. Or Caroline, as you once *were*.'

Posie swallowed hard. She didn't want to speak ill of the dead, but an idea had come to her which didn't seem altogether unlikely:

'This is hypothetical, Mr Steinhauser. But did it ever cross your mind, sir, that Lord Glaysayer *himself* murdered your wife and your other, Swiss, business partner? That he did it deliberately in order to take over all three shares of the mine and to offer his wife a baby daughter they couldn't otherwise have had?'

Steinhauser nodded quickly. 'Of course it did. But how could I prove it? I still don't know to this day what happened. But I *do* know that Robin Glaysayer was guilty of robbing me of my life, however he did it. Which is not to say he didn't get his comeuppance.'

'How so, sir?' Posie declined the offer of a fancy cigarillo which Mr Cardinal was offering her, and instead she stood, absolutely riveted, staring at the Swiss man.

Steinhauser laughed his wild laugh.

'Robin Glaysayer was always reckless with money, so I'm not surprised to hear tonight that he had money problems, that this fine house has to be sold. That he probably leaves no inheritance for "his" girls. He always had his fingers in various dodgy schemes as a way of making extra money on the side, but it never got him anywhere in the end. But Robin Glaysayer's problems with money started a long time ago; around the time he had forced me to abandon my livelihood and my life.'

Steinhauser got out a small blue bottle from his pocket and dabbed at his eyes with the handkerchief soaked in liquid from the bottle. He continued miserably:

'Glaysayer had mistakenly thought that Stefan, our business partner, would not have organised anything like a Will or a Testament regarding his share of the diamond mine; that he was just a hopeless drunkard. But, although Stefan was a drinker, he was sharp as a tack, and he had made specific provisions for his son back in Switzerland to inherit his share. The son was sharp too, although he was only a child, and when profits started to mysteriously "dwindle" at the mine the son sent out agents to check what was going on. The son detected fraud and had old Glaysayer outed, threatening to have him up in court in Switzerland, promising imprisonment and worse. The son ended up buying Glaysayer's "two" shares at a fraction of what they were really worth in an out-of-court settlement. And then the son turned the mine into a real, rip-roaring success story. It's a huge enterprise now, and the number one diamond mine in the whole of Africa, outside of Kimberley in the South, of course.'

Jocasta was eyeing her 'real' father curiously, and Posie had the uncomfortable sensation that she was trying to assess how much he was worth to her now, financially.

'What do you want me to do, sir?' asked Rainbird softly to the Inspector, the pair of handcuffs discreetly tucked inside his inner jacket pocket, hidden from view but there all the same. 'Arrest the man?'

The Inspector almost growled. 'On what grounds, Sergeant? I'm wracking my brain for anything which will stick but all I can feel is dashed sorry for the chap. Where's Binny? I said we were all to stay close.'

'Wandered off, sir,' replied Rainbird dejectedly. 'He was carrying the Sales Particulars for this house, that purple brochure of the Duke's. Most odd, sir.'

'Golly,' said Posie brightly. 'I don't know about you, but I could murder a coffee. And the last one is still soaking its way into that poor zebra's hide. So shall I do the honours? I'll make enough for everyone.'

'I'll come with you,' said Jacinta, looking relieved to get up and leave the hall and the company of her sister for a bit. 'Show you where things are kept.'

'Follow them.' Inspector Lovelace glared at Sergeant Rainbird. 'And keep a close eye. I don't trust *anyone* in this place.'

He sniffed a bit. 'Besides, Posie is too valuable an asset to lose.'

* * * *

Nineteen

The coffee made, Posie started to load up one tray with cups and Sergeant Rainbird the other with biscuits and cheese and oatcakes. Posie had kept up a banal flow of conversation with Jacinta in the huge and well-equipped kitchen while she was boiling the big service kettle, but all the time she had kept thinking about Mr Cardinal: about how he had hinted that he didn't trust anyone.

Why, he had even cast doubt on brave Mr Goodman earlier that night, saying how calm the man was being in the circumstances, singing his cheery songs in the Library; how he was unlike someone who had just risked their life sailing over the Channel.

And now it looked as if the Duke and Lenny, *and* Mr Steinhauser, however sinister, were all somehow innocent of Lord Glaysayer's murder, which only left Jacinta and Jocasta as the remaining viable suspects. Posie felt as if she had been dealt a particularly bad hand of cards, and even these were at risk of slipping through her fingers.

So did that mean that Posie should be suspicious of Jacinta right now? Of the hunched, poor figure of a girl adding milk and sugar calmly to the cups beside her? Try as she might Posie couldn't see it: she didn't feel the least bit scared, for one thing. But perhaps the famous Posie Parker gut instinct was distinctly off-kilter tonight?

It was true that Jacinta seemed unusually quiet, much quieter than earlier, as if she were brooding on something. Could she remember that strange premonition from earlier? Or was she 'seeing' something new? Or was she simply the murderer, after all?

It didn't add up, and Posie was left feeling none the wiser. She hated the fact that nothing here at Maypole Manor was adding up; that nothing was coming together as easily as things had done before, on other cases.

Revisit the crime scene in your head, she said to herself grimly.

Pore over the details. Sure as bread is bread something will leap out and help you there: give you some sort of answer.

She sighed, and made herself think again of the horrible dead figure of Lord Glaysayer collapsed over the desk in his study: of his strangely-arranged pistol; of the old framed photo he had fallen onto, the picture of Jacinta together with her mother. She thought of the Will which Jocasta had so gleefully read to herself. And then, randomly, Posie thought about the Duke and the purple-covered Sales Particulars for the house.

It came to her quickly. It wasn't the solution to the murder, but it was the answer to something which had been puzzling her all night; something which didn't add up.

There *was* a link, a recurring link.

It was the tiger. It had to be.

Somehow, in some way, it kept cropping up. And Posie had known the photograph was important the minute she had seen it, too.

Puzzle pieces were coming together in her head, but slowly; frustratingly slowly, as if through a mist or fog which showed no sign of clearing.

And then Posie realised just how and why the tiger was important. Amory Laine herself had almost stumbled upon it accidentally.

But it was crazy. Totally mad.

At the very last minute Posie grabbed a huge pair of yellow rubber gloves which were carefully hung on a nail above the sink in the kitchen, together with a matching plunger. She managed to stuff them both up Alaric's huge jumper without either of Sergeant Rainbird or Jacinta seeing and then the three of them set off, laden down. Stepping through the kitchen doorway into the main service corridor, Posie spoke to Jacinta in a nonchalant, chummy fashion as a prelude to what she really wanted to ask.

'Are you feeling okay, Miss Glaysayer? I know it's a rough night for you, and I'm so sorry about your father, but you need to stay strong. You seem very out of sorts.'

Jacinta winced. 'I am out of sorts, as it happens. I was just thinking that actually JoJo was right for once: she told me earlier tonight that I was a very poor clairvoyant, that I was a fraud. I'd never considered it before and I certainly didn't try and con people deliberately. But I've missed so much here, not *seen* as much as I should have done. I should have kept our father alive tonight. Perhaps I'm not so great after all. I'm a rotten failure. I was just thinking that it might be time to shut up shop on Lamb's Conduit Street, that "Mystic Mirabelle" may have had her day. I have to be good *all* of the time; not on and off. Who wants to come to a clairvoyant who doesn't deliver the goods?'

Posie glanced at the girl. Privately she agreed: she didn't believe in all that fortune-telling guff, but if you were paying for it you'd probably want a fairly consistent service, no doubt. Posie smiled and tried to reassure her. 'I wouldn't be so hard on yourself, Miss Glaysayer. At least, not tonight. Think of something else for now.'

She waited for a few seconds.

'Could I ask you something a little unorthodox while we are alone?'

'Fire away.'

'You receive the old tiger under your father's Will, don't you?'

Jacinta nodded, frowning. 'Why?'

'It seems a funny bequest to me. But does he mean something special to you, Bobbie, I mean?'

Jacinta eyed Posie with surprise, and then shrugged.

'No. Not really. He actually belonged to my mother. He was shot accidentally while we were all out in India once; she was trying to shoot at something else – a bird I think – aim was never her strongpoint. She was very upset about it, but my father insisted that Bobbie was stuffed and brought back with us. He said it was a real waste otherwise. And after a few years I think my mother got used to him. Bobbie was always in our hallway, wherever we lived; guarding us. I loved to sit on him when I was a child, a bit like a rocking horse, even though I wasn't really allowed to. Once, when we were burgled out in Africa, and all held up at gun-point, my mother had the foresight to stuff all of her jewels in Bobbie's mouth. Of course no-one thought to look in the tiger's mouth, so they were safe. She was quite rich, my mother, in her own right, you know. But Father used up all of her money too; it went on travelling and high-living.'

Jacinta laughed as if at something very funny. 'Do you know, when she died, my mother left *me*, just me, her whole estate. That was a lovely gesture, but there was quite nothing left to give. Not a jot. So it was an empty gesture, too.'

'I see. How sad. But why were *you* the sole beneficiary of her Will and not your sister, too?'

Jacinta shrugged. 'I wondered that. Perhaps my mother saw which way the wind was blowing and realised that father was likely to leave everything to JoJo. Maybe she wanted to "even" things up a bit. But if I had received anything at all I would have split it with JoJo fair and square, as would have been right.'

'I believe you. But dash it all, your sister wouldn't have done the same with Maypole Manor, would she? Even if it *had* been hers to own, without the mortgages and debts which need to be settled. She wouldn't have given you a half-share. Doesn't that make you mad?'

'That would have been her decision at the end of the day. She's a different character to me, I suppose. I wouldn't have held it against her.'

They were now in the entrance hall, and hard up against the tiger.

'I say, Sergeant, can you stop a minute? Let's put these trays on the floor here.'

And Posie was swiftly turning herself and Jacinta around, away from the room and towards the tiger itself, away from the view of anyone who happened to look over. Rainbird eyed Posie quizzically, but, used to her often crazy methods, he stood firm, and formed a screen with his body, pretending to mess around with the coffee things, so that Posie and Jacinta were quite out of view.

'Miss Glaysayer, I have an idea. It may be wildly wrong, but I ask your permission to try, anyhow. It concerns this here beast, Bobbie. I need to touch it.'

'You can't touch him. You know he's saturated in poison? Dripping in the stuff. I told you that earlier.'

'Mnnn. So you say. But I'll take my chances, if I may.'

And quick as a flash Posie had pulled on the large rubber gloves and delved inside the tiger's mouth, past the teeth and fake tongue. Amory had been right when she had said that it was a very strange sharp feeling inside, almost like…

Almost like…jewels.

Packed haphazardly but tightly into the throat of the beast.

Posie drew out what she could feel: firstly, a huge diamond necklace, and secondly, a misshapen, bent-up tiara, which must have been pressed out of shape in order

205

to fit the tight confines of the tiger's gullet. It glittered with many diamonds in the electric light. Posie recognised both of the items from the photograph in Lord Glaysayer's study. Both had been worn by his wife.

Posie passed across the two items to Jacinta, who took them wordlessly, her mouth fallen open. She was breathing slowly, shallowly, and seemed momentarily incapable of speech. Sergeant Rainbird emitted a low exclamation of surprise:

'Well, I'll be jiggered, Miss!'

And then Posie took the sink plunger and started jabbing wildly down the neck of the tiger, as far as she could reach. Jacinta seemed to pull herself together with a visible effort, and then she stared at Posie aghast.

'Don't destroy poor Bobbie! There isn't any more, you know, Miss Parker. You're wasting your time. These two items *were* my mother's fortune after father had frittered away her cash. I really thought he'd sold these, too.'

Jacinta took the heavy, spiky handful and dumped it into Sergeant Rainbird's surprised hands.

'You'd better take these, Sergeant. They don't belong to me, nice though it is to hold them for a while. I know my father owed vast sums of money to the government, for taxes he hadn't paid. So you'd better take these. They should make some inroad into the debt, at any rate.'

'No,' insisted Posie, puffing with effort and indicating that the Sergeant should hand the jewels back. 'Legally, I think they *are* yours. It's all been managed most cleverly; you'll see. Hold onto the jewels please, Miss Glaysayer.'

Posie pulled something else out from the tiger's mouth. 'Aha! That's what I thought might be here! An explanation.'

She shook out a cream-coloured envelope, thick with dust, addressed to Jacinta in a round, curved black script. Posie handed it over and started to strip off the rubber gloves.

'Hadn't you better go and wash your hands, Miss

Parker? We've had quite enough deaths here tonight. We don't want you to come down with a nasty case of arsenic poisoning.'

'*What* poison?' scoffed Posie. 'I don't believe there was any: I think your father asked you to spread that news about so that no-one came near, so his inheritance for you would remain hidden. Just like it had remained hidden these last few months.'

'But how on earth would I ever have found the jewels?' whispered Jacinta in a low, quivering voice. 'I don't have premonitions about everything, you know. It's patchy at best.'

'I think that your father would have told you on his deathbed; if you had been there at the hospital. But it's my belief that, although the poison story is fake, he did leave specific instructions with a friendly restorative taxidermist about the jewels and the letter. The man would have come and taken the beast apart after your father had died, and would then have informed you about what was inside it. You told me that your father had had the taxidermist up here just a few days ago, didn't you? He was probably just prepping the man for what was required of him. Aren't you going to read the letter?'

Jacinta nodded, shaking, tearing open the envelope. She read the enclosed letter quickly, her twisted shoulders trembling all the while. At the end she winced, but didn't look surprised. She had gone very, very pale. She passed the letter over to Posie wordlessly.

It was dated six months previously, and it read:

My darling girl,

You will be reading this when I am dead, and probably because Mr Luckie, the taxidermist, has just handed you this missive. Even you with your magic talents couldn't have foreseen that, eh?!

On a serious note, these were, of course, your mother's jewels. And now they are yours, as she wished; as is right legally. Good old Bobbie has been guarding them for you; both from me and from your sister. For, as you well know, both of us would have sold them a thousand times over to make some extra cash.

The jewels are not part of my estate; they were your mother's alone and are therefore outside of my estate. They cannot be collected in and used to pay off the many, many debts which you know I have. So enjoy the jewels, or sell them, or do whatever you like with them. But, I pray, do not let them anywhere near your sister.

You will be wondering why I left her Maypole Manor, and why I left you absolutely nothing in my Will, I suppose. The answer is that I knew you would receive your mother's jewels, which are worth a fortune anyhow, and, very simply, I wanted to bring your sister down a peg or two. Maypole Manor has so many mortgages upon it that Jocasta will emerge with nothing at the end but a sore head and many sittings in the bankrupt's court.

I am even considering selling the house before my death; so the gift for her in my Will really will be an empty gesture.

But why do I behave like this, you ask?

We have to look at the past for a moment.

I 'acquired' your sister in dubious circumstances out in Africa. To put it bluntly, I killed for her. I am not proud of what I did, and if I could change what happened out there I would go back in a heartbeat, but what is done is done. I am, unfortunately, a very bad, very greedy man, and I know I will be judged for it by some higher justice.

Your sister was always a difficult child. Your mother tried to love her, and God knows, she was a saint of a woman, but it was as if your sister knew how I had acquired her, that she was bathed in bloodshed. I pandered to her on all matters, guilt suffusing my common sense, wanting to 'make up' to her for depriving her of her real parents at so early an age.

Jocasta seemed all the worse compared to you; you who had

been born with a physical disability and who bore it so bravely. I do not exaggerate when I tell you that you were the apple of your mother's eye. And mine too. I look every day at the painting you made for me when you were a child and it brings me such happiness. We adored you, but we had to show affection and love to Jocasta, too. Your mother barely managed it; she had convinced herself that Jocasta was accursed. I think she was scared of the child. And I, as I said, went the other way and spoiled the girl rotten to compensate for my previous actions.

So what did your sister do which was so bad?

The answer was, everything. We tried to hide it from you, but Jocasta stole; she lied; she stole some more.

She killed animals for pleasure. She showed no love or loyalty to any living thing; not for you, not for your mother, and certainly not for me. She seemed absolutely incapable of love.

She tried several times to steal your mother's jewellery, and regularly took money from everyone's pockets, frequently my own, and often from the servants. When questioned about the thefts, she would simply shrug and walk away, smiling, not bothering to defend herself. At your mother's deathbed she showed absolutely no emotion; no remorse for her behaviour.

Since your mother died I have 'managed' Jocasta by keeping her close. I expect you thought she was a favourite, but I was just trying to contain the damage she caused and causes. Each time she was expelled from a school, then jobs, I hoped against hope that she would find something she liked, that she could enjoy, that she could throw her energies into. That she might change. But it didn't happen.

The last three years have been a struggle, I'll admit. Your sister is, as I am sure you know, a first-class drug addict. It started up in 1918. Sometimes it's heroin, but it's more often the oblivion of cocaine which she seeks out. It breaks my heart.

I am, as I said, a terribly bad man, but I simply cannot endorse the use of drugs. I live wildly beyond my means, but drugs have never been part of that.

Recently I have found out something which makes my heart break even more. Do you remember the central heating system I had installed here, at Jocasta's request, three years ago?

I went to check on it one afternoon recently when I thought it was playing up; I hadn't been to see it since it was installed, as a matter of fact.

There is a central boiler and, you remember, mini-tunnels snaking through the house which contain very large water pipes for transmitting the heat. If you turn off the heating it is possible for a man to walk through these mini-tunnels which are tacked on to every room. In fact, they connect up with the old smuggling tunnels which were part of the house before I bought it.

I got the shock of my life to realise that I was walking into a drugs emporium. And that it was your sister who was running it. In my own house!

There were cannabis plants growing everywhere in the warm dark tunnels, with Jocasta's writing affixed to labels stating when the plants could be harvested. And, not only that, but stacks of what looked like heroin and cocaine were piled up all over the place, awaiting collection.

I had known that your sister had got herself mixed up with a bad bunch for a while, that the parties she throws here were not really of the legal kind, but what shocked me was the scale of the thing. It was a professional operation, linked to a top-class smuggling racket.

I tried to talk to your sister, to get her to stop whatever madness she was involved in, but she lied and lied. Refused to speak about it. I have often been on the brink of calling the police and asking them to come here and take her away: but how can I do that to her, really?

There is, of course, a man at the bottom of all of this.

Your sister is wildly in love with a rogue by the name of Larry. I have never met him, and I do not want to, but it is my belief that he is the mastermind behind what must be this drugs racket here, and that he is simply 'using' your poor sister because *of her ties to Maypole Manor and the convenient spot it is in. I cannot believe he loves her, and if he says he does, he is lying.*

I write all this to get it off my chest, but also as a means of explanation. You deserve to know this. You may have to know this, as it may all blow up when I am dead. You may have to look after your sister in the future, or you may choose to walk away and never see her again. That is, of course, your choice. It is not as if there is any real blood between you.

Forgive me if it seemed that I loved Jocasta more than you. Nothing was further from the truth.

With much love and a thousand apologies.

Your father,

R. Glaysayer.

Posie looked up, stunned. The letter explained so much.

She spoke automatically: 'We'd better get this over to the Inspector for him to have a look at it.'

But her mind was working overtime.

So often at this horrid party she had heard about the wretched central heating system and dismissed it as being unimportant, when actually, it had been important all along. Key, in fact.

Amory Laine had been right when she had said that people were creeping about in the walls; that the walls had ears. The smugglers mentioned by Lord Glaysayer had been creeping about all night long. They had been creeping around even as Inspector Lovelace had gathered his small team together at the start of the evening for a briefing, probably creeping right past them, eavesdropping. And that was why the heating had gone off, why it was so wretchedly cold; it had been switched off deliberately so that the smugglers could go about their usual business. The letter from Lord Glaysayer also pretty much explained the flashing lights outside.

'Shall we get this here coffee out, Miss? Otherwise it will be as useless as the last brew.'

'Yes, yes, Rainbird. Of course. Here, let me help you.'

But she spoke absent-mindedly, for she was looking at Jacinta intently.

'You know,' said Posie gently. 'I'm not sure if you remember anything about your premonition from earlier tonight, but I'd say that you were a very good clairvoyant. Unwittingly you described exactly what was happening in this house. You described it very clearly.'

Jacinta looked up, confused. 'Did I?'

'You spoke about *snow* inside the house. We all thought you were quite dotty at the time but "snow" is the nickname for heroin, isn't it? And you mentioned tunnels, too. Tunnels with a precious cargo. And *disguises*. Well, that all fits. We should have listened more carefully to you. *I* should have listened more carefully. I saw your sister's face after you had finished speaking and she was scared; scared that you were speaking the truth aloud for everyone to hear.'

Mr Steinhauser came over and offered to help pass around the coffee and Posie nodded her thanks very quickly, somehow unable to meet those haunted eyes, now that she knew he had spoken the truth about what had happened out in Tanzania.

But just then there was a sudden commotion.

'HELLO! I say, Inspector! INSPECTOR!'

Everyone swung around at the shouting. And then the tall figure of Sergeant Binny came sprinting through the entrance hall, carrying several brown-paper packages. He was very excited and his voice was gleeful.

'Look at this little lot!'

He deposited the packets at Inspector Lovelace's feet like a faithful Labrador bringing home a prize to its owner.

Posie marched over with Lord Glaysayer's dusty letter in her hand.

'What the blazes…?' The Inspector was looking confused; his gaze jumping uncertainly from Binny to Posie and then back again.

Posie spoke up quickly, quietly. 'It's *snow*, sir. Top-class heroin to you and me.'

Sergeant Binny looked at Posie gobsmacked, then swallowed. Then he looked rather annoyed at her stealing his thunder. He nodded anyhow.

'She's right, sir. There's masses of the stuff, too. You have to come and see! Just like the Glaysayer girl said when she was writhing around in a fit! Customs and Excise are going to be thrilled, sir. This is a major drugs ring operating here.'

By now everyone was staring, as Sergeant Binny hadn't managed to keep his voice down.

'*Where* did you find this, Sergeant?'

'It was in the tunnels. I took these here Sales Particulars and used the diagram in them and I found where the old tunnels are. They're not bricked up anymore, sir: they're well lit up with electricity and everything! And they link back to the heating tunnels in this house.'

'And there's more of this you say?'

'Yes, sir. This is just the tip of the iceberg. There's more than I've ever seen before. Heaps of the stuff. More than I *will* ever see in my lifetime as a copper. Come now, sir! Please!'

Lovelace shook his head steadfastly, looking around at the assembled group.

'I can't. I can't leave my position here. What's this now, Posie? Goodness gracious, me: it's all happening tonight.'

Posie had passed over Lord Glaysayer's letter.

'I think you'd better read this, sir.'

She stood waiting meekly at his side while Lovelace started to read, at what seemed a painfully slow speed. People had begun to drink their coffee, and out of the corner of her eye Posie saw that Jacinta seemed busy scribbling some sort of note on the back of her father's old envelope.

At the end Inspector Lovelace whistled quietly in disbelief, and folded the letter into his inner jacket pocket.

'What will you do now, sir?' Posie whispered.

'There's not much I *can* do, but hold tight. This isn't evidence anyway, unfortunately. It's almost akin to hearsay; and a *certain person* could just say it's the ramblings of an old, sick man, off his head on strange herbs and pain medication. Which is not to say I don't believe the contents of this letter. I'm positive it's all true. Every word. By Gad! There's nothing more you can do, Posie. Go and sit and have your coffee and we'll get through the night. It's past three o'clock now. It seems like the longest night on earth, doesn't it?'

Posie returned to where she had been sitting before, to the empty space next to Mr Cardinal, who was smoking away and looking sleepy. Posie tried not to look over at Jocasta, who was obviously angry and scared and terrified at being 'found out' as being part of the drugs operation, but Posie could still feel a strange sort of hatred radiating out from her, which she felt had nothing to do with Jocasta's smuggling activities having been discovered.

'I say, Posie. May I call you that?'

It was Jacinta, a frown on her face, her blue eyes troubled again. She bobbed before the sofa, twitching. Posie felt Bryn Cardinal's hand lightly caress her shoulders, the weight of his arm resting there, proprietorial, the slight smell of Dolly, Lady Cardigeon, so nice and close and familiar.

Posie nodded.

'Of course. What's up?'

'There's something wrong. I can't say what it is aloud. But please read what I've written here for you. I think it might be important. I'm afraid it's only just come to me.'

But they were interrupted. Just then there was an almighty droning sound overhead which rendered everything else unimportant: a huge, terrifying mechanical grating sound roared above them.

'Jeepers!'

Edwin Goodman was on his feet, terrified. 'What is heaven's name is that? It sounds like the end of the earth!'

Lenny and the Duke dived for cover behind the settee. The Inspector had gone ash-white but held his ground. The local men, Ellacott and Protheroe and Cleghorn, all came running at once and stood together uncertainly in the entrance hall, looking at the ceiling as if it might cave in at once.

'What was that?' demanded the Inspector, to no-one in particular.

Mr Cardinal was still sitting down, but Posie could swear she saw pure excitement on his ruddy pink face when he announced, in tones of absolute wonder:

'It was an Avro!'

'A what, sir?' asked Sergeant Binny, confused.

'An Avro of some sort. A biplane. I flew one in the last war; a 504, as it happens. It sounded just like that. But it beats me who would be flying one out on a night like tonight. In the snow! He'd have to be absolutely crazy! There's only three men I know of in the whole of Britain who would dare to fly out on a night such as this. And I'm one of them.'

And Posie's stomach lurched.

For surely one of those three men had to be Alaric.

* * * *

Twenty

The sound had died away, leaving no-one any the wiser, and for a moment everyone was side-tracked by Lenny, suddenly announcing to the room at large that she felt very sick, and clutching oddly at her stomach.

She went away with Sergeant Rainbird to the bathroom, the Duke gazing after Lenny's retreating figure wretchedly.

Posie's thoughts were miles away however.

Was it possible, was it just possible that Alaric might be flying to Maypole Manor tonight on a mercy mission?

But then Posie laughed at herself, for her foolishness; her mind and heart were just playing tricks on themselves. Right now Alaric was in South Africa, enjoying the warmth and the wine and the good company and probably a glamorous party somewhere too...

Instead Posie opened the note from Jacinta, expecting to read something about a premonition, or about the tiger again. Or about something not quite relevant.

But what she read made her sit up, stock-still, and very gently and slowly get to her feet.

Posie read the note over again, and then tucked it up her grey woollen sleeve, all the while her heart, a ball of fire and ice in her chest, was beating ten to the dozen, fear palpably running through her veins. She felt like she couldn't breathe.

'What's wrong, Miss Parker? You feeling funny, too? You look a mighty odd colour, if you don't mind my saying so.'

'No, Sergeant Binny. I'm right as rain, thank you. Right as rain…'

But she wasn't. That was far from the truth. Posie cast around quickly for Bikram, Alaric's unfaithful pointer dog. Her panic subsided when she saw that he was sitting right next to Mr Cardinal. He was snoozing peaceably and seemed unusually happy being petted by Mr Cardinal's non-smoke-holding hand.

Posie swallowed and tried to remain calm. Between her juddering heartbeats which she swore the whole room could hear, she tried to get a grip and remain professional; to try and process the new information which had come to her so late in the day.

She walked to a window and looked out, regarding the now-calm, snow-caked landscape with unseeing eyes.

Get a grip.

A confused series of images and thoughts played through Posie's mind, all of which somehow, tonight, in the back of her mind hadn't made sense. But now a solution to them all was coming together jaggedly.

A plan of the most daring kind. That was what this whole night had been about.

Could it be? Was it even possible?

It was absurd, and ridiculously high-risk. And it was downright lucky, too. Not to mention spectacular in its results.

The whole dashed thing had been undertaken by a chancer whose luck never ran out. 'Planned' was too strong a word for it: there had not been much planning involved. Just a lot of risks.

For, despite the best efforts of Posie and the Inspector, the blueprint for 'the Guillotine' was destined to end up in the wrong hands anyhow.

Posie exhaled, as if in need of oxygen. She noticed that now the Duke was being sick near the fireplace and that Father Moriarty was bending over him with a look of some concern on his face, offering water.

Things were falling into place.

Slowly.

Surely.

Horrifyingly.

Posie pulled the envelope out of her sleeve again. There were a few panicky points on it in Jacinta's writing. The first read:

POSIE,

YOU MENTIONED DISGUISES.

IT JUST JOGGED MY MEMORY. BUT TOO LATE, I FEAR.

Posie stared and stared at the words until they felt like they were imprinted on the inside of her eyelids, and would be forever. The whole horror-story was now fixing itself into place; a kaleidoscope of mismanagement and sleight-of-hand whirring together in a terrible circle in front of her, as if to taunt her, as if to tell her how bad a detective she really was.

Disguises.

Posie read the rest of Jacinta's note again, and every word cut just as sharply as the first time she had read it:

I MET A MAN YESTERDAY HERE BY CHANCE. HE WAS SPEAKING WITH FATHER IN THE STUDY ABOUT CODES FOR THE SAFE AND 'TIMINGS'.

HE SAID HE COULDN'T DRIVE AT ALL, BUT

HE KEPT IT QUIET: HE HAD WALKED FROM ST MARTIN MILL TRAIN STATION WITH A HEAVY BAG. HE SAID HE COULDN'T TRUST ANYONE TO DELIVER IT HERE SAFELY, ONLY HIMSELF.

HE WAS IN A RUSH: SAID HE HAD TO GET BACK TO LONDON BUT HE WOULD BE BACK AGAIN THE NEXT DAY, IN TIME FOR THE PARTY.

HE LAUGHED AND CALLED HIMSELF A CONTROL-FREAK, FOR HIS SINS. SAID HE HAD AN ASSISTANT, TOO, BUT HE COULD NEVER BOTHER BRINGING HIM ALONG, EVEN THOUGH HE WAS SUPPOSED TO. HE WAS A TINY, FEEBLE LITTLE MAN BUT HE EXUDED POWER: HE MADE ME FEEL QUITE FRIGHTENED, LIKE YOU'D DO AS HE TOLD YOU.

HE SAID HIS NAME WAS MR BRYN CARDINAL.

LATER, WHEN I ASKED FATHER WHO THE MAN WAS, HE TOLD ME HE WAS A SECURITY EXPERT WHO WOULD MAKE SURE THE SAFE WAS ALL IN ORDER AS FATHER WAS EXPECTING TROUBLE, PERHAPS AT THE PARTY ITSELF.

I DIDN'T ASK ANY FURTHER QUESTIONS. BUT PERHAPS I SHOULD HAVE DONE?

I ONLY REMEMBERED THIS JUST NOW. SORRY.

Bryn Cardinal.

Sure as bread was bread the Bryn Cardinal she had been – but *had* she been? – so entranced with all night was not the real one. He was an imposter.

A chancer. A spectacularly, brazenly, impossibly charmingly good one too.

Thinking rapidly, Posie saw where the whole mess had started. She had just *assumed* that Inspector Lovelace had met, or at least *seen* the MI5 man before. That they perhaps shared a history, or work experiences.

But as Posie tried to remember her briefing with the Inspector on the train, she realised that she had just taken this for granted. All the Inspector had had to go on was a series of notes, drafted by the real 'control-freak' Bryn Cardinal; the notes originally intended for Assistant Commissioner Scabbes.

And bearing in mind the MI5 man's seniority, and eminence, and (but had they got that wrong?) his status as a war hero, the Inspector had obviously not, as he had done later with Constable Cleghorn, liked to ask for any identity checks or papers to be supplied.

Besides, that most senior Scotland Yard policeman, Assistant Commissioner Scabbes, was a personal friend of the real Bryn Cardinal, and it wouldn't do to annoy a friend of a boss. So the Bryn Cardinal who had presented himself at Maypole Manor had happily been accepted as the real deal.

The last-minute nature of the whole thing was spectacular!

Inspector Lovelace had only been drafted in at the eleventh hour because Assistant Commissioner Scabbes had become poorly. If the Commissioner had been running the show right now instead of Inspector Lovelace, the real Bryn Cardinal would be sat here instead, not this imposter. There was no way on earth that the imposter could have got away with the deception.

Which meant that somehow, cleverly, the imposter had managed to keep up to date with the fact that Scabbes was being replaced by Inspector Lovelace at the last minute. And he had capitalised on that fact.

The only way in which that could have happened was for the telephones to have been tapped; for Scotland Yard telephone lines to have been compromised.

It made Posie wonder what the original plan had been. For sure as bread was bread there had been some original plan to steal 'the Guillotine' blueprint, albeit in another way. If the *real* Mr Cardinal and Commissioner Scabbes had presided at tonight's party, perhaps the real Mr Cardinal would have been ambushed on his way back to London and forced at gun-point to give up the blueprint?

It didn't bear thinking about.

Posie tried not to remember the formidable sight of the blueprint and the Luger strapped expertly to the imposter's chest with black bandages. She suppressed a shiver and tried not to think about *who exactly* the imposter might be. It didn't help matters.

The imposter had also been extraordinarily lucky in that the snow-storm which had enveloped Maypole Manor had meant that Scotland Yard, even if they *had* learnt that something was wrong, were not able to contact anyone in the house.

Presumably the imposter was sitting here biding his time until a break in the weather meant he could flee.

But where was the real Mr Cardinal?

And then Posie almost snorted aloud with laughter at her ineptitude.

It had all been before them the whole time! Terrifyingly so. For, yes: this was about disguise, but it was about murder too.

She remembered the strange little scene on the train the day before which no-one had thought much about: the nosing around she had done in the small bathroom, and Sergeant Rainbird reporting a strange occurrence which had been dismissed as nothing more than an amorous liaison at the time:

'A fella went in, but didn't come out. A woman came out who must have been in there the whole time and now she's gone back in there again.'

Posie remembered too the mess in the bathroom: the splintered mirror, the broken make-up, the burning black cigarillo stub. The detritus of a drug-addict's tantrum, which they had all been so keen to attribute to Amory Laine. Poor, dead Amory Laine.

And the smaller details on the train, too, which had seemed boringly insignificant at the time. They all came back in a horrid rush, taunting Posie: the blind which had been up in the corridor, flapping about, cold air streaming in. And the polite middle-aged man with the blue eyes and the beard who had passed her so benignly.

Sure as bread was bread Mr Bryn Cardinal, the *real* Bryn Cardinal, was dead. He was dead by the time Posie had made it to the bathroom to change into her frivolous fancy clothes. She didn't know exactly what had happened, of course. But she could hazard a pretty good guess at it.

Posie pictured the scenes running very clearly through her mind.

The real Mr Cardinal, who couldn't drive, caught the train, the Golden Arrow, at 12.15 from Platform 3 at Victoria, the same as Posie had done. Supposed to bring an assistant, the man liked to go things alone and travelled by himself.

Perhaps he had received a cryptic or coded message, but somehow or other the real M15 man had been asked to meet someone in the lavatory in Posie's carriage. No fool, he had been suspicious but had gone along anyway, perhaps armed. Sergeant Rainbird had probably seen the real Mr Cardinal go into the bathroom.

Waiting in there already was the imposter, dressed as a woman. What passed between them was anybody's guess, but the imposter had had to get the real Mr Cardinal out of the way, and the two men, so ill-matched physically, would have fought, thus splintering the mirror and dropping the make-up. The real Mr Cardinal must have ended up either dead, or near-as, and whether dead or alive he had been thrown out of the bathroom window. If he hadn't been dead when he was thrown from the train he would have been when he landed at high speed. The force alone would have killed him.

The imposter had then waited in the bathroom for a

bit and then come out briefly, perhaps to grab a change of clothes from his carriage which was next to the bathroom, all curtained-up and hidden from view, or perhaps simply in order to be noticed, as indeed Sergeant Rainbird had done; to throw people off the scent later with reports of a woman being seen at the time.

The imposter had then gone back into the bathroom, would have had time for a very quick smoke, and then changed into his suit and prominent black hat. He would have added his false beard carefully before throwing his women's clothes out of the bathroom window. He had then exited the bathroom and passed by Posie in the corridor, calm as anything.

That must have been it. She was still unsure why the window was wide open in the corridor itself, but that would resolve itself, or not, later.

Posie looked around herself now, very much back in the present. She knew she probably looked wild-eyed and terrified and she tried to appear calm and unruffled.

Both Lenny and the Duke were squirming in pain on one sofa, the priest looking worried. Sergeant Binny had run off somewhere, too.

Posie looked over at 'her' Bryn Cardinal and saw that he was smoking a black cigarillo, exactly like the butt of one she had found in the bathroom. *How brazen and calm and collected he was!*

What ease he had radiated throughout, and what an aura he had of being in control: him with his little notebook full of lists, his pretend 'knowledge' of the house guests and the background checks M15 had run, and his annoying way of constantly putting the Inspector in his place; reminding him who was really calling the shots.

Posie cursed herself for not having spotted the imposter a mile off. There *had* been signs, but they were very subtle: the fact that the imposter had been happy from the start for Inspector Lovelace to take the lead during the handover, never really adding anything concrete or factual; the fact that he had not known the code to the safe, and had let Inspector Lovelace open it.

And that *smell*. The familiar scent. Into Posie's mind came a sudden remembrance of Dolly again. And she realised what it was. It was *eyelash glue*. Stage glue. Dolly always stank to high heaven of the stuff as she wore fake lashes by the bucketload. Even now that she didn't have to work in a theatre as a Wardrobe Mistress.

It was the exact same smell.

It was the smell of stage glue which had been used to keep the imposter's beard in place earlier, when he had been 'playing' at being a random stranger. And when she casually glanced over now, even from this distance, Posie could see that tiny little tell-tale smudge of something which must be old glue on his one good cheek.

For it had been important that the fake Mr Cardinal had never been seen on a train. It was important for the imposter to be able to say that he had driven to the party, and that he would leave that way too. With the help of his 'man', Evans.

Posie started: where the blazes was Evans?

If 'Cardinal' was an imposter, then Evans had to be, too. It was a double-act.

Evans who had supposedly gone for firewood and been gone an age.

Her heart thumping, Posie stood again at the window and as she did so she saw the bright, small light from earlier, pulsing through the darkness. The same sequence of flashes.

FLASH. PAUSE. FLASH-FLASH.

Could *that* be Evans outside in the darkness? Signalling?

Thinking about it, Posie realised that often that evening Evans had been missing or otherwise engaged, and sometimes his disappearances had been at the same time as those lights were being set off. Was he somehow communicating with his boss, the imposter? If so, it was ineffectual. For the man still sat calmly over on the sofa.

Posie had thought enough alone now. Time to share.

Feeling angry, and scared, and also a little bit stupid, Posie marched over to Inspector Lovelace and presented him with Jacinta's rough little note.

'Something else,' she muttered under her breath. 'It's awful, so prepare yourself. In fact, it's unbelievable.'

She couldn't bear to watch the Inspector's face, or to witness the poor man as he realised he had lost control of the whole thing, so she continued to stare out of the window as the lights went on and on, unanswered. Posie folded her arms and thought through everything again.

The nub of the situation was this: the imposter had the blueprint. Right now. And the imposter also had a gun. He was, no doubt, a highly dangerous man. And it seemed to Posie fairly certain that the man wanted the blueprint as he was either a spy for some other country, or, perhaps worse, a highly unprincipled mercenary type who would sell the blueprint to whoever would pay the most for it.

The imposter had, likely as not, killed the real MI5 man he was now pretending to be. The snow had helped the man with his horrible work tonight, but, in a way it had protected everyone in the house, too. For, as long as it snowed heavily outside and no-one could get information from the outside world, the house guests at Maypole Manor were none the wiser and everyone was safe. Even the arrival of the clueless and uninformed local policeman and his two buddies earlier had not presented a threat to the imposter; he was content to sit it out and he had even been calm enough to engage in friendly banter with them all.

But who knew what he would do now that the snow had stopped, now that information might find a way of trickling through to Maypole Manor?

Who knew what he might do if he learnt that they, Posie and the Inspector, knew he was a dud?

And then Posie covered her mouth in horror: for in all the plotting and thinking she had been doing she had forgotten that in fact two of the party at Maypole Manor were already dead.

Amory Laine and Lord Glaysayer.

So no-one was really that safe, after all.

Without turning to look at him, Posie clutched at her elbows beneath the big jumper in terror, and wondered if somehow – *but why?* – the imposter had had to kill both the film star and Lord Glaysayer too in his quest for the blueprint.

Stealing a glance over at the Inspector, which wasn't a very good idea, Posie was brought back to earth suddenly when she heard the priest speaking in a dangerously calm, low, authoritative voice to the assembled party. The voice of a doctor breaking bad, bad news:

'I don't want to worry you people. But it seems to me pretty certain now that we've all been poisoned.'

* * * *

Twenty-One

So far, Lenny, Duke Del Angelo and Sergeant Rainbird had all been taken very ill. The priest was pacing about, unable to do anything. Constable Cleghorn went down next, as did his two local reinforcements.

'It *must* have been the coffee,' the priest was saying, his arms crossed tightly over his Fair Isle cardigan, almost at his wits' end. 'We haven't all drunk or eaten anything else in hours.'

Father Moriarty looked in the coffee pot desperately, smelling and sniffing and frantically trying to work out what the poison might have been. Inspector Lovelace, leaving aside the issue of the fake MI5 man for a minute, was at the priest's side, trying to be helpful, horribly aware that the nightmare of the New Year's party was only getting worse.

'What do you think it could be?' he was saying, uselessly.

'I don't know. I can't tell you that. I'm thinking arsenic, or cocaine, like that which was given to Amory Laine. But perhaps a lesser dosage?'

As if on cue, Julian Carter started to vomit and curl up in pain, and the priest dashed to be at his side. Sergeant Binny collapsed on the floor next, rocking backwards and forwards. Then Jacinta started to look queasy, too.

'Dropping like flies,' muttered the Inspector. 'But *why*? What's the point?'

And then, as if in a dream, there was an immense banging at the front door. Everyone who wasn't poisoned sat or stood up, shocked into bright watchfulness. Posie stole a quick look over at the imposter, but he continued to sit on his sofa, calm, the dog now sprawled over his lap, another cigarillo in his hand.

'OPEN UP! OPEN UP! THE LAW REQUESTS YOU TO OPEN UP!'

It was a familiar voice, and not one Posie would ever have imagined herself grateful to hear, but she could have run over and kissed Inspector Oats, for it was he. By some miracle. How had he managed to get here from Deal in all this snow?

Inspector Lovelace was over at the door in seconds, and Posie went with him. Relief was written all over the Inspector's face. He managed to draw back the bolts and open the door, and for a second he crumpled like a wet rag, but then he recovered himself.

'Dash it all, Oats,' he whispered. 'I'm bally pleased to see you. Come in.'

He drew Oats through the door and into a little alcove where a small desk and seat were located, almost but not quite hidden from view of the other party guests by the fire.

'Come here, away from prying eyes. And keep your voice down for goodness' sake!'

Oats looked around the room quickly, his fishy eyes taking everything in. He was somewhat incongruously wearing a flying-suit and carrying what looked like a pair of wooden skis.

But there was someone else behind him.

'Posie! My darling!'

Posie suddenly found herself caught up in a strong pair of arms, lifted clear off the ground. A wild smothered moan died in her hair; lips pressing themselves against her own.

'Thank goodness you're all right! I was more than a bit worried about you there. This is some serious nightmare you've gone and got yourself mixed up in this time, isn't it?'

It was Alaric.

Of course.

* * * *

He was gorgeous: all golden-brown from his trip to South Africa, and he seemed god-like in the way he filled up the doorway with his Belstaff-jacketed bulk. He also looked ridiculous because he was still wearing his flying helmet and goggles. Snow covered him all over like a liberal dusting of icing sugar.

Posie almost burst into tears. The Inspector was wringing his hands as he drew Alaric into the alcove.

'Boynton-Dale, jolly good of you to come here like this.'

Alaric ripped the goggles off at last but kept Posie in his arms. A look of immense worry was stamped all over his sun-tanned face and his famously changeable eyes were the colour of dark gold. He smelt overwhelmingly of petrol. Not of lemon and cardamom and the trade winds, but at least he was *here*. A girl couldn't have everything, after all.

Posie held onto Alaric's bulky jacket sleeve. *Just how on earth had she ever thought to play him false?* She pulled back a bit from him to drink in those lovely eyes.

'But *why* are you here? You're supposed to be in…'

'South Africa? Yes. Well. I was. But if truth be told I felt bad about leaving you in the lurch like that over Christmas. You *said* you didn't mind, but it nagged at me every day. I vowed to myself I'd make it back to England for New Year's Eve and make it up to you…and here I am. A bit late, but better late than never, eh?'

'But how did you know to find us here?'

'You'd left a note at the Grape Street Bureau for Len and Prudence. It mentioned a job with the Inspector. So I called Scotland Yard and they jumped on me like a starving man runs after a crust of bread in a famine: just about begged me to fly down here. It was a government order, actually. They couldn't get here otherwise. Do you really think I'd fly out on a night like tonight if I didn't have to? We had no choice. Came from old Trenchard himself, right at the very top. I couldn't say no to the Head of the Air Force now, could I?'

Inspector Lovelace was murmuring a hushed thank you.

'Not at all,' reassured Alaric in a whisper, his eyes still clouded with worry. 'Reminded me of the good old days. I would have come sooner but I had to wait for the blizzard to blow itself out. Oats here was recalled from his holiday and he managed to make it up to the Croydon Aerodrome before the trains stopped running. We set off as soon as we could, but it took the best part of an hour to get here. Bally fine beast I was flying. Only her second flight out.'

The Inspector frowned. 'It must have been very dangerous. How did you see to land? There's no air-field here.'

'I used the South Foreland lighthouse on the clifftop as my guide. I landed her up there and then we skied down. Your Inspector Oats here wasn't half bad, as it happens. First-time flying; first-time skiing. There's a medal in that somewhere, I'll warrant.'

Inspector Oats had drawn himself up proudly to his full height and had managed to climb out of his flying-suit. He didn't look half as frightening as he did usually, somehow; his standard Scotland Yard uniform of homburg hat and beige trench coat having been replaced instead by off-duty flannel trousers and a Fair Isle tank top.

'Well, well, well,' Oats whispered, his eyes flashing with

excitement. 'What have we here, then, Lovelace? A mare's nest, by all accounts.'

'That's right, Oats. Of the highest order.' Inspector Lovelace recapped the events of the night for the newcomers, while Alaric held onto Posie's hand tightly, finding the green paste ring on her finger there and absently playing with it, over and over, until he seemed to realise what it was and ripped it off, frowning.

'What the infernal blazes…? No, never mind.'

Inspector Lovelace was concluding. 'So we're in a devil of a mess here. And now it seems we've all been poisoned too. Half have gone down already. Although, touch wood, I'm feeling absolutely fine so far. And Posie seems fine, too.'

Inspector Oats gulped nervously, but he was not to be put off his stride by such trivial matters as a poisoning. He fished in his pocket and for a moment Posie thought he might be about to draw out a gun, but then she remembered that Scotland Yard policemen were forbidden from carrying firearms, and Inspector Oats was nothing if not law-abiding.

Instead, he drew out an official-looking paper with red stamps all over the top. He whispered aloud, somewhat pompously, summarising as he went:

'At six o'clock last night, 31st December 1921, a body was found outside the railway sidings at Bromley, just outside of London. It was found by a woman walking her dog. She wasn't sure at first, as the body was covered in snow, but when she managed to uncover it properly she called in the police. By the time the local force had manged to get the thing reported up to Scotland Yard last night, it was gone nine o'clock. By the time Scotland Yard discovered it was an MI5 agent called Bryn Cardinal and that he was supposedly down *here* on a secret assignation, it was gone eleven o'clock and all communication with this house and this whole area was down. That was when I was recalled for duty, and Mr Boynton-Dale was ordered to fly us here as soon as the weather permitted, as there was no other means of transport for getting here. It says here that another M15 agent, Jimmie Maloney, Mr Cardinal's assistant, who was supposed to be here too, is also missing. Presumed dead, but a body has yet to be found. Know anything about him, do you?'

'*Another* agent?' Posie frowned. 'We haven't come across anyone, real or fake, pretending to be a Mr Maloney, have we, Inspector Lovelace?'

Lovelace shook his head. 'What we know of the real Mr Cardinal is that he liked to work alone. Perhaps he left Maloney behind. Like he did yesterday when he travelled down with the money. It seems he might have inadvertently saved the fella's life.'

'*How* had Cardinal been murdered?' Posie found herself asking, almost against her own will. She fancied she was beginning to feel sick now herself.

Oats flashed her a glance which told her exactly what he thought of her time-wasting antics, sighed huffily and checked his statement again.

'Knifed,' he said, almost casually. 'Throat slit, but the man had been drugged, too. Enough chloroform used to drown a dog. Stunk to high heaven apparently.'

Posie blanched but nodded, understanding now the need for the open window in the train corridor. *Poor man.* Posie almost trembled to think that she had been sitting next to such a brutal killer for much of the night.

'Right.' Inspector Oats was chomping at the bit, almost springing into action.

'So you say this chap pretending to be Bryn Cardinal is that large chappie over on the sofa with his back to us, with the dog? He's got this 'ere blueprint? Right. Well, well, well. Let's be 'avin''im.'

Posie almost rolled her eyes at Inspector Oats' dramatic turn of phrase, and wanted to warn him of the danger he might be facing, but she saw he was busy getting out his handcuffs. He also had his baton at the ready. But they were all suddenly galvanised into action by Alaric, who all at once threw caution to the wind and shouted aloud:

'By Gad, that man's got my bally dog! Bikram! Bikram! I say! Come here!'

Alaric suddenly and recklessly marched into the heart of the room, and the Inspectors and Posie were forced to bob along behind.

'I say! Who the very devil are you? That's my dog! Infernal unfaithful creature! But…'

His ranting was cut off midstream.

Alaric stood, silenced, as Bikram at last leapt off the fake Bryn Cardinal's lap and pawed the carpet, moaning softly. But the dog didn't leave the imposter's side.

'It can't be… I don't believe it.'

The fake Bryn Cardinal threw back his head and laughed uproariously, as if Alaric had just said something very funny.

By now everyone who wasn't very sick was staring at the man, mightily confused.

'Would you care to explain, Mr Boynton-Dale?' asked Inspector Lovelace, curtly. 'Do you know this man?'

'I'll say!' roared Alaric. 'And so will you!'

Both Inspectors goggled, first from the imposter to Alaric, and then back again.

'This is Larry 'Nine Lives' Crozio. You know? The famous flying ace? He was even more famous than me and poor old Hugo Catchpole.'

'Larry Crozio?' repeated Inspector Oats stupidly. 'Crozio? The pilot who was shot down in a ball of flame right at the end of the last war, but who was then sometimes seen, on and off, for the next couple of years by members of the public who thought they'd recognised him? Of course, nobody believed them for a minute!'

Posie's mind was whirring. She remembered the stories

in the newspapers which especially filled the silly season in the summer. One year one particular newspaper had even run a competition offering prize monies if Larry could be found.

Larry Crozio smiled cheerily all around. 'Yes, that was all quite amusing. But since then I've been very careful to go undercover. I couldn't risk being found out and brought in.'

'Why not?' whispered Posie. 'You'd done nothing wrong. Had you?'

Crozio turned to her and smiled what seemed a genuine smile of regret. But he stayed silent.

Alaric was pulling over and over at his hair. He laughed bitterly.

'What most people didn't know about Crozio, other than the fact that he was a national hero, of course, was that he had become a liability. The government wanted him brought in. He was, at his "death" suspected of being a double agent, and would fly missions for anyone who'd pay him the most, especially the Germans, who'd lost the Red Baron by then and were in sore need of another flying ace. No-one knew for sure of course if he had managed to parachute out of that burning plane, but most of us on the inside thought it was highly likely that he had faked his own death. We were all well rid of him. Aside from the fact that it was almost certain he was a traitor, Crozio was always causing difficulties; with ground crew, with other pilots, with everybody's wives. You name it: the man was famous as a cad.'

Alaric shot a warning look here at Posie, but Posie was skilled at knowing when to react and when not to, and here she just looked mildly surprised.

'The only decent thing Crozio ever did was to raise this dog, Bikram.'

Posie was flabbergasted: 'Bikram is *his*?'

Alaric nodded unhappily. 'I took him when Crozio didn't return from a sortie one night. He was in the same squadron with me at Biggin Hill. Bikram has been with me ever since.'

'That's all absolutely correct, Posie.' Mr Crozio was nodding suavely. He turned again to Alaric.

'I thought I'd stay and meet the man who decided to fly tonight. I was just on the verge of leaving, as it happens, but I simply *had* to see who it was. For old times' sake. I had a bet with myself it was either you or old Hugo 'One-Eye' Catchpole, but if I'd put money on it, it would have been you. Tell me: what was she? Humour me, Alaric. An Avro, but not one I've ever flown in, I'll wager. A new model? She sounds divine.'

'An Avro Bison,' muttered Alaric reluctantly. 'Only her second flight out. Brand spanking new.'

'Sweet.' Mr Crozio smiled, unhurried. He patted his chest, and a crackle of paper could be heard there.

'And now, if you don't mind, gentlemen, I'll be off. I have some rather important business to attend to. It was lovely to see you again, Alaric. And to *meet* your enchanting lady friend, too. We got on *very* well together.'

Alaric took a sharp intake of breath and put his arm defensively around Posie. Larry Crozio began to walk sharply towards the front door, stepping first over Sergeant Binny on the floor, and then over Jocasta, who was now also groaning in pain. Posie noted that Jocasta's anguished gaze never left Mr Crozio, although he had walked right past her without a second glance. And then Posie saw it, but too late.

Larry.

Larry Crozio was the 'Larry' of the letter from Lord Glaysayer; the man behind the drugs ring and the smuggling. A man who probably knew this place better than the back of his hand. Jocasta was in love with him; was crazily, madly in love with him.

Which explained the looks of pure hatred which had been directed at Posie for most of the party, as Larry Crozio had made it increasingly obvious over the course of the night that he liked her, and had been paying almost no attention to Jocasta.

'STOP!' shouted Inspector Oats, darting over with his baton and handcuffs. 'You're under arrest, you blighter! Of course you can't just leave!' Lovelace was there in a jiffy, too, scrabbling around for his gun. He found it and pointed it at Larry Crozio who put his hands up.

Posie continued to look at Jocasta; at this silly, stupid girl who had got herself into such murky waters that she could never possibly understand them. She realised how Jocasta had more than likely helped Larry Crozio with tonight's plan: how she had perhaps been responsible for drafting Larry in in the first place as things had changed and Inspector Lovelace had replaced Scabbes at the last minute, opening up possibilities.

But there had been errors too.

Jocasta had not been at Maypole Manor the day before the party when the *real* Bryn Cardinal had unexpectedly shown up to deliver the money, so she didn't realise anyone would spot there was a difference the following day. But Jacinta had been there earlier, and she had realised, albeit too late. And Lord Glaysayer had met *two* different Bryn Cardinals, and he must have realised too.

So what had Lord Glaysayer been playing at?

And then into Posie's mind came a sudden remembrance. She remembered Robin Glaysayer bobbing around in the Inspector's room, nervous as anything. She remembered how she had felt there was something vitally important he was about to tell them. He had even mentioned that 'your man' had dropped off money the previous day, as if testing if the Inspector had harboured any doubts as to Mr Cardinal's true identity.

So why on earth hadn't he said something? What had been his game?

Posie bit her lip, but she was suddenly conscious of Edwin Goodman, who seemed to have escaped the poisoning, standing, and dragging the heavy bag with him.

He made as if to loop back through the hall, towards the Library.

'Sir, can you stay where you are. Are you all right?' shouted Inspector Lovelace, keeping his gun trained on Crozio. 'Are you ill, too, Mr Goodman?'

Inspector Oats looked over briefly. He was attempting to restrain Larry Crozio, who was laughing and looking as if he were enjoying himself, despite the gun held at his head.

But then Inspector Oats' shrieked in a sort of horrified triumph.

'That's not a Mr Goodman!' he bellowed. 'Lovelace, you fool! That's Bertie Bunce, the music hall star who murdered his wife a few years ago and ran away from the crime scene! He's changed the way he looks but not that much; same old slippery rogue as before, I'll warrant. I was on the case back in my Whitechapel days. He's famous in the East End of London! Never been seen since. By Gad! We're cleaning up here!'

Posie gasped in horror, her body shaking uncontrollably beneath Alaric's strong grip. She could see Inspector Lovelace's pale white face had turned even ashier, his mouth set in a grim line, and his large hands were shaking uncontrollably as he held onto his Webley. Poor, poor Inspector Lovelace... But she had been fooled, too. She cursed herself for her stupidity.

Posie was astounded at the staggeringly clever nature of the thing. For not only was Bryn Cardinal a fake, but so too was the American. *Had he ever even existed?* So now this motley bunch of criminals had both the precious blueprint *and* the money.

They had worked together as a double act; a *triple* act, if you counted Jocasta in, too. It simply couldn't get any worse.

But just then Larry Crozio seemed to change. He stopped laughing, and a quiet, deadly calm seemed to descend on him. He ripped open his shirt and calmly withdrew his Luger, turning it on the two Police Inspectors.

'Drop it or I'll shoot you!' shouted Inspector Lovelace angrily, waving his Webley. 'I promise you! It's not an empty threat!'

'I'd like to see you try, my man. For at least an hour now your gun's cartridge has been empty of bullets. Bunce removed the gun from your back pocket and took out the bullets in all the fuss when Miss Glaysayer was having her funny turn earlier. You should take more care in future. *If* there is a future for you, that is.'

The very room seemed to hold its breath. Alaric tightened his grip on Posie's arm, but Larry Crozio suddenly marched over, gun at the ready, to where they were both standing and took Posie by the hand, not roughly exactly but certainly not as gently as before.

'Sorry, old girl. I don't like to make you a hostage, but needs must, I'm afraid…'

'I say!' shouted Alaric, helpless.

He aimed the gun at Alaric, and then at the Inspectors.

'Come here, both of you. And give me those,' he said in a low voice to Inspector Oats, indicating the handcuffs. 'Or else I'll shoot the girl.'

The handcuffs were duly passed over.

'And yours, too, Lovelace.'

Larry Crozio then stepped over to Constable Cleghorn, who was still curled up on the floor, sick, and neatly stripped him of his own pair of handcuffs.

'Now then, you three. You all sit in a circle with your backs to each other. No funny business, mind, or I'll shoot Posie first up, followed by all three of you.'

Within seconds Alaric and the Inspectors were handcuffed together, incapable of moving at all. Out of a pocket in his jacket Mr Crozio grabbed a white silk flying scarf and, ripping it into three, gagged the men. Posie's heart juddered and she felt the acid rise in her tight throat as Crozio kept his gun trained on them. Crozio then called out to Bertie Bunce.

'Fine, Buncey-boy. Get out of here now. You know the way. Evans is down where he always is. Take what you can and get the blazes out of here.'

'What about me?' wailed Jocasta suddenly. 'Aren't you taking me with you? After all I've done?'

Larry Crozio was looking all around the room, mainly at the people who still weren't ill, which was only the priest and Mr Steinhauser, as if he was wondering if he could leave them alive without their causing him any trouble. He focused eventually on Jocasta, who looked terrible.

'I'm sorry, poppet. I'm not taking you anywhere. It's been a blast, all this, but, you know, all good things come to an end. Don't they?'

He seemed about to leave, and so Posie risked it. She spoke up:

'Jocasta. You're better than this man; you deserve better. He killed your father, didn't he? I saw your face in that study tonight and I saw that you were scared. You *knew* it was Larry who had killed your father, and you were upset about it, weren't you? You shouted out that he was a first-class idiot; making it look like a suicide with all those clumsy, badly-arranged "clues". You hoped to hurt him with your words but I fear that this man is beyond hurt. He simply doesn't care. But Jocasta, help me; why did your father have to die tonight? I don't understand. Because he had twigged that both parties to the transaction were fakes?'

Jocasta remained silent, her face quite shut-up with hatred for Posie.

In the end it was Crozio who spoke. He sighed wearily.

'If you *must* know, Jocasta hasn't a clue. She can't help you. But I can, of course. Old Glaysayer must have realised pretty quickly we weren't the real deal, though he was chummy as anything and played along very nicely. He even caught me cutting the telephone wires in his study after the early reception and he said nothing; just walked out of there as if *he* had been disturbing me. I didn't know what he was about; whether he was going to tell the Inspector or not…'

'So what happened?'

'He must have been wrestling with his conscience for a bit. But, when it came down to it, old Glaysayer was just a very bad, very greedy man. Just like us. He called us early to the rendezvous, at quarter-to midnight, and said that he knew we were fakes, but that Lovelace didn't. He wouldn't tell, but could we cut a deal?'

'What did he want?'

'He didn't want the blueprint, that's for sure. He was a man in dire need of cash, and he had plenty of it, albeit not his own, sitting in his safe. He wanted half. I said it was too much. He said he would blow our cover. That was it. The end. Game over.'

Posie swallowed. She saw Father Moriarty standing, swaying, sick now too. She turned back to Crozio, tried to focus.

'So then you "staged" it to look like suicide, but you did it badly. And to add even more confusion to the scene, one of you sprinkled Jacinta's perfume about the place, crushing the vial, just to suggest her involvement if the whole suicide story wasn't believed. Clumsy, or desperate, I'd say.'

Crozio nodded, his patience wearing thin. 'That was Bunce's idea. He had taken the vial earlier in the evening, as well as a lot of other people's things. Man's a pickpocket; one of the best: he's had to be, living off his wits for several years before he met me. Handy, though; especially when it comes to stealing bullets from inconveniently-loaded guns.'

Inspector Lovelace made a squealing noise from behind his gag on the floor. And then Julian Carter staggered up from the floor. He seemed a bit better.

'You devil!' he managed. 'Did you kill my wife, too, you monster? Or was it that simpering old nag of a music hall star, who I recognise *now*, of course. Although he's wearing an orange tan and he's tried to fix his teeth, to no avail, might I add. Bertie Bunce of the many accents! He always was third-rate! He used to carry a candle in the old days for Amory when she was still Brenda Brown in Whitechapel. I suppose she didn't recognise him tonight and he was mad about it and thought he'd kill her, just like he killed his wife years ago. Was that it?'

Posie looked at Mr Crozio and saw a frightening lack of remorse in his eyes. She remembered snippets of her conversation with Amory over the evening, before she died.

'No.' Posie shook her head certainly. 'It was *you*, Mr Crozio. Wasn't it? I thought at first that she had been killed because she said she had seen someone coming out of my room; but how wrong I was! You killed her because of something far simpler: you heard her tell me that she felt like she was hallucinating; that she thought she had seen someone from her music hall days…And you wondered how long it would be before she realised that she was right and it was, in fact, Bertie Bunce, although much changed by his years on the run, just *playing* at being the American, Edwin Goodman.'

Posie shook her head in frustration.

'Bunce was good at the accent, but he wasn't that good: he kept slipping up. I can't believe I didn't see it sooner, myself: so much was wrong about his being an "American." His knowledge of British movie stars and music was simply too good, for a start. And then he slipped up big-time when he was talking about sailing to America and feeling sea-sick, when he was supposed to be a good sailor.'

Mr Crozio was looking exasperated, but amused, too.

'I'm right, aren't I, sir? You did kill Amory Laine. It was easy as anything to slip cocaine into the water you gave her out on the terrace. You always carry a large stash with you, don't you, sir?'

Mr Crozio stared at Posie for a second and then nodded. He turned his gun which had been trained on the policemen on her at last.

'I knew you were a smart cookie, darling. You got it in one there. I hate to do this to you darling, but you leave me no choice.'

He clicked the slide forward on his gun. There was a horrible silence in the room, but every eye was on Crozio and his gun. Posie was trembling violently, and she didn't dare look down at Alaric, but suddenly Crozio was distracted by Father Moriarty hauling himself to his feet weakly, over by the fireplace.

'I say,' he mumbled in a hollow voice. 'I think I've worked out what we all have. The fact that we are all still alive and some are already feeling better just confirms my thoughts. I'd say that we have all been poisoned by boracic acid.'

'What the devil is that?' whimpered Julian Carter, still holding his stomach. 'And will we be okay?'

'You'll all be fine. In a day or two, or three. It causes sickness and stomach aches when used in low doses. Which is what has happened here. But you won't be able to do much in the meantime. Certainly no sprinting off over cliffs and running away, Mr Crozio.'

'What do you mean?' the man shouted. He tugged at Posie's arm, marching her over to the front door, gun still aimed at her head. 'I'm perfectly fine.'

'You don't look it, sir. You've gone quite blue in the face, which is one of the signs.'

Sure enough, Mr Crozio was suddenly bent double, although somehow he was still able to keep his gun trained on Posie.

'There's something else,' the priest continued to speak to anyone who fancied listening. 'Boracic acid is often used as eye drops. And there's just one person here who I've noticed using eye drops quite liberally all night long.'

And just as Posie turned to stare at where Mr

Steinhauser had been, she saw Mr Crozio drop to the floor, violently sick. He had dropped his gun and started to lurch all over the place.

But before Posie could reach down and grab the Luger, she felt a forceful arm grab her from behind, and then a cloth with a very strong smell on it was being pressed to her face.

And then Maypole Manor and everyone in it disappeared, and the world went black.

* * * *

PART FIVE

A Means of Escape

Twenty-Two

When she came to, Posie heard the sound of huge waves crashing on the shore.

She opened her eyes blearily. She saw only darkness. Her head ached badly, promising a migraine, and for a second she remembered the strange party up at Maypole Manor and the poisoning of everyone. *Had she dreamt it? Was she dreaming now?* Or was she in some terrible nightmare which had no end?

Her hands were bound tightly but her legs were not and she was positioned in a sitting up position, next to some damp sandbags and what smelt like seaweed. A small light flashed through the darkness into her eyes and Posie winced. It was a pocket torch.

At her side was movement. The light came on again and Posie saw Mr Steinhauser's face lit up ghoulishly from below by his torch. He didn't wear his hat anymore, but his fancy Rolex watch glimmered in the artificial light. Posie wondered with a sharp pang how Inspector Lovelace was doing; *if* indeed he was still alive.

She found her voice and when she spoke it sounded as if she were a hundred years old; hoarse and raspy. She was very scared, but tried not to show it.

'What's this all about, Mr Steinhauser? Have you gone

quite mad? I thought it was Jocasta who you were after. Not me. What do you want with me?'

The man laughed, but it was touched with a slight sadness.

'That was all a most convenient front, my dear. I never actually said my motive in being at the New Year's party was purely for Jocasta. That was secondary. A horrid little thing, isn't she? What a disappointment. I'm glad I've met her the once but I certainly won't want to be pursuing that relationship, thank you very much. Why, she basically sold old Glaysayer down the river! Poor devil! A lifetime of trouble is what I'd get if I promise that girl a home and help now. They say the apple never falls very far from the tree, though. Don't they?'

'You mean because Lord Glaysayer was a bad man, that meant his daughter had to be, too? I think that only applies to blood relationships, sir.'

'I'm talking about a blood relationship. Mine, and hers. Just because Robin Glaysayer did me wrong out in Africa thirty years ago doesn't mean that I'm a good man myself, does it?'

'I don't think I follow you, sir.'

'Think of me like a mercenary, Miss Parker. I would have worked for anyone who paid me the most; like our friend Mr Crozio did in the war. And since I had to renounce my identity all those years ago, I needed work, and work which came from people who didn't ask too many questions. Some would say I chose to work for unscrupulous people. People who paid me a great deal.'

He shook his watch in Posie's face. A knot of fear was twisting itself ever tighter in her stomach as he went on, but she tried not to show it. She remembered Inspector Lovelace telling her the evening couldn't get any worse, and she felt like laughing hysterically. It just had.

'Hang on a minute. You're seriously telling me that you have been paid, somehow, to attend Robin Glaysayer's New

Year's Eve party? That you weren't just there for Jocasta?'

Steinhauser shook his head. 'No. It was nice, and a good coincidence, but I was there to work.'

Posie's voice was barely audible to her own ears, but she pushed on hopefully.

'Were you involved in the smuggling, too, sir? Or were you after the blueprint?'

'Good grief, no! That's not what my master requires at all. That's all a fairly low-key, petty business for him. He wouldn't deign to get involved.'

Again the knot of fear tightened.

'*You* were my work, Miss Parker. My master has been listening in on your conversations and your telephone calls at Grape Street for months now.'

Posie gasped. So *her* telephone line had been compromised too. She remembered the taps and hissings on the line when she had spoken to Sergeant Rainbird, arranging the details for the visit to Maypole Manor. She shuddered. But was she really so surprised?

'When this 'opportunity' arose at the last minute, it seemed too good for my master to miss. I was called for: by remarkable coincidence I had a link to the host, and to his daughter, so I was deemed the best person to carry this out. My master has many such men as me, you see: men who do his business.'

Posie's heart was pounding, her hands shaking. Blood was rushing in her ears, just as loud as the waves outside. She tried not to let her fears reach their logical, terrifying conclusion. Steinhauser continued:

'And it was simplest. There was no need for any elaborate lies or disguise. Robin Glaysayer and I already had a back history together, albeit a bad one. Besides, Glaysayer never was a man who could refuse a great sum of cash, and my master had arranged a fantastically large payment for the 'favour' of letting me attend his New Year's Eve party at the last minute in the guise of an old friend.'

'Tell me. What is your master's business?'

'Oh, Miss Parker. For one of such intellect, surely you know *that*? I gave you the clues earlier; I said that I had been in mining for many years. Just because I was forced out of my own diamond mine doesn't mean I bowed out of the whole business, does it? I think I mentioned a third partner, a chap called Stefan. When he died his assets and shares in his mines went to his son, who was still a child. I started to act for the child, to manage his affairs until he was old enough. And I still get involved from time to time. Like now. He tasked me with following *you*. And so I followed you around in London yesterday, to make sure you actually came down here and to see what you looked like, although I didn't much like snooping about on you, I'll confess: it felt dirty, somehow. And I raided your room here yesterday, for which I hope you will forgive me. I made a mess. I'm sorry, I didn't have much time. I was tasked with finding one piece of evidence that proved beyond a doubt that you were really *you*, but you had gone to a great deal of trouble not to bring anything. So I was grasping at straws with that photograph, I'll admit it.'

'Why did you need it?'

'My master wanted to make sure I had the right girl. He likes *proof* of things first. He didn't want to be seen snooping about in that ghastly house with all those tunnels; he couldn't spy on you himself what with all those policemen everywhere. So he met me just once, agreed that it was you who were in the photograph, and then he left again, taking all my belongings with him to make it easier for me to get away later. You must understand that it was a *hugely* risky undertaking for him to come to England in the first place for this rendezvous. My master cannot move quite as freely as he would like to, so everything needs to be planned out very carefully. But you were a prize worth the effort, it seems.'

Steinhauser checked his wristwatch. 'He told me to

bring you here. Now. Thank goodness the others are all now indisposed with the coffee I managed to drug and I got you away on time.'

Posie remembered with a sickening feeling the story which Amory Laine had told of a tall man disappearing into a hidden doorway and meeting a very small man there. So it hadn't been the Duke at all. It had been Steinhauser, and his 'master.'

'What was his name, this third partner?' Posie's voice was almost a soundless whisper and her throat and lips felt very dry.

'What did you say he was called?'

But she knew the answer before it came and the words had already died on her lips. Fear gripped her like an all-consuming paralysis.

'I didn't say, Miss Parker. But you know it. The man out in Africa was an aristocrat, too. A Swiss aristocrat of the very highest pedigree. His name was Count Stefan della Rosa. His little son, who is now one of the most powerful men in all of the world, is already known to you, I think. His name is Caspian.'

'And he wants *me*, sir?'

'Yes. Still.'

Posie felt like screaming: Caspian della Rosa was probably the wealthiest, cleverest, most calculating criminal the world had yet known, not to mention the most unscrupulous. Back in February he had declared at gunpoint that he would take Posie with him on all of his future crazy illegal adventures, expressing a desire for her to share his bed as well as his life's work. She had managed to escape from him in the nick of time but he had made it clear to Posie that he would seek her out and come back for her one of these days.

It looked like that day had come.

Mr Steinhauser swung his torch about a bit, and squinting, Posie saw that they were sitting in a cave, very far back, and that she was almost at the bottom of some wide, roughly-hewn steps cut into the soft chalky cliff-face. There was a closed wooden door at the top of the steps with new-looking bolts across it.

The cave was fairly big, and the floor was hard, but covered with little pebbles and stones. They were obviously well above the sea level, protected from the swell of the tide and the crashing waves.

'We haven't come far, have we, sir?'

'Sorry?'

'We're still at St Margaret's Bay in Kent. Aren't we?'

'Spot on.'

Posie saw that where the cave ended, at the front, a crack of a slightly lightening sky was just visible. She realised that there must be steps cut down at the front of the cave, too, leading to the cove she had glimpsed the day before with the Inspector.

That seemed so long ago now. An impossibly long time ago.

As her eyes adjusted to the torchlight, she saw that there were things scattered all around them on the floor: a few cigarette packets and loose cigarettes; an American movie magazine; a French newspaper. There was a leather satchel containing what looked like a set of folded evening clothes. There was an odd black shoe, smart and shiny in the dim light. There was a thin blanket and a waterproof sheet, and there was a compass.

There were the remnants of a simple meal; bread and cheese and a slab of butter. And there was a hand.

A hand…

Posie screamed in the darkness and she felt Mr Steinhauser startle next to her.

'A hand! A dead body! Oh my days! Did you? Did you…'

He grabbed hold of her. She could feel herself whimpering on and on as Mr Steinhauser tried desperately to silence her.

'For goodness' sake, be quiet! Of course I didn't kill the man: I'm many things but I'm not a murderer, I can promise you that. We need to wait for our lift and I don't want to draw unnecessary attention to ourselves from the wrong quarter. I know it's horrible and that it's not at all ideal. I wouldn't be choosing to share a space with a recently-dead corpse, would I? But that's what we've got to do. I almost tripped over him actually as I dragged you down here. Gave me quite a turn…'

He let Posie go again.

'Who is it? Is it… Is it?'

'Yes. I think it's your American, Edwin Goodman. The *real* American. Poor beggar. He's had his throat cut. A dangerous lot, up there. I was glad to get out, I don't mind telling you. I could feel something wasn't right the whole night long: made me nervous as anything.'

In the distance there sounded the roar of a boat's engine. Posie and Mr Steinhauser sat in a horrible brooding silence, Posie thinking constantly about the corpse at their feet.

A few minutes later a very powerful light came from the steps at the front of the cave, and footsteps could be heard ascending. The light shone inside the cave, and Posie squinted at the very small figure she could just make out silhouetted behind the bright torchlight.

'Aha!' She recognised a familiar, slightly raspy, low voice. The accent barely there.

It was Count Caspian della Rosa, and he sounded gleeful, almost like a small child.

'Miss Parker! We meet again. As I told you we would. You belong to me. Don't forget, will you?'

Posie couldn't see his face at all but she knew that the man would be wearing his cool, calm smile. And she knew too that his benign, kindly exterior concealed a ruthlessness like no other.

'Tonight has cost me dearly, my darling, but you were worth it. It's time to go. By my calculations we have approximately four minutes more to take advantage of this tide and my boat is parked just below. Now, if you could come this way, my man Steinhauser will assist you down the steps. They're very steep. And don't try and run, my love. This time there's no escape.'

Posie knew there was no point resisting. She had seen the Count kill men in cold blood before, and she knew he wouldn't have changed. So she got to her feet painfully and walked towards Caspian della Rosa. She stood at least a head and shoulders taller than him, and she saw that, master of disguise that he was, he seemed to be dressed in casually expensive sailing clothes. She also saw that, for the second time that evening, she had a gun trained directly upon her.

'Where are we going?' she asked, faux-innocently, stalling for time. Her mind clicked through many gears; desperately seeking a way out. For to go with this man now was to spend the rest of her life with him.

'My darling,' he said, taking her arm calmly but very tightly as if for all the world like they were just a normal couple, 'we will go to France first of all. It's closest and I'm not a wanted man there. You know I have places everywhere. You can choose where we live, but later. Just now I need to get us to a place of safety. And that is not here. I am not supposed to be in England, you know, so I'm afraid you'll have to say goodbye to these shores, too.'

Posie gulped and followed the small, stocky man down the rocky steps. Caspian della Rosa shone his torch ahead of him and half-pulled her after him. She was aware of Mr Steinhauser behind her, ostensibly making sure she didn't fall, but really making sure she didn't try and jump into the water or try anything stupid like trying to get away.

It was still very dark outside, although streaks of light were starting to ripple through the dark winter sky, and as Posie's eyes adjusted to the darkness she saw that masses of dark boats were bobbing around. One boat, a small yacht, had a few lights on and was waiting for them, its engine still running. She exhaled sadly.

The game was over.

But just then there was a shout and a huge commotion erupted behind them. What sounded like a door banged shut somewhere, and a dog was barking madly. It sounded like Bikram.

Could it be?

Suddenly a gunshot snapped out through the darkness.

Posie saw Mr Steinhauser turning around behind her, and falling uselessly, tumbling over the rocky cliff edge into the dark, dark sea below.

Then there was another gunshot.

Caspian della Rosa, ever cool under fire, had stopped in his tracks, still as a cat, hidden on one of the precarious stone steps below Posie. He was looking carefully all around him. He let go of Posie's arm and grabbed her instead by her pearl necklace, forcing her uncomfortably close to him.

'Now,' he hissed. 'Now! Follow me. This is my boat here.' He tugged at the necklace insistently.

But Posie twisted her head to look back, and in that instant she saw the large figure of Larry Crozio emerge from the cave, his gun outstretched.

'Bunce!' he was shouting. 'Evans! Where the blazes are you? We've got intruders here! Cover yourselves! Did you get much of the snow out?'

From somewhere far down in the cove a tinny voice replied:

'Here, sir. Yes, we took what we could carry, sir. But we had to leave a lot behnd. We've nearly finished loading up tonight's deliveries. With you in a second, sir.'

'Forget that, you fool! I need you now! Which boat are you on? Flash your torch so I can see you.'

Caught between two very bad men, Posie was on the verge of jumping over the rocky cliff edge into the foaming sea below when out of nowhere a flying, snarling shadow emerged at break-neck speed out of the darkness, bounding past her and hurling itself at Caspian della Rosa on the step below her.

In his panic to retain his balance the Count pulled hard at Posie's necklace, and the string broke, pearls scattering everywhere in the dim light, rolling down the jagged steps, plopping over the edge and down into the black waters.

Bikram was barking madly, and biting furiously at Caspian della Rosa who tried to remain balanced on his precarious foot-hold, and in all the chaos the Count pulled the trigger of his gun.

Posie threw herself on the ground as best she could. The Count's shot echoed in the night air.

'Who is that?'

Larry Crozio lurched forwards, and sensing rather than seeing an intruder, he started to fire his gun too, to which the Count retaliated.

Among the gunshots and reverberating bullets and amid all the barking Posie saw her chance and she took it. She kicked off her shoes and crawled around Crozio on the rocky outcrop and back into that frightful cave. She stood up and just about made out the wooden door at the back of the cave, hanging open, an electric light shining within. She knew it must lead back up to Maypole Manor.

Posie hated tunnels, but she would take her chances on this one.

Just as she was through the door, she heard the sound of a man's scream and the distinct sound of a body falling into the water. But just *who* had succeeded in shooting who was a mystery.

And she didn't hang around to find out any more.

* * * *

Twenty-Three

As she was puffing her way up through the last section of the claustrophobic tunnel Posie suddenly sensed Bikram next to her. Panting, he padded along beside her, very close.

Posie put out her hand to pat his head. 'Never let me or Alaric call you unfaithful ever again,' she muttered. 'I can't believe I owe my life to a dog!'

She came out somewhere deep in the very heart of Maypole Manor, in the cellars near the servant's quarters, and it took her several minutes to orientate herself.

But when she came out into the big entrance hall, she was surprised to find the room deserted. All the windows and doors were wide open, and the strong sea breeze was blowing through the house. The entrance hall still smelt terrible, however, and she tried not to look too closely at the detritus of Steinhauser's handiwork.

Bemused, Posie wondered where everyone could have gone to. And then she heard a low muttering sound coming from along the corridor, from the direction of the Library. She walked soundlessly up the corridor in her stockinged feet and peered in.

Alaric was sitting on the edge of a sofa, smoking nervily, running his fingers through his hair ceaselessly. The two Inspectors were sat dejectedly on another sofa, while over on the platform with the piano, Jocasta Glaysayer was sitting in handcuffs, fast asleep, with Rainbird and Binny firmly stationed on either side of her.

The clock was just chiming six o'clock. Posie hadn't realised she had been gone that long. She stepped into the room.

Alaric looked up at her, his tanned face as white as a ghost.

'Posie! Oh thank the Lord!'

'Anyone fancy bacon and eggs?' she asked blithely. 'I'm starving. And I promise I won't make anyone coffee this time round.'

* * * *

After Posie had described Caspian della Rosa's involvement in the night's activities, she was met by a stunned silence, then a barrage of cursing from Inspector Lovelace. And then, after she had recounted in detail what had happened out on the steps to the cove, all from the safety of Alaric's arms, she was told what had been happening up at Maypole Manor.

Just after Mr Steinhauser had left, followed shortly by Crozio, Sergeant Binny had roused himself and managed to unpick the locks of the handcuffs which had bound Lovelace, Oats and Alaric together.

Desperate, and realising how futile it probably was, Alaric and Lovelace had located the tunnels leading down to the beach, but had not been able to enter them, as they had been locked by Crozio from the inside as he had departed. Oats had remained behind, guarding Jocasta and the sick house guests.

They had then regrouped, and, after some consideration

Inspector Lovelace had sent everyone who was sick back to their own beds, save for Jocasta.

Inspector Lovelace sat with his head in his hands, a broken man.

'I can't believe it,' he muttered. 'This is very far from my finest hour. I've been swindled by a bunch of crooks! I'm so very, very sorry Posie, that I put you in this much danger. I simply had no idea. And you *thought* there might be a connection with Caspian della Rosa at the very start and I just pooh-poohed it all out of hand! Told you to get real! I'm so sorry. Can you forgive me? I've been blind throughout this case. If it's any consolation, Scotland Yard will be receiving my resignation letter first thing tomorrow morning. I've messed up bigtime on this. I wouldn't be surprised if I'm the subject of a prosecution now.'

Inspector Oats harrumphed in what sounded like triumph, but could have been regret, while Posie shrieked her indignation.

'But *why*, Inspector? They pulled the wool over all our eyes, including me. Don't feel bad. It's not just your fault.'

'Try telling that to Assistant Commissioner Scabbes,' Inspector Oats muttered darkly.

'Oats is right,' nodded Lovelace dejectedly. 'I'll be hung out to dry for this: not only was I hoodwinked, but now the plans *and* the money have disappeared yet again. We're back to exactly the same position we were in a few months ago. And who know who will get hold of the blueprint for 'the Guillotine' now?'

'It seems to me that the plans for that plane would be better off lost, or even better, destroyed,' said Posie decisively.

'And there's a good chance that that may indeed have happened tonight, you know. When I heard a gunshot and a body falling into the water as I left, it was fifty percent likely to have been Crozio, wasn't it? In which case the plans will be washing around in the surf at the bottom of the cove right now, or else lost forever at the bottom of the ocean.'

'You don't know Crozio!' muttered Alaric. 'There was a reason he had the nickname 'Nine Lives', you know. Although I think he must be on about his twelfth life by now. Most of the poor blighters who drank that coffee will be sick for days, but oh no, not Crozio! It only seemed to affect him for a couple of minutes, then he got up, right as rain and ran off. We couldn't believe it.'

'Well, *you* don't know Count della Rosa,' retorted Posie, almost with a warped sense of loyalty to her kidnapper.

'I'd say he's not the sort of chap to get himself killed on a staircase at St Margaret's Bay! And *one* of them definitely went in the water!'

'I suppose we'll find out in due course,' said Inspector Oats in a resigned fashion. 'Besides, Lovelace, don't feel too bad about things. I'll attest to Scabbes that you did all you could here in limited circumstances, and that you've managed to bring in a major drugs ring, too. They were even operating tonight, on New Year's Eve, if Miss Parker is to be believed! It's outrageous! They can't get rid of both of us, can they?'

'Thanks, Jimmie,' murmured Inspector Lovelace dejectedly.

'For what it's worth, I appreciate it.'

* * * *

Two hours passed slowly, a low fire burning in the grate, a horrible sense of defeat and tiredness hanging over the occupants of the Library.

At just after eight o'clock and as it grew light outside an unfamiliar voice was heard shouting out repeatedly from the entrance hall.

'I say! Sir? Sir? Are you here, sir?'

Alaric and Posie and the Inspectors went along together to see who it was, hopeful that it might be the police from Dover or even someone with a working vehicle which had somehow got through the snow.

But instead they came across a bespectacled, pin-striped-suited young man with greasy skin and a worried expression. He was carrying a smart briefcase and wore an inadequate trench coat. He was virtually blue in the face and shivering profusely. He looked very nervous.

'And who are you?' blurted out Inspector Oats rudely.

'My name is Maloney, sir. Is my boss here, sir?' The young man was craning his neck, looking all around in vain.

'A Mr Bryn Cardinal? He snuck off without me on New Year's Eve, but I knew he needed me to bring him back to London. He doesn't drive, you see, although he manages to keep that fact hidden well under wraps, as I think he's ashamed of it. So I came along in my car, of course, to pick him up, just like I always do; like he *expects* me to. He's a rum one to work for, I can tell you! But I've been stuck in a snow drift along the lane here all night long. I only just got out now, dug myself out with my briefcase here. We've got some top-secret information to take back with us to London, apparently. He'll have my guts for garters for being so late. So where is he then? And why are you all staring at me like that, anyhow? Like you've all just seen a ghost?'

But before anyone could answer him, the mercifully loud tones of the telephone could be heard ringing out through the house, and then there was a commotion outside as local policemen started to swarm through the snow-packed grounds, some medical men in attendance, bearing stretchers.

'Better late than never, I suppose,' said Inspector Oats, scowling.

And for once Posie found herself agreeing with him wholeheartedly.

****

Four Months Later

Epilogue

The weather had become much warmer, and the seemingly endless April showers had given way at last to bright blue skies devoid of any clouds. The scent of cherry blossom wafted through the air.

Posie Parker stood on the roof terrace of Museum Chambers and breathed in a good lungful. She closed her eyes.

'Mnnn. The smell of London in Maytime... That definitely beats the smell of the sea any day. Smugglers or no smugglers.'

'Really?'

Alaric was wielding a small pickaxe, bare-chested, sweating profusely, but he looked over at her now in disbelief. It was safe to say that he was not in the best of moods.

'All *I* can smell is frying onions from that chap outside the British Museum, with his bally little cart illegally selling bacon rolls to weekend tourists. More fool *them*, is what I say. Guaranteed stomach aches.'

Posie sighed and stared out. The roof terrace was very high, at least ten storeys up. From here you could be forgiven for thinking you were on top of the world. The view over Bloomsbury and beyond was spectacular: the great grey beached whale of the British Museum of course, the flags flying proudly from the Department Stores on Oxford Street and the Tottenham Court Road, the strange and ancient steeple of St George's Church with its fighting lion and unicorn, forever at odds.

Posie turned to Alaric, who was now heaping bits of chopped wood together in a big pile.

'You're just put out about the hives. Don't be such a sourpuss. Be nice, darling. It's not *my* fault that all but one of them failed. Maybe there just aren't enough flowers for them to feed on around here, or maybe the winter was just too tough this year? It took ages to get warm, after all.'

Alaric just winced and Posie left it; she was obviously probing a raw nerve. Alaric continued to pile up his broken beehives silently. One beehive had survived the winter and bees were now swarming out of it all over the place. Posie batted one away from her face as she tried to think of how to make the best of the situation.

Just then Ted, the Chief Porter, came charging out of the little box-like structure which covered the very top of the stairs onto the roof terrace.

'Ah, Miss Parker! Thought I'd find you up here. And good morning, my Lord.' Ted doffed his bowler hat respectfully in Alaric's direction, even though Alaric wasn't technically a Lord anymore, and then he did a double-take at the sight which met his eyes. The Porter pulled his gaze away with a visible effort. He proffered a silver salver.

'Telegrams for you. Brought them up here straightaway, Miss.'

Posie fished in her pocket for the tip which was expected of her and took the two cards from Ted without further comment. Turning at the staircase, Ted obviously felt he couldn't hold his tongue any longer and he looped back on himself.

'I say, Miss,' he muttered in an undertone, hitting out impatiently at a bee which was buzzing around his head, 'need that wood, do you, Miss? Only it would be the best sort of firewood imaginable. It would burn a treat in my hearth in Bethnal Green. Seems a pity to just chuck it out…'

Posie nodded. 'I'll see to it that you get it. But I'd come and collect it later this afternoon, if I were you. And don't let Mr Boynton-Dale hear you talking about *burning* the hives, it would bring back very painful memories. He isn't in the best of moods right now. Understandably, perhaps.'

Ted flashed Posie a look laden with meaning: he had never understood the logic behind trying to cultivate hives of city bees up on his nicely-kept roof. He had never thought it would work, it was *unnatural* somehow, and now the proof was in the pudding.

'And I'd get his Lordship to put his shirt and vest back on, if I were you, Miss,' the Porter said as a parting shot to Posie, still in an undertone. 'It's only just May, and there's a cruel nip in the air. We're not on Margate beach here, you know.'

'Mercifully,' muttered Posie, under her breath, ripping open the first of the telegrams.

The telegram was quite long and contained the news that Inspector Lovelace's wife Molly had had a little baby girl, Phyllis. All were doing well, and would Posie like to come and visit them at home in Clapham sometime soon? And would she consider being Godmother?

Posie smiled, genuinely touched. She had never been Godmother to anyone before, and she had always thought she would make a fairly good one: prime opportunities for present-buying and general treats and spoiling loomed ahead.

She read on.

Oh, and by the way, the Inspector was now a *Chief* Inspector, and this was due to the discovery of the vast smuggling network down at St Margaret's Bay. The achievement had been recognised by those at the very top at New Scotland Yard, and Chief Inspector Lovelace had written that he owed this latest development in his professional life in part to Posie.

She smiled and ripped open the second telegram.

'Oh! Goodness!'

She read it quickly. Dolly, Lady Cardigeon, Posie's friend and general confidante, had given birth early. A month early. And to twins! All was well, although the babies were tiny.

'Girls!' Posie said, laughing. 'Lots of girls!'

'What's that, darling? What "girls"?'

Posie told him. Alaric leant back and lit a cigarette, crinkling his eyes up against the strong sunshine. He blew a smoke ring into the air, and pulled on his old linen shirt haphazardly.

'That's old Cardigeon's hopes of an heir down the drain, then. Isn't it?'

'Oh, Rufus and Dolly won't care two hoots about that!' said Posie genuinely, a note of anger in her voice.

'I know. I meant old Cardigeon, Rufus' father. The old buffer.'

'Mnnn. Maybe. They want me to be Godmother to both of them. And Inspector Lovelace just asked me too, for his daughter! It never rains but it pours, eh? Isn't that lovely?'

'Well. That depends. Yes, if you like babies. And buying presents. I don't like either of those things. I hate buying presents especially: I'm bad at it, too. Just look at that lovely green chair I got you. You use it as a clothes-line in your bathroom most of the time. Don't say you don't!'

Posie had had enough. She marched up to Alaric and put her hands on her hips.

'For goodness' sake, darling. Just pull yourself together and stop saying nasty things.'

'I *mean* those things. Just because I happen to mean them doesn't mean they're nasty.'

Posie stared at Alaric aghast. 'I'll see you later. I'm going to the office.'

'But it's a Saturday! You can't go in on a Saturday!'

'I can and I jolly well will. I've got stacks of work on as it happens. And I need to be away from you for a bit. To think about things.'

She stalked off and took the stairs from the roof double-quickly, jumping into the birdcage lift at the bottom which was conveniently waiting empty for her. She stuffed the telegrams into the pockets of her deceptively simple smock-style designer dress and pressed the button.

As she emerged into the Reception Hall of her block of flats she realised she had nothing with her; no bag, no keys, no coat, no money. Just an optimistically-summery dress and a headful of simmering, angry thoughts for company.

'Ted,' she called out brightly, just stemming the tears she could feel gathering behind her eyes. 'Do you happen to still have my spare key for my office on Grape Street? For when you feed Mr Minks when I'm away?'

'Of course, Miss.'

The Porter darted forwards with the key on a ribbon and Posie took it with a small smile, giving no explanation, dashing quickly outside onto the sun-bleached pavement, thankful to be alone with her thoughts for a bit.

* * * *

Grape Street, as ever, was shadowy and cool and welcoming. Posie sat at her desk and felt her resentment simmer away. She held Mr Minks gently and he purred in her lap. She thought about Inspector Lovelace and his good news. And then she thought about Maypole Manor.

That had been a very strange case.

After help had come at dawn, the Dover Coastguard had been put on alert for both Caspian della Rosa's yacht, or any suspicious small boat which might be carrying Larry Crozio, Bertie Bunce and the man they had known as Evans. But nothing matching those descriptions had ever been sighted.

The Coastguard was also tasked with trying to locate the body of Caspian della Rosa or perhaps Larry Crozio, but, perhaps unsurprisingly, neither were found. Both had just disappeared into the night.

The body of Mr Steinhauser, however, *was* found, but it was his Rolex watch, rather than the man himself, which became an object of some fascination in the newspaper reports about his death. He was generally described as a 'Swiss man of business', which sounded boring enough, and no-one bothered to dig any deeper as to what he had been doing on New Year's Eve. Having no relatives on record in England, and no Will, his fancy watch and his London flat and all of his vast riches were sold, the proceeds going to the government.

There were other, wider repercussions of course.

News of Amory Laine's death leaked out within hours of her body being removed from Maypole Manor, and hordes of distraught fans braved the ice and snow to come and lay flowers in Kent at the spot she had been found in.

Her death filled the newspaper front pages for a good few days, and the Icon Film Company were quick to capitalize on their investment and re-released all of Amory's films in an attempt to make a quick buck, before swiftly moving on and finding a new star to replace her with.

Most significantly perhaps, a top-secret government Inquiry had been set up to investigate just what exactly had happened at Maypole Manor.

Everyone who had been in attendance at Maypole Manor that night was called for in the second week of

January and grilled within an inch of their lives; none more so than Inspector Lovelace, who had, as promised, resigned in the days following the party.

Inspector Lovelace was being hung out to dry, and, despite Inspector Oats being as good as his word and sticking up for him, things didn't look good at all.

Posie found it strange to see everyone gathered again in such different circumstances, in a small grey room in a government office in Victoria: strange to see Father Moriarty in a smart pinstriped suit; odd to see Jocasta without make-up and dressed in a rough grey prison shift and handcuffs; odd to see Lenny with a huge diamond engagement ring on her finger, the Duke at her side.

At the end of the government Inquiry Posie had run into Lenny in the women's bathroom, whether accidentally or on purpose she couldn't tell. Lenny had been applying dark maroon lipstick in the small institutional-looking mirror and looked up just as Posie came out of a cubicle.

Posie got the distinct feeling that Lenny had been waiting for her. It was the first time they had spoken since New Year's Eve, and then they hadn't really *spoken*.

'Doesn't look good for your Inspector out there, does it?' Lenny had said, matter of factly.

Posie shook her head as she dried her hands on a green paper towel. The room smelt overpoweringly of bleach. She looked at Lenny's finger, at the jewel she had first seen amongst the Duke's things at Maypole Manor in his jewellery roll.

'Congratulations,' she said politely. 'I hope you'll be very happy. And is it 'Lenny', or 'Lehni' now?'

Lenny had looked at Posie in the mirror without any expression showing on her artfully made-up face. She put her lipstick down slowly, tucking it carefully away in a handbag.

'I called myself Lenny all the while I was growing up in London,' she said quietly. '*You* try having a German name when the country you live in is at war with Germany and you feel as English as the next girl. *Not* easy. I changed back again to my real name when I needed to switch identities; I need proper documentation for one thing, for the marriage to Luca. Besides, Luca doesn't care two hoots about stuff like that. And we're not at war with Germany anymore. Never will be again, thankfully.'

'I see. Well, it all seems to have worked out just fine.'

'I know you wonder how I can do it,' she said in a low, dead voice. 'And I know you found my Leica lid.'

Posie shrugged, and turned to go.

'The thing is,' whispered Lenny in an insistent voice, 'I was very badly affected by what happened out in Luxor, you know. I almost fell apart. I was in love with Harry Redmayne, actually, although the feeling wasn't mutual. But anyway, I was haunted for weeks, months, by images of it all: the fire; the deaths; the carnage. When we got back to London I couldn't work anymore. I didn't have the heart to work, especially not for the British Museum, it reminded me of Harry over and over. And I've always supported myself; I don't have a private income or anything. My parents weren't rich and they didn't leave me a bean. So no photographs means no food on the table. I was in a bad place when I saw that advert. Which is why I replied.'

'Look, you don't need to explain this to me…'

'Oh, but I do. I can see what you think of me. The look in your eyes.'

'You mistake me, Lenny. As I said, I hope you'll be very happy together. Will you still move to Maypole Manor? After all that happened there?'

'Of course. But the Maypole has already gone. It's called 'Casa Veneto' now, you know. After the area Luca come from in Italy.'

'Ah, I see.' Posie tried not to look astounded. 'Well, good luck with that…I must dash.'

****

As it happened, the Inspector had been fine; *more* than fine. Days after the Inquiry had ended the government declared that no-one was to blame in the affair, and that the whole thing, while highly unfortunate and dangerous and not at all desirable, would probably have no lasting consequences for the country as it seemed highly likely that Larry Crozio had been killed, and that the blueprint was now lost forever. For everyone.

Inspector Lovelace's resignation letter had been ripped up and he had, puzzlingly, been reinstated at Scotland Yard on a slightly higher salary. But when the Inspector saw the monetary value of the drugs hoard they had found at Maypole Manor he had understood immediately.

He told Posie all of this in the first few days of February, sitting in a Lyons Corner House on the Strand, eating hot crumpets and drinking coffee. He told Posie that the real Bryn Cardinal was being honoured posthumously with yet another medal.

'So he *was* a war hero, then, sir? After all?'

Inspector Lovelace nodded. 'The man was a desk pilot: he stuck to office work all the way through the Great War, made some big contributions apparently which he was rewarded for. He was a lone wolf all the way through, though. The man was going to come a cropper at some point, carrying on like that…'

Posie took another crumpet and licked her buttery fingers, 'What will happen to Jocasta now, sir?'

'She's awaiting trial as we speak. I'd imagine a good long sentence will be what she's facing. Key player in a drugs ring. It doesn't look good.'

'Mnnn.'

'Surely you don't feel sorry for her, do you?'

'No, sir. Not really. It's just that she's so immensely

unlovable. And it does seem unfair, sir, doesn't it? Old Crozio and that awful man Bertie Bunce managed to escape with a good deal of the drugs and all the loot, and never got called to justice, and yet Jocasta gets all the blame pinned on her.'

'Life *is* unfair, Posie. As well you know. You make your bed, and she made a particularly spiky one for herself. Just as well she's not been implicated in the murder of her father. That *would* be a hanging offence she'd be facing. The forensic reports are all back now: Glaysayer *was* murdered, and with a bullet from a Luger, too. So old Crozio used his own gun and then just used Glaysayer's pistol as a sort of prop for general effect. And the priest was right: Amory Laine definitely died of a huge cocaine overdose, although there's nothing directly linking Crozio to her death, so it will be recorded as an 'accidental' death, unfortunately.'

'Speaking of the priest, Father Moriarty. There's still one thing I don't understand, sir.'

'Yes?'

'I know he was a German doctor, and all that. But just what was he doing at Maypole Manor on New Year's Eve? Was he doing something dodgy? Why was he there?'

The Inspector grinned. 'Depends what you mean by dodgy. No, but seriously, the man was who he said he was; he really was working as a priest under his new "English" name. It seems that Conan Doyle used to be a great favourite of his. Apart from the dodgy name he was all genuine.'

'So?'

'I don't usually betray secrets, Posie. But I'll tell you this. When I had to take his statement, days after the event, I asked the priest the same question you just asked of me; said I couldn't understand why he had been there in the first place. In answer, he pulled out a photograph of a little boy, and I could see at once that Father Moriarty was the boy's father. Unmistakeable. It was the usual story. Priest meets married rich woman who can't have children; they have an affair – scandalous, naturally – and a son is born, a son who is much treasured by the married woman and her rightful husband. And the priest, whom the woman still loves, can only come by her house in St Margaret's Bay at random times, when the woman's husband is away, to see her and his little son. The husband was away on New Year's Eve, and our Father Moriarty thought he would take his chances and brave the weather on his old bicycle. Foolish, but when was love anything *but* foolish?'

Before they had left the café, Inspector Lovelace had handed Posie an envelope.

'These are for you,' he said, smiling. 'I'm sorry again for the danger I put you in, and the fact that you weren't formally paid. I hope I haven't put you off working with me in the future.'

And when Posie had opened it later she had discovered a formal letter of thanks from the British government, together with a little coupon. Pulling the coupon open, she had read:

This entitles the bearer, Miss Rosemary Parker of Museum Chambers, WC1, to one outfit (including shoes) per month, for one year, from the House of Harlow. Valid until February 1923.

Laughing, Posie put the letter back inside the envelope and discovered yet another voucher inside. This one was gold-edged.

Surprised, she pulled it out. And then she saw that it was Inspector Lovelace's voucher for the Ritz Hotel in Paris which he had won at the New Year's Party.

He had scrawled a note on top:

Thought you deserved a weekend away.
  Sorry again..
  Lovelace.

* * * *

And now, back at her own desk in her own office, Posie thought briefly of the other house guests.

She had seen a wedding notice placed in the newspapers in March for Duke Del Angelo and Lenny, or Lehni as she had called herself. The address given for flowers and gifts was 'Casa Veneto', St Margaret's Bay, Kent. Posie had sent flowers but hadn't heard anything back. It was entirely possible that the couple were on a long, extended honeymoon. Perhaps in Italy, where Lenny could pretend everything was new to her, and where the Duke could show off his old castles and not visit any of his tomato factories.

Posie guessed they wouldn't be visiting Sicily.

Posie yawned and stretched.

She still felt cross and unable to face Alaric. Really, he was *impossible*. She started to gather some money together from her desk drawer, fancying a walk around Bloomsbury and a coffee or an ice somewhere.

She was fine walking around on her own again now, although it had taken some weeks of looking over her shoulder at every given step, checking for Caspian della Rosa, before she had become calm again and realised that Caspian della Rosa wasn't about to ambush her at any given moment on the streets of London.

Besides, he had said himself that he wasn't able to be in England at the moment. So surely she was safe? And that was assuming he was still alive. Which was itself questionable.

As she locked the glass-stencilled front door to the

office, Posie could hear a heavy, padding tread coming up the stairs. At the second landing the strange steps continued up, towards her.

Surprised, for she never had clients on a Saturday, Posie waited. And then she saw the twisted figure of Jacinta Glaysayer emerge.

'Posie! What luck! How glad I am to catch you!'

Jacinta was wearing a dusky pink travelling suit and she looked very smart. Her hair was now worn bobbed and there wasn't a gypsy scarf in sight. She was holding a big bunch of daffodils.

'Oh, how lovely!' exclaimed Posie.

'I'm embarrassed to say they aren't from me, actually. They were on your doorstep below, so I brought them up. I just happened to be passing actually. I'm leaving today.'

'Oh?'

'I was taking out the last few bits and pieces from my flat and my office on Lamb's Conduit Street. I'm off. For good. "Mystic Mirabelle" is a thing of the past for me. I want a fresh start. I decided to sell those jewels of my mother's; I think that's what she would have wanted, and with the money I'm going travelling first, and then I'm going to open a small guesthouse for English tourists in Tuscany. I fancy the sun, and the food. It will be good for my poor old bones, too. And oh, I just want to get away from all of *this*.'

She unwrapped a newspaper she had been holding which carried a story about Jocasta's trial on the front page. Jocasta had just received a sentence of twenty years' imprisonment for fraud and smuggling offences. Jacinta shook the paper angrily.

'Jocasta still refuses to see me. Whenever I visit her she pretends I don't exist. She only spoke to me once. And when she did she said: "Unless you have news from *him*, or a premonition concerning *him*, don't bother coming." So I stopped going. It's sad but what can I do?'

Posie agreed that there was nothing much to be done.

'I was just heading out. Shall we walk together?'

The two women walked down the stairs with its embarrassingly old blue runner, and they left the building. They stood together under one of the big London plane trees in the avenue outside.

'So I'll wish you good luck then,' said Posie, genuinely. 'And when you have your hotel, send me the address. I'd like to come and visit one day, if I may. I adore Tuscany, but I was only ever in Florence with my father. I'm sure I'd love to see your guesthouse, wherever it will be.'

'Of course.' Jacinta nodded, but then looked embarrassed.

'You know, I'm trying to give up all this clairvoyant stuff. But this morning I got a picture of you so clearly, I thought I had to come and see if you were really here; if I was *right*.'

'Oh, what was it?' Posie was interested, but incredulous.

'You were sitting alone in your office, with a cat for company. The man who loves you was nearby, standing high up, angry at himself for having hurt you. He wanted to tell you he didn't mean anything that he said, but he couldn't, as you had stormed off. The man loves you, Posie. More than you know. More than *he* knows. And he will do anything to make you happy. He'll give you anything; even things he doesn't like. I hope that makes sense to you.'

Posie stared at the girl, dumbstruck. Jacinta turned and walked away in the direction of Shaftesbury Avenue.

She didn't look back and she didn't wave.

Posie stood, uncertain, on the street corner. She fingered the jagged edges of the lush yellow daffodils. Suddenly a pearl dropped out, loose, running away over the pavement. It was creamy and lustrous and reminded Posie a bit of a necklace she had once owned. She didn't chase after it.

Posie absently pulled the florist's note out from the expensive wrapping paper, all the while thinking to herself;

re-running Jacinta's words through her mind. She read the note.

And then Posie saw Alaric's tall, loping figure coming towards her across the street, crossing in front of the crowd of people gathered by the old Rag and Bone Man.

Posie smiled and waved, her heart suddenly very full.

When Alaric came across and hugged her and suggested a tea out somewhere together, she laughed easily. She threw the bunch of daffodils into the nearest bin with their cryptic little note:

See you soon, my darling. Or should I say, my PEARL? All is fine here except for the fact that you are not with me.
   Soon.

C.D.R.

Alaric hadn't been bothered by the note or by the flowers.

And despite a chilly shivery feeling which had come and gone in an instant, neither was Posie.

Not much, anyhow.

* * * *

Thanks for joining Posie Parker and her friends.

Enjoyed *Murder at Maypole Manor* (A Posie Parker Mystery #3)? Here's what you can do next.

If you loved this book and have a tiny moment to spare I would really appreciate a short review on the page where you bought the book. Your help in spreading the word about the series is invaluable and really appreciated, and reviews make a big difference to helping new readers find the series.

Posie's previous cases are all available in e-book and paperback formats from Amazon, as well as in selected bookstores.

You can find all of the previous books, available for purchase, listed here in chronological order:

www.amazon.com/L.B.-Hathaway/e/
B00LDXGKE8 and

www.amazon.co.uk/L.B.-Hathaway/e/B00LDXGKE8

More Posie Parker books will be released in late 2016.

You can sign up to be notified of new releases, pre-release specials, free short stories and the chance to win Amazon gift-vouchers here:

www.lbhathaway.com/contact/newsletter/

Historical Note

Needless to say, the characters in this book are all fictional. So too is Maypole Manor, which is a creation of my own, although the place it is located at, St Margaret's Bay in Kent, England, is very real. For a note on the location, see the end of this Historical Note.* I have used artistic licence far more here than I have in previous Posie Parker Mysteries, although where I have strayed a good deal from the accurate historical situation or conditions at the time I have noted that below.

In the main, the historical timings, dates, background and detail described in this book (including the terrible weather conditions and gales suffered by the UK at the end of 1921) are accurate to the best of my knowledge, save for the following exceptions:

1. Fry's chocolate-covered 'Turkish Delight' which is still sold today and mentioned in Chapter One was actually marketed as 'Fry's Turkish Bar' in 1921. The packaging was not pink foil as we know it, but golden foil. I have used the current day incarnation as it is a personal favourite.

2. The American furniture made by Lloyd Loom was only just becoming available in England in 1921, and

it was not until 1922 that it really became crazily fashionable and easy to buy. So I think for Alaric to have got his hands on a piece for Christmas 1921 as is mentioned in Chapter Two would be slightly testing the boundaries of probability. Possible, but not hugely likely.

3. Amory Laine, the film star in this story is, of course, fictional. However, she is (in her dark and beautiful looks alone) partly inspired by the English film star *du jour*, Madge Stuart, who starred in a smash hit (now lost) silent film of 1921, *Innocent*, which was produced by Stoll pictures in London. My movie star, Amory, makes a name for herself in this story in *Innocent and Naïve*, a film which is inspired by Madge Stuart's hit film. (Referred to in Chapters Two, Three and Ten.) Needless to say, Amory Laine's character and vices are uniquely her own and a creation of mine, and were not inspired by anyone, living or dead.

4. Geo. F. Trumper on Curzon Street in Mayfair which Posie visits in Chapter Two existed back in 1921, but was, as now, solely for men.

5. While the precision bomber nicknamed 'the Guillotine' in this story is totally fictitious (first mentioned here in Chapter Five), Hugh Trenchard *was* a real historical figure; as well as being a war hero in his own right, he later went on to become Head of the Royal Air Force (and he was in this position at the time of this novel). He was hugely interested in the development of strategic bombing in the period between the two World Wars. My suggestion, however, that he encouraged the government to pay for the blueprint of 'the Guillotine' from its American creators is of course an invention of my own.

6. The suggestion by Inspector Lovelace in Chapter Five that the government were hugely wary of spies during the inter-war years (and thus the growing rise and importance of MI5) is an accurate one.

7. Dover Marine Station, where Posie and Inspector Lovelace arrive in Chapter Six is now part of the Dover Western Docks. This huge station is now decommissioned and disused, and all the more interesting and evocative for it. However, it is still being used occasionally (at time of writing) as a Cruise Liner Terminal.

   On the subject of trains, Dover Marine Station was served by the South Eastern and Chatham Railway (SECR) during this period. For a dash of twenties glamour rather than historical accuracy I have placed my characters as passengers on the luxurious Golden Arrow, but all good train buffs will know that this particular train was not introduced on this route until 1929, when it left London at 11.00 am every morning, syncing with its Paris counterpart. It took a speedy 98 minutes to reach Dover Marine Station.

8. As mentioned in Chapter Six, Tanzania was part of German East Africa until just after the First World War.

9. The reference to Fred Astaire in Chapter Eight (by Inspector Lovelace) is a personal flight of fancy on my part. He was only really becoming known in London one year later than this story is set (in Jerome Kern's *The Bunch and Judy* at the Globe Theatre, London).

10. The songs performed in Chapter Ten were all contemporary. 'And Her Mother Came Too' by Ivor Novello would have been a raging hit by the time this novel took place, as it had been recorded at Hayes

studio in November 1921, by rising English singing star Jack Buchanan.

11. The reference in Chapter Eleven to Sir Frederick Kenyon and his daughter Kathleen's assistance in the pursuit of knowledge about 'Lenny' Brandenberger on New Year's Eve 1921 is purely fictional, although Sir Frederick Kenyon was the Director of the Museum at this time, and did live in a house attached to the British Museum in Bloomsbury with his daughter, Kathleen. The redoubtable Dame Kathleen Mary Kenyon would indeed have been twelve at this time. She went on to become a photographer and famous archaeologist in her own right (some say the most influential female archaeologist of the twentieth century). It is not inconceivable that this bright, precocious child would have been interested in the goings-on and work of employees at the British Museum at this age, and I have stretched this possibility here to include a girlish idolisation of the older, glamorous Lenny.

12. The address given for the Italian Embassy in Chapter Eleven was not actually in use until several years later, starting in 1931.

13. The snowstorm suffered at Maypole Manor and in the surrounding areas of St Margaret's Bay on New Year's Eve 1921 is entirely fictional and a plot device of my own, and although the weather that year was bad, it was certainly not *that* bad.

14. In Chapter Seventeen I mention a leather Belstaff motorcycle jacket, and while these *were* made by Belstaff, it would have been impossible for Alaric Boynton-Dale or for Lenny Brandenberger to get their hands on one until 1923, three years later, when they were mass produced.

15. The diamond mine I describe in Chapter Eighteen is fictional, as diamond mining was not taking place in Tanzania properly until the 1930s, rather than in the late nineteenth century, as this novel suggests. The oldest and most prolific diamond mine in Tanzania (like the mine in this story) is located south of Mwanza, and is the Williamson Diamond Mine, established in 1940.

16. The Avro Bison (biplane) which is mentioned in Chapters Twenty and Twenty-One was not actually in use by the British RAF until 1922, but it is possible that, in very special circumstances (and on government business) a pilot could have got his hands on one a couple of months early.

17. The German pilot, the Red Baron, referred to in Chapter Twenty-One was, of course, real, although his exploits were and have become the stuff of legend. He was Manfred Von Richthofen and he was killed in 1918.

* Note on St Margaret's Bay

I am not the first and will certainly not be the last writer to use this wonderful location as the setting for a story. Among others, Ian Fleming, of James Bond fame, both lived here and used it as a setting and inspiration in his writing.

St Margaret's Bay is a remote beach near Dover, Kent. It is located in the eastern foothills of the North Downs. Very steep chalk cliffs surround a tiny enclosed shingle bay, which has a small promenade.

The closest part of England to France (a distance of some 20 miles of sea), this tiny bay and its village (above) is justly famous for its stunning and treacherous surround of white chalk cliffs. These natural defences have made the place at various times a focus for smuggling, for high-end tourism and as a frontline of attack in World War Two.

The place has always attracted tourists (the Bay Hotel, demolished in the 1940s, always had a good custom and was massively extended to keep up with demand in the late 1930s) but when Noel Coward moved in, in the 1930s, he and his clutch of glamorous friends (including Katharine Hepburn, who apparently swam in the sea no matter the weather) made the place a playground for London's most glittering stars and a weekend haunt for the rich and famous.

There is no train station at St Margaret's Bay, as in this story, and visitors, now as then, have to travel from Dover train station, or from St Margaret's Mill (as does our MI5 representative in the story).

St Margaret's Bay, as mentioned in this story, was also the last place in Britain where bombs were dropped at the end of World War One.

****

Acknowledgements

Thank you to my parents who have taken me to the places in East Kent which are mentioned in this story, the most memorable being the hauntingly empty and desolate Dover Marine Station (as was).

Thank you to Wendy Janes for her comments on the manuscript, and also to J.S. for his help in supplying aeronautical information regarding accurate flying times, navigational difficulties and what would have been achievable in a 1920s biplane in snowy conditions. But this is a novel, and therefore I have stretched things to the bounds of all probability, and any mistakes remaining are, of course, solely my own.

* * * *

About the Author

Cambridge-educated, British-born L.B. Hathaway writes historical fiction and contributes to a number of popular history magazines and websites. She worked as a lawyer at Lincoln's Inn in London for almost a decade before becoming a full-time writer. She is a lifelong fan of detective novels set in the Golden Age of Crime, and is an ardent Agatha Christie devotee.

Her other interests, in no particular order, are: very fast downhill skiing, theatre-going, drinking strong tea, Tudor history, exploring castles and generally trying to cram as much into life as possible. She lives in London and Switzerland with her husband and young family.

The Posie Parker series of cosy crime novels span the 1920s. They each combine a core central mystery, an exploration of the reckless glamour of the age and a feisty protagonist who you would love to have as your best friend.

To find out more and for news of new releases and giveaways, go to:

http://www.lbhathaway.com

Connect with L.B. Hathaway online:

(e) author@lbhathaway.com

(t) @LbHathaway

(f) https://www.facebook.com/pages/L-B-Hathaway-books/1423516601228019

(Goodreads) http://www.goodreads.com/author/show/8339051.L_B_Hathaway

19819904R00175

Printed in Great Britain
by Amazon